THE POISON APE

ALSO IN THE SERIES

Shinjuku Shark

THE POISON APE

ARIMASA OSAWA

Translated by Deborah Iwabuchi

Copyright © 2008 by Arimasa Osawa

All rights reserved.

Published by Vertical, Inc., New York.

Originally published in Japanese as *Dokuzaru Shinjukuzame II* in 1991
by Kobunsha, Tokyo.

ISBN 978-1-934287-24-8

Manufactured in the United States of America

First Edition

Vertical, Inc.
1185 Avenue of the Americas 32nd Floor
New York, NY 10036
www.vertical-inc.com

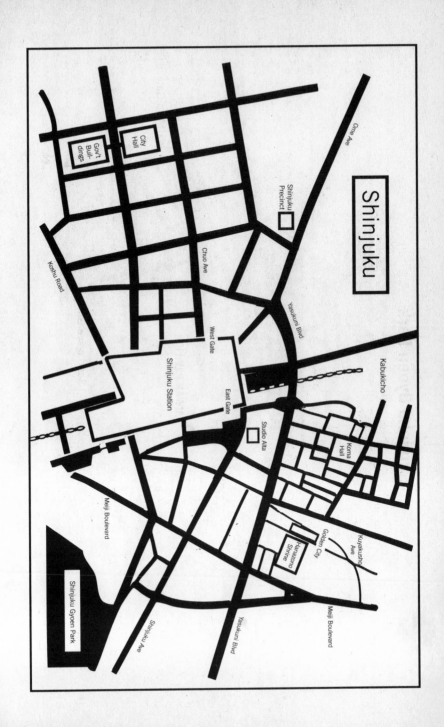

Shinjuku Gyoen Park

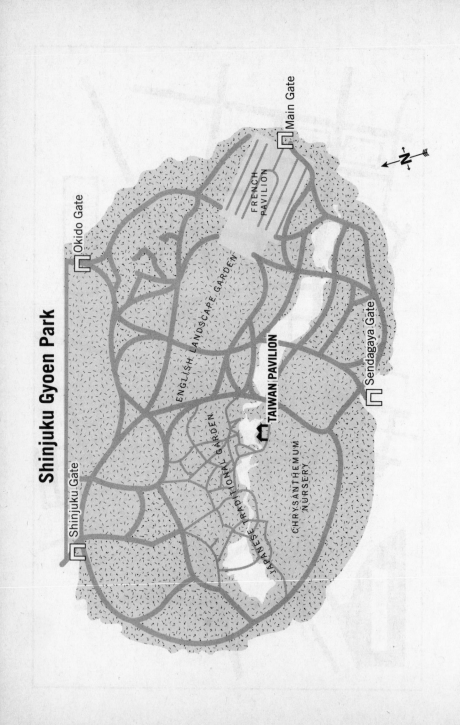

Note on Names

With the exception of widely-known historical Chinese figures such as "Chiang Kai-shek," whose names the reader is presumably accustomed to seeing in the Eastern order, all Japanese and Chinese names are given family name last in this translation, i.e. in the Western order.

When a name appears alone, it is usually the surname, as in "Samejima"; the notable exception to this is the appellation for club hostesses, which are (false) given names.

THE POISON APE

1

The dealer was wearing a navy blue jacket and yellow chinos. His hair, which was long enough to cover half of his ears, stuck out underneath his baseball cap.

Samejima guessed him to be twenty-three or four. The dealer stood against a pillar as if he were waiting for someone. The west entrance of Shinjuku Station was beginning to crowd with the evening rush. The dull silver color of his aviator sunglasses shone beneath the brim of his cap.

Samejima, crouched down and posing as a slacker, was in the shadows of another pillar seven or eight yards away. He was wearing jeans and a t-shirt, with a sweater tied around his waist. He also wore sunglasses that Sho had bought for him at a night fair. The lenses were perfectly round circles. When he wore them with a suit she said they made him look like a hit man for the Chinese mafia in some B-movie.

Dealers rarely worked alone. It was customary for them to use a lookout man, someone who would pretend to be a stranger, to watch for patrolling policemen or undercover cops who might stake out the operation. Samejima had managed to discover the lookout. A man in a gray suit and a red tie was reading a tabloid in front of a shop about twenty yards away. Samejima watched as the man took his eyes off the paper from time to time to peer around. Both the dealer and the lookout were new to the Shinjuku scene, and were probably connected to Hongo, a racketeering gang that had recently begun to deal paint thinner. Their specialty was "luxury brands" known as Three Nine and Juntoro.

It had been about two months since Samejima had first heard that Hongo was backing a Juntoro dealer at the west gate of the Shinjuku Station. Nowadays the high quality Juntoro was hard to find, and a tiny bottle went for up to five thousand yen. It was said that once you tried the good stuff you could never go back to the cheap thinner sold at craft shops because it burned more than the Juntoro. There were plenty of users hooked who were willing to cough up the money for the good stuff.

The dealer didn't look as though he was worried that he was being followed, but Samejima was still cautious. He regularly changed his outfit and his hairstyle to make sure neither the dealer nor his lookout caught on to him. He fought back the craving for a cigarette. Lighters and cigarettes would draw too much attention. Plus, there wasn't an ashtray anywhere nearby. If a pile of ashes collected at his feet it would look suspicious to anyone.

Samejima glanced towards the lookout, who held his folded magazine in his left hand while he drank out of a small energy drink bottle in his right. Samejima suddenly wondered if he would take the empty bottle home with him. All he had to do was fill it from his stash of thinner and he was set to earn another five thousand yen.

Samejima had taken down a group of amateurs dealing toluene after he noticed a boy going through the recycling bins next to vending machines, removing only the small energy drink bottles. The boy was sixteen, still in high school. Someone had told him about a place that would give him five thousand yen for a hundred such bottles.

Samejima had asked the boy where the place was, staked it out and tailed a man who showed up there. He discovered his hideout. The man was the youngest son of the owner of a liquor shop. He used the shop's light truck to collect all the small bottles he bought from scavengers. He had amassed a huge pile of bottles. A twenty-year-old nightclub hostess was also at the hideout. She had met the man at the liquor shop and lured him into working as a dealer.

She had already recruited a childhood friend of the shop owner's son. The friend was the delinquent son of a house painter. It had been their first foray into criminal activities for both of the young men. The woman, however, was a pro. She had joined a gang at the age of thirteen, and had extensive experience in shoplifting, extortion and prostitution. She had an impressive criminal record.

Although she was the youngest, this woman was the leader of the group. When Samejima had arrested them, she went all wide-eyed and feigned innocence, saying she was just helping the guys out on a part-time basis. But when the two young men went pale and confessed to everything it quickly became clear who was in charge.

She had "relations" with both of them, and each had been fooled into believing he was the one she really loved. It turned out she had yet another lover, a man doing time for an assault conviction.

To Samejima's surprise, the lookout tossed his empty bottle into the trash. While watching him, he almost failed to notice a prospective customer approaching.

The customer came from the corridor leading to the east side of the station. He was a young man of about twenty. He wore a red vinyl jacket, and most of his face was hidden with a white cotton mask—the type Japanese wear to keep from spreading the flu. He sported a bad dye job and the ends of his hair stuck straight out at his neck. A crop of bad acne poked out around the mask.

Samejima had realized about a week ago that the white mask was the signal. Traditionally in thinner and toluene deals, the customer would hang out in the dealer's area and use the signal—a fist held close to the mouth in a feigned cough. The dealer would spot the signal and sidle up to his client, asking him in a whisper how many bottles he needed.

The police had eventually caught on to this system and made so many arrests that the addicts had been forced to come up with something new. Now there were lots of different ways to contact dealers, and the white cotton mask was the one used to signal intent to buy Juntoro at the Shinjuku west gate.

Dye Job walked hunched over with his hands stuffed in his pockets. The dealer glanced at his lookout, who then quickly checked the surrounding area and touched his tie to indicate that the coast was clear.

Once, when an officer on patrol walked by, the lookout had run his hand through his hair. Samejima had wanted to burst out laughing. The usual symbol for a cop was forming a circle with thumb and forefinger and bringing it to the forehead, but it would have been foolish to actually do that as a cop walked by. The lookout would have blown his cover on the spot. However, bringing his hand to his forehead must have been a reflex, so he fussed with his hair to signal danger.

The dealer, who had been lounging by a pillar, straightened himself and approached Dye Job as he passed in front of him. The dealer's lips moved slightly, and Dye Job responded. Samejima watched as money changed hands. The dealer put his left hand around the young man's shoulders while his right hand took the proffered paper envelope of money. Next he handed his customer a key that had been hidden in his left hand. The key probably opened one of the thousands of coin lockers located inside Shinjuku Station.

Then the dealer whispered something else—probably the location of the appropriate locker. Dye Job turned on his heels, separated from the dealer and walked back in the direction he had come from. Now all he had to do was find the locker, open it, and get the Juntoro—a tiny bottle carefully wrapped in a brown paper bag.

As the customer melted into the crowd, the dealer began to walk slowly away. The lookout stayed put.

Samejima stood up. This was what he had been waiting for. The dealer had traded a key for money. But he wouldn't be stupid enough to keep dozens of keys on himself. If he were ever caught, all of the lockers would be opened and everything in them confiscated. Plus, lots of keys would give away the fact that he was a dealer. That was why he never carried more than two or three keys at a time. He would get more as needed. If a dealer gets arrested, his lookout usually gets nabbed too, so they would use a third man to hold the keys.

The dealer was headed for the lower level of a department store at the west gate of the station. A number of steel wagons were lined up at the entrance for a wagon sale. Sweet pastries, kitchen utensils and jewelry were on display, the sellers hoping to catch the attention of department store customers passing by.

The dealer stopped at the last wagon, which had necklaces and brooches on display. The salesman was a short man in his forties with thinning hair wearing a three-piece suit. The dealer walked up to the wagon, picked up one of the pendants hanging from it, and said something to the salesman. A stool was squeezed into the small space between the wagons and the department store display window. On the stool was a small cash box to hold the proceeds from the jewelry. The salesman turned around and opened the lid of the cash box.

The third man.

Samejima began to run. At the edge of his vision he saw the lookout go into a panic, raising his arms. The dealer had his back to Samejima and the salesman was busy with the cash box. The lookout waved his arms around like a lunatic. When he realized his efforts were useless, he began to edge away from the scene, ready to run off like a scared rabbit as soon as he realized Samejima was a cop.

By the time the salesman had closed the lid to the safe and turned around, Samejima was right behind the dealer. Panic spread over the salesman's face.

"Hands up!"

Dumbfounded, the dealer turned around. He went white when he realized his lookout had fled. Samejima showed the two his police badge, and began to speak in a calmer tone.

"Samejima of the Crime Prevention Unit of Shinjuku Precinct. Would you mind showing me what you have in your hand there?"

The salesman was expressionless. The dealer held out his hand. He had three locker keys.

"What's your deal? What's wrong with a couple of keys?" sputtered the dealer, swallowing hard.

"Oh, I think you know. I've been watching you," Samejima replied coolly. "I've seen what you're up to."

"Whaddya mean? What have I been 'up to'?"

"These are keys to coin lockers. What's inside them?" Samejima asked like he was just making conversation. He had all the proof he needed to nab this one. The only problem was the little salesman.

"Just p-products," said the salesman.

"Why don't we go take a look at those products?"

At that instant the dealer yanked himself out of Samejima's grasp and turned to run.

"Do not resist!" Samejima bellowed, knocking him to the ground.

The air around them turned icily silent as pedestrians stopped in their tracks. The dealer's sunglasses clattered noisily to the floor. He bit his lip and moaned in frustration.

"Goddamn..."

"You want the handcuffs or not?"

"No! Please, man, gimme a break."

"Then stand up like a good boy." Samejima dragged him to his feet, and spoke to the salesman. "Show me the cash box."

Expressionless, the salesman held out the box.

"Open it," Samejima said, gripping the dealer by his right wrist.

The salesman opened the lid. There was a small box inside along with coins and cash-filled envelopes.

"Take out that box."

The salesman gingerly held it out, all the while avoiding Samejima's gaze. There were more than twenty keys inside.

At Samejima's command, four uniformed policemen were soon on the scene. Two railway security officers arrived after.

The seven of them moved through the station, a small mob with the dealer and his key man at the center. The salesman, knowing that the station security could quickly locate the lockers anyway, navigated the way to each location.

The police confiscated the thinner from the lockers. They had to move quickly to look for the "factory" where the thinner was being bottled, and they didn't have much time now that the lookout had escaped.

The seventh locker was at the east gate; the busiest spot in the station, which meant that locker got a lot of use. The police had already confiscated more than twenty bottles. Two officers carried large plastic bags and filled them with every last bottle. The area was packed with people taking their belongings from their lockers. It was the second busiest time of the day for Shinjuku Station. Only the morning rush was busier.

"Where's the next one?" Samejima asked the salesman as they opened two lockers and collected the bottles inside.

The salesman only spoke as little as possible. Samejima knew that the man could see his own future closing in on him. This couldn't be his first arrest. He might even be a bonafide member of the Hongo gang. If so, he was probably thinking about what kind of punishment would await him. He was also busily trying to figure out how to minimize the damage his arrest and confession would have on the gang.

17

Samejima noticed that the salesman still had all of his fingers, but had no doubt that he would be missing at least one before long. The gang would put on a show and tell him that he was being punished for hurting their reputation by selling illegal substances, but in reality he had endangered one of their most important sources of revenue.

The salesman would almost certainly claim that he worked independently, and deny any connection to the gang. If he confessed that he was working on the gang's orders, most of the gang's important members would be hauled away in handcuffs. If that happened, it would mean losing more than just a finger or two.

Samejima was pulled out of his reverie by a faint cry that came from the crowd. A figure burst out of the circle of onlookers that had formed around the uniformed officers. It was a tall, dark man with something shiny in his hand.

He's not Japanese, thought Samejima as he looked at the man's dark complexion.

He was wearing a dark blue anorak and work pants covered with pockets. He wore thick work boots that were caked with white clay-like dirt. The pants he wore were too short, and half of his brown socks stuck out under the cuffs.

His expression was blank, but his eyes shone with a dangerous gleam. A second too late, Samejima realized the shiny thing he held was a steel carving knife. It was too late to shout out a warning.

Screaming something in what must have been his native tongue, he rammed into the salesman, who stood facing the lockers. The salesman cried out in pain, and the officer right next to him looked down at his face in surprise. The salesman arched his back in agony and gripped the officer's shoulders.

Samejima finally sprang into action. He rammed into the dark-skinned attacker with his shoulder, knocking him to the floor. The police and rubberneckers finally realized what was going on.

All at once, a cry went up from the crowd when they saw the

knife thrust into the right side of the salesman, buried almost to the hilt.

The salesman let out a deafening scream.

"It hurts! Oh my god, it hurts!"

His eyes bulged out of their sockets and his mouth opened wide enough to shove a fist in. Blood gushed from the wound and quickly pooled around his feet.

"Help me, officer! It hurts! It hurts, it hurts!" he continued to scream, gripping desperately onto the policeman's collar with both hands.

A railway security officer at the edge of the group gave a yell and jumped on top of the dark-skinned attacker who had toppled to the ground. Two more officers followed suit, and they piled on top of the man on the station floor.

Another officer brandished a nightstick and was about to jump into the fray when Samejima yelled at him, "Call an ambulance!" He dropped his nightstick and fumbled with the microphone of his wireless transmitter on his shoulder.

"Hang in there!" Samejima said. He grabbed the salesman under his armpits as his knees buckled. The officer he clung to stumbled from the sudden shift in weight.

The salesman's mouth was still wide open, but he no longer cried out. His lips began to tremble. His face went pale and his eyes rolled back in his head. Samejima, holding him from behind, was instantly soaked with the man's blood.

"Sit him down, sit him down," he said. "Lower his heart." The salesman slumped over like a rag doll. His head fell between the officer's legs.

"What's going on? What the fuck's going on?" the dealer mumbled to himself, his eyes staring.

The police piled on the attacker pulled apart, and dragged the dark man to his feet. The attacker's bloodless lips continued to move soundlessly. Samejima knelt down in front of the salesman.

"Hey. Hey, can you hear me? Hang in there, understand?"

The man's eyelids were beginning to close. His face had gone from white to ashen.

"We're losing him."

The policeman supporting the salesman went pale. His blood-spattered gloved hands searched for a pulse.

"Keep talking to him," Samejima ordered. "Make sure he stays conscious until the ambulance gets here."

As Samejima turned back to the attacker, he bumped into the knees of the dealer. He was trying to distance himself from the police and the dark-skinned attacker. He had squatted down and started to bawl. It sounded like a cat crying.

"What the fuck, what the fuck, what's happening, what the fuck!" He wrapped his arms tightly across his chest as he cried, all the while staring at the dark man. He was terrified.

Three policemen had grabbed on to the attacker's arms and hair. The man's lips were still moving and the corners of his mouth had dried white spittle on them. He had enormous eyes and a bulging Adam's apple.

Samejima took a deep breath, stood up, and went over to the attacker. He didn't show the slightest hint of resistance.

"Enough. Handcuff him."

Even when handcuffed, the man's lips never stopped moving. He looked past Samejima, his eyes fixed on the small, dying salesman.

Samejima took another deep breath. A whiff of the man's body odor stung his nose. He finally realized what the man was mumbling. It was a prayer.

2

The salesman died of massive blood loss in the ambulance before reaching the hospital. As Samejima had suspected, he was a card-carrying middle-rank Hongo member. His name was Saji. He was forty-one.

The man who stabbed him was an Asian who gave his name only as "Ali." He barely spoke any Japanese. When asked in English why he had done it, he replied in his native language. Ali was temporarily taken to the Shinjuku Precinct.

Samejima called the police headquarters and ordered an interpreter. They had a translation center with staff who could provide interpretation and translation in English, French, Spanish, Portuguese, Russian, Mandarin Chinese, Cantonese, Korean, Tagalog, Thai, and Urdu. There were two types of interpreters—those who majored in a foreign language in college before joining the police force, and those who learned a language after they entered the force. The employee who answered the phone got an idea of where Ali was from and said an interpreter would soon be on the way.

At the precinct, Ali and the dealer were put in neighboring interrogation rooms. Police usually preferred to wait to question a dealer until he had calmed down from the shock of the arrest, but Samejima couldn't waste any time. The lookout was on the move and they did not know how Ali might be involved in thinner trade.

They had to wait for an interpreter for Ali. If the interpreter showed up while Samejima was busy with the dealer, Momoi, the chief of the Crime Prevention Unit, was available to question him along with a detective from the Criminal Investigation Unit.

Samejima sat down in a chair between the dealer and the table. A newly transferred detective was there to record the proceedings.

"Your name?" Samejima began. The dealer had no form of identification on him. Saji had had on him his driver's license along with a card with a seal identifying him as a Hongo member.

"Kawasaki," the dealer said flatly. He didn't know that Saji was dead.

"First name?"

"Ichiro."

"Are you saying 'Kawasaki' because that's your hometown? Whatever. We'll know who you are as soon as we get your prints."

The dealer sulked, staring up at Samejima from under his brow.

"You know you're in trouble, right? Are you expecting Hongo to come to the rescue?"

The dealer shook his head.

"All right then, let's try it again. What's your name?"

"Toda."

"Full name."

"Haruki Toda."

"Haruki, how much have you been selling?"

"How much?"

"How many bottles, how long, customers, all of it."

"Today was my first time."

"Hey, now. Do you really think I just happened to notice you while strolling past?"

"How long were you watching?"

"How long do you think?"

"A week?"

"You had quite a sleek operation going. Do you think I could bust you in just a week?"

"Two weeks?"

"I'm the one asking the questions."

Toda went silent. He was probably wondering how badly Saji had been hurt. If Saji confessed, he'd be caught if he lied. He'd still be in trouble if his partner in crime blabbed even if he himself didn't say a word. On the other hand, if Saji clammed up—or was dead—the only information the police could get would be from him. The less he said the better.

"How is, uh, how is Mr. Saji?"

"Not too lively."

"How bad is he?"

"That man tried to kill him."

"Why?"

"Good question. Have you ever seen him before?"

"No. Never."

"Now that's strange," said Samejima, but Toda kept his mouth shut. "The attacker saw all the police around. He saw you and Saji with all those uniformed cops. Why did he stab Saji? He could plainly see that you were under arrest."

"How should I know?"

"Maybe if I put the two of you in a cell together you'll remember him. It's awfully crowded downstairs."

"Gimme a break, man."

"He saw that you and Saji were arrested. He had gone there to stab Saji. Think about it for a few minutes."

Toda kept his eyes lowered, but he gulped loudly enough for Samejima to hear.

"He's not—not a silencer..."

"Silencer?"

"Nothing."

"I'll know if I put you two together."

"No, please! He might have come to kill both of us."

"Why would he do that?"

"We got caught, right? Another gang member might have seen us and paid him to kill us to keep their secret."

"I see."

"First Saji, then me. That's it. Megi got away. He must have notified the gang. That rat…"

"Megi? You mean your lookout?"

Toda nodded.

"How do you write his name?"

"I don't know."

"I'll just take a look at the Hongo membership file."

Toda nodded. So, this Megi was also a member.

"Is Hongo putting so much into thinner sales that they have to kill you to keep you quiet?" Toda nodded again. "Yeah, I guess so. How much did you sell yesterday?"

"Seven."

"Bottles? Or yen?"

"Yen."

Seven hundred thousand yen. That meant 140 bottles.

"That's quite a payday. Where does the Juntoro come from?"

"I dunno."

"Who's going to believe that? You're the one selling the stuff."

"It's true. I'm just their gopher."

"So they'd really go to the trouble to bump off their errand boy? They'd pay an outsider to kill you?" Toda looked up at Samejima, and Samejima glared down at him as hard as he could. The dealer's eyes filled with fear.

"It's collateral for some kind of gambling debt."

"What kind?"

"I really don't know the details. Some old guy's factory went bankrupt and he couldn't pay. He brought the stuff to the boss. That's what Megi told me."

"By 'boss' you mean the Hongo leader?"

Toda nodded.

"Say 'yes' or it won't be on the record!"

"Yes," said Toda in a slightly surprised voice. Up until then, Samejima hadn't mentioned the nodding.

Samejima took out a cigarette and put it in his mouth, and thrust the pack in front of Toda's face. He bobbed his head slightly and took a cigarette.

They might be able to nail the Hongo boss. It might not have turned out this way if Saji was still alive. He would have told the judge that everything Toda said were lies. Even if Megi, the lookout, vanished without a trace the boss would still have to hand over one of his higher-ranking subordinates in exchange. The only gang members with the power to negotiate an exchange of goods to settle a debt were the boss and those close to him.

"How is Mr. Saji?" After a cigarette, Toda seemed relaxed enough to ask the question again.

"We don't know yet. Listen, are you sure you never saw that foreigner before?"

"I never saw him with the gang."

"So you spend a lot of time at their office?"

"No. I just went once."

"Did they take you out to eat?"

"Yes."

"What about women?"

"Just once. They took me to a soapland."

"Who took you?"

"Mr. Saji and Megi."

"What's your cut?"

"Five per."

"Five hundred yen per bottle?"

"Yes."

"70,000 yen a day. Not bad. You must have a lot saved."

"Well, I like playing mahjong, and…"

"Are you a user?"

The poor state of Toda's teeth and the way he spoke with his mouth full of spit gave Samejima a clue.

Without saying "yes," Toda just nodded. Thinner and toluene eat away at the gums until the roots are exposed. Users have a hard time closing their mouths, get halitosis and eventually begin to drool uncontrollably.

"Did they give you a discount?"

"One thousand off."

"Rough. Who made that decision?"

"Megi."

"So, of the three of you, Megi was in charge?" Samejima had thought Saji looked to be the older of the two.

"Mr. Saji was older, but Megi was always putting him down because he made mistakes. He called Mr. Saji an idiot, a klutz."

"So that's why he was involved with thinner smuggling."

In most gangs, members over forty were rarely directly involved in dealing. It was usually left to younger men in the lower ranks who were counted on to be quick on their feet. If Saji was working directly with dealers it meant that he had no other way to make money.

"I heard that Mr. Saji likes to bet on horses and had gotten into a ton of debt. He asked them to let him work in sales to pay back his debts," said the dealer.

"Debt, huh?"

"Yeah."

Yakuza organizations didn't let their smarter members get involved with dangerous business. Any young member was used as if he was disposable, but once a member distinguished himself things changed.

Saji hadn't made it with all his fingers intact so far because he was smart. He had just been lucky. But instead of losing a finger, he had lost his life.

"Does Hongo use foreigners?"

"I don't know."

"How about daylabor procurement?"

Toda blinked and then thought for a few moments. "Megi recruited some a while ago. He said he had a few working in construction."

"So he might have been one of those construction workers. Do you try to get those guys into gambling?"

"Dunno. I hear they don't like to gamble. They send most of their money back home."

"Why would such a serious, dedicated guy kill someone?"

"Who knows? Maybe they paid him a ton of money."

"How much would *you* do it for?"

"Huh?" Toda forced himself to smile. "I would never…"

"Really? What if you needed some badly, and you were broke. What if they promised you all the good stuff you wanted?" Samejima saw sweat forming on Toda's upper lip. "Maybe he was feening for the good stuff."

"I wouldn't do it. I wouldn't kill anyone, even for money."

Samejima looked Toda up and down.

"What you're doing is the same thing as killing someone. That stuff you sell destroys people. It messes them up. They start fires, they beat their parents to death. Ever think of that? Thinner, uppers, they're all the same. You're a user yourself. You ought to know. They're all as bad off as you, or even worse. If you didn't sell that stuff, they'd stay out of trouble! Use your head for once, you fucking moron!"

Toda went pale. Samejima stood up. With Megi on the loose, the gang had most likely already moved the stockpile of Juntoro from wherever it was held before it made its way to Shinjuku. If he dangled Toda's testimony in front of the Criminal Investigation Unit, Section Four, they would gleefully set about crushing the Hongo gang.

Samejima decided to take a break and left the interrogation room.

Momoi was standing in the hall. He was a police inspector in his fifties, and everyone referred to him as "the cadaver." Momoi had lost his only son in a car accident fifteen years before. He himself had been at the wheel. Ever since then he had been like a walking corpse, lacking enthusiasm or interest in anything. In truth, the only reason Samejima was in the Crime Prevention Unit was that Momoi, his superior, had raised no objection to taking him on.

All of the other sections at the Shinjuku Precinct had refused to have anything to do with Samejima. The main reason was the fact that he "disrupted" teamwork within the force. Samejima was ranked as an inspector, the same rank as the chiefs of the seven main Shinjuku sections.

Momoi had dry, graying hair. He wore a brown suit. He always had one of two expressions on his face. Or rather, he was either expressionless or absorbed in depression. But Samejima knew that no matter how burned-out his boss looked, there was a true policeman somewhere deep inside. He had once risked life, limb and backlash from the police force by shooting a violent criminal to save Samejima's life.

"How goes it?"

Samejima saw that Momoi had just come out of the interrogation room next to Toda's.

"Did he sing for you?"

"Yes, he did. He told me that the Hongo leader had taken the thinner as collateral for a gambling debt."

"What do you plan to do?" asked Momoi.

"I'll let Section Four handle it."

Momoi almost grinned. "They'll take all the credit for it, you know."

"I don't mind. At least we'll have closed down the Juntoro route

28

at the Shinjuku west gate."

"How long did you stake them out?"

"Now and then for the past three weeks."

"Nice job." Momoi nodded slightly in recognition, and Samejima nodded back. It was all he ever required in the way of praise.

"How about the other guy?" Samejima asked.

"When the interpreter arrived he still didn't talk until we offered him a meal in exchange for his confession."

Samejima nodded. It wasn't uncommon for desperate people to talk for food.

"He's in tears now. The interpreter is a real nice guy, doing his best to comfort him."

"What happened?"

The two walked together into the Crime Prevention office. Momoi took off his jacket and hung it on the back of his chair.

"He and his brother came to Japan as migrant laborers. His brother is two years younger, probably nineteen. He's not sure of either of their ages. They both started working and sent their earnings home, but his brother started huffing thinner. There was a guy in the workers' barracks who taught him how to use it. His brother got totally addicted. It was so bad he refused to work anymore. One day Ali dragged him to work, but his brother slipped off the scaffolding and broke both his legs so badly they say he'll never walk again.

"He found out where his brother got the stuff. He figured out that if he waited in front of the lockers at Shinjuku Station, the dealer would come around stashing the bottles. He was waiting there to stab the dealer. He felt that both he and the dealer were responsible for ruining his brother's life. That's what he said."

Samejima nodded. Thinner and drugs. That sort of tragic story was all too common. Addicts are only focused on getting a fix. Inevitably someone close to them ends up getting hurt, or worse.

Parents killing their children to make them quit, or getting killed instead. An addled man beating up his own sister, a deranged user burning his own house down, in the worst cases torching the entire apartment building where he lived, burning innocent neighbors to death in their sleep. And yet, despite the havoc they wreaked, dealers never faced murder charges.

Both thinner and drugs were efficient sources of income for criminal organizations. It was very profitable, and they couldn't resist such easy money even if it came at the cost of countless numbers of lives.

There were more plainclothes detectives dedicated to crushing drug dealers than thinner dealers. Cases involving drugs—usually speed—would be written up in the paper. It looked good on your record if you nabbed a drug dealer. Thinner and toluene were usually left for uniformed officers to deal with. Thinner was seen as just a child's toy. Even so, there were inevitably more victims of thinner than of drugs.

It took a great deal of time and patience to first locate the dealer, then track down his supplier, usually someone selling the stuff wholesale.

Informants usually exposed the hard-drug smugglers and dealers. Most of these informants were criminals themselves, and had their own motivations for helping out the authorities. Perhaps they had money problems and were removing a competitor who had cheaper stuff on the market. If the police tried operating without these informants they would have to put in a lot more effort when tracking down smuggling routes.

The same was true for thinner. The cops all knew that as long as thinner and toluene were not classified as drugs, it was very difficult to track down and catch the wholesalers, which is why investigators put far more emphasis on hunting down drug dealers.

The big difference was that if someone was caught with drugs, they could be arrested on the spot. If they were caught with paint thinner, they couldn't be arrested since it wasn't technically an illegal substance.

Samejima refused to differentiate between drugs and thinner. He had no patience for gangs that put impressionable young men at risk by getting them to work as dealers. The big players in the gangs got the lion's share of the profits, using the money to buy expensive cars and dine in fancy clubs.

Indeed, Samejima was not known as the Shinjuku Shark because he was hard on younger yakuza out peddling their wares. He was known for his sharp fangs that hunted the fat cat gangsters who thought they were safe in their comfortable, cozy lives.

3

According with Samejima's wish, the Hongo gang investigation was handed over to Criminal Investigation, Section Four (Marubo). One morning at six-thirty, two days after the transfer paperwork was done, Samejima was standing in front of an apartment building in Okubo. He had come straight from his apartment in Nogata, not even stopping in at the precinct first.

There was no elevator in the building, just a staircase that went up the four flights. Most of the inhabitants in the area had late-night jobs in bars and clubs in Shinjuku. More than half of the residents in the building were Taiwanese and Korean.

Samejima climbed the stairs up to the third floor. The entire building was quiet. Most of the residents didn't get home until three or four in the morning. Six-thirty was the middle of the night for them.

Samejima headed towards the apartment at the end of the third floor. The steel door that had recently been painted, and the clean cream color contrasted oddly with the dingy hallway. The previous resident, a bartender, had vacated a couple of weeks ago, and the Shinjuku Precinct was renting it for a month.

Samejima opened the unlocked door without knocking, and was hit by the strong smell of cigarettes and male body odor. It was a tiny apartment with two small rooms, one of which served as a combination dining room/kitchen. There were four men huddled in the larger Japanese style living-room/bedroom. Two were from the

Crime Prevention Unit of Shinjuku and two were from Public Safety Section One.

In the entrance was a pile of plastic bags filled with empty convenience store meal boxes and drink cans. Two of the four men squinted when Samejima walked in, the light from outside spilling in behind him. He raised his right hand in a silent greeting.

Three of the men sat in a circle staring at a small television monitor. The cord extending from the monitor was linked to a VCR with a surveillance camera set in a narrow gap in the curtains on the window. Samejima didn't know the fourth man. He wore a dress shirt, and stood next to the tripod on which the camera was set.

Samejima carefully closed the door and joined the men. Saito, a member of the Crime Prevention Unit, stood up. At twenty-nine, he was one of the youngest officers in the unit.

"Shinjo is out sick. I'm here to replace you," said Samejima. Saito nodded and then stretched his stiff muscles. He was dressed in a gray sweat suit with a red stripe down the sides. His hair was short and permed. He could pass as a yakuza.

"Is the west gate business taken care of?"

"It is as far as we're concerned."

Samejima looked down to find Kawada, another officer from the Shinjuku Precinct, asleep on the job with his arms folded and legs crossed. Samejima nicked his knee with his fingernail. Kawada woke with a start.

"Samejima…"

"Shinjo's not coming. Time to switch out. You can go home now."

Kawada was thirty-five, not much younger than Samejima. He was deeply surprised to see Samejima in the room.

"Are you sure?"

"Yeah, go on."

Kawada's beard had grown in. It made a rough scratching noise when he rubbed the greasy stubble with both hands. He looked at the oil that had transferred from his face to his palms.

"Thanks," he said as he stood up.

Samejima turned to the other two in the room. He recognized Yoshida, a sergeant from Public Security Section One. A veteran in his mid-forties, his glasses and his fair complexion made him look more like a teacher than a policeman. The man standing by the tripod looked to be a little older than Samejima. He was tan, handsome and had a look of fearlessness. His hair was sun-bleached to a reddish-brown.

"Samejima from the Shinjuku Precinct. Here to take over the shift."

"Thanks," said Yoshida.

"I'm Araki," the tan man simply said before turning back to the window.

Samejima pulled off his thin jacket and sat down in front of the monitor. "What's going on?"

"They started at two a.m. with four men. There was a couple at three-forty, and two women and a man at five-twenty-four," Yoshida read from his notebook.

The monitor displayed a view of the second-floor walkway of the apartment building next door. There was a ceiling and a hand railing in the walkway, but no wall to block the view. The camera angle showed the faces and torsos of everyone who came and went. In the center of the screen was a door to one of the apartments, and everyone who entered or left the apartment was caught on camera.

"Mahjong?" asked Samejima. Saito and Kawada were busy getting ready to leave.

"Yeah. The day before yesterday the guy who delivered ramen to the place next door said he could hear the sounds of the tiles," Yoshida replied.

"Do you know how many tables they're running?"

"Two or three. Business is slow," said Araki.

Conditions had to be just right to use a surveillance camera to expose a gambling operation during business hours. There had to be viable spot where the camera could be set up without the customers noticing it.

Public Security Section One had told the Shinjuku Precinct about information they had of a gambling operation catering to Taiwanese. Section One requested the assistance of the Crime Prevention Unit of the Shinjuku Precinct. Crime Prevention found the apartment that was well suited for a surveillance operation, and collaborated with Section One to create a surveillance squad.

The squad leader from the Shinjuku Precinct was Assistant Inspector Shinjo, advisor to the chief of the Crime Prevention Unit. He was supposed to be on surveillance duty this morning, but Momoi received a call that he was ill, so he sent Samejima in his place.

The majority of mahjong gamblers arrived in the middle of the night and the small hours of the morning. That meant they could use fewer personnel to run surveillance during the day.

"We're heading out, then." Saito and Kawada had collected their things and headed towards the entrance.

"Good work."

"Thanks."

They quietly opened the door and slipped out. They'd go home to sleep or nap back at the office, and then would return at four in the afternoon.

"Is headquarters sending a replacement for you?" Samejima asked as he pulled a pack of cigarettes from his jacket pocket.

"I'm staying," answered Araki. Samejima looked at him.

"Araki was supposed to come this morning, but he came early late last night. 'Early late last night' sounds funny, doesn't it?" smiled Yoshida.

"Insomnia," mumbled Araki. "I have a hard time getting to sleep.

35

Probably because I drink too much."

Samejima nodded. There was something about this man that made him uneasy. "Does there seem to be a lot of money involved?" he asked.

"Two hundred thou or so a night," answered Yoshida. "Things aren't good here for Taiwan, either." By that, he meant Taiwanese who worked in Shinjuku.

Taiwanese people began coming to Japan in waves starting in the 1980s. Large numbers of Taiwanese girls suddenly came to work as barmaids and hostesses, and so-called Taiwan clubs and bars were thriving. There were more than two hundred such establishments in Shinjuku alone.

The majority of the clubs were not large, with usually just a *mama*—a female owner—with several hostesses working for her. Most of the club's profits were earned by getting the hostesses to work as prostitutes.

There were two main reasons for the recent decline in such establishments. One was the improvement of the Taiwanese economy and the other was the transfer of Tokyo government buildings to Shinjuku.

With the economy turned bullish in Taiwan, citizens could make a decent living without leaving the country. Also, the presence of bureaucrats and businessmen in Shinjuku increased the demand for larger, glitzier places to entertain clients. They shunned the small-scale Taiwan clubs for the newer Korean establishments that had recently cropped up. The Korean places were well appointed and spacious with over a dozen hostesses working in each club. They were very friendly towards the newly transplanted bureaucrats.

"They really love to gamble, don't they," Yoshida said.

"Taiwan has outlawed mahjong, so they all come here to play," Araki muttered. He had a careless way of speaking.

"But business has really been slow recently," Samejima said.

The Taiwanese certainly loved mahjong. There were over two hundred gambling halls in Shinjuku alone at the height of their popularity. The Taiwanese mafia ran most of those gambling places.

"There's been a drop in the number of yakuza crackdowns," Araki said. "From 1984 to '85, there was Operation Cleansweep, where the government cracked down on major crime syndicates. The gangsters, flushed from their holes, fled to Japan and set up shop in Shinjuku. They pimped Taiwanese prostitutes and earned a modest living running gambling joints. There were a few gangsters who made a pretty penny."

Samejima had heard of Operation Cleansweep.

The government ferociously hunted down gangs, and all the violent criminals ran to Japan and Hong Kong to hide. As illegal immigrants, they had no legal means to earn a living, so they leaned on prostitutes for money. Eventually they gathered a group of hostesses and set up gambling joints.

Yakuza—gangsters—were the same in any country. Once they knew there was money to be made, they were all over it like white on rice. During the boom in Taiwan clubs, there were more than two hundred Taiwanese yakuza in Shinjuku that leeched onto the establishments and collected "protection money" from them.

The Japanese and the Taiwanese yakuza had had the occasional quarrel, but it never escalated into major disputes.

This was due in part to the peculiarities of Shinjuku amusement quarters.

The Kabukicho district alone had at least two hundred Japanese yakuza offices, and there were twenty organizations that claimed certain areas as their own turf. So why was the appearance of foreign gangsters in this overcrowded area met with so little resistance?

It was because there were no demarcation lines for their turfs. When it came to protection money, the gangs collecting the fees could differ from one club to the next. Sometimes there were several establishments on the same floor of the same building, each paying fees to a different gang.

Accordingly, any time a new club set up shop, there was no organization that could automatically claim it as its own. It was first come first served. No gang would make demands of a club that was already paying protection to someone else. That would start a turf war, which would immediately draw the attention of the police. It was this sort of "local culture" that kept the Japanese yakuza from challenging the Taiwanese bars paying off the Taiwanese gangsters.

As Taiwanese bars began closing and the pool of gambling customers began to dry up, the Taiwanese gangsters also dwindled in number. There were some who stuck around, however, having found other ways to make money while the going was good.

During their time in Shinjuku, Taiwanese gangsters made the acquaintance of their yakuza counterparts. As with organized criminals in any country, they had an extremely strong sense of honor when it came to returning favors and, conversely, to staking claims on favors they were owed.

Once the Taiwanese gangsters repatriated, they felt obliged to invite their Japanese yakuza friends to their home turf, and entertained them lavishly in Taiwan. The Japanese, in turn, saw Taiwan's amusement districts as investment opportunities. Samejima knew that Japanese yakuza had provided funds for high-class clubs, restaurants and coffee shops in Taipei. Most of those operations were headquartered in Shinjuku. They installed puppet locals as titular heads of operations. They made tidy profits from their investments. The money was laundered through Chen Tsuan, an underground bank, before making its way back to Japan in the form of amphetamines and small arms.

In short, Taiwan had become the route of choice for smuggling drugs and guns into the country.

Samejima wondered why, at this late date, Public Security Section

One was so interested in Taiwanese gambling operations. It would make sense if they had a rat or an informant, since gambling was still illegal. But it seemed like overkill to set up such a lavish surveillance operation just for a small gambling joint. Samejima suspected that the brass that ordered the stakeout had something in mind other than cleaning up a few rounds of mahjong.

"Here comes someone," said Yoshida. Samejima turned his attention back to the monitor. The door to the apartment opened, and two women, apparently hostesses, appeared with a man.

"We saw them go in a while ago," breathed Araki.

One of the women looked to be in her early thirties, and the other one maybe twenty-one or twenty-two. The man was solidly built and wore a brown double-breasted jacket. His torso was long but his legs were short. He had a thick neck and the start of a potbelly.

Araki adjusted the camera to zoom in on them. The man turned to wait for the younger of the two women to catch up, and then turned back and looked straight into the camera.

"He's got a fat face," mumbled Yoshida. Samejima agreed that he didn't have normal features. His small, unusually sharp eyes were sunk deep into the sockets in his square face, and his jutting jaw gave him an obstinate look. "That one's a piece of work. You can bet he's knocked off a man or two."

Samejima had to agree with Yoshida. His piercing gaze was incredibly unusual. When he looked towards the camera, Samejima felt like he and the man were staring at each other.

This guy means business, he thought. He used those few moments to burn the image of the man into his brain. If he was a Taiwanese gangster based in Shinjuku, Samejima was bound to run into him again. The man looked as though he could see the surveillance camera. It was almost as if he was looking at Samejima through the camera. He flashed his white teeth for an instant.

Was he laughing? Samejima wondered, but in the next moment, the man closed his mouth and turned to the side. Standing between the two women, he put his arms around their shoulders and walked down the hallway.

Samejima asked Yoshida if they'd seen him before.

"No, it's the first time for me. What about you, Mr. Araki?"

Araki readjusted the zoom and then he looked back at the other two. He seemed to be on the verge of saying something, but only stated bluntly, "No, first time."

"So he's a new guy? Maybe he's here as a tourist. Some big shot from the Sihai gang, perhaps." Samejima noticed that Yoshida used deferential language with Araki. Once Yoshida got to know someone he didn't bother spending a lot of energy figuring out which level of speech to use. Samejima outranked him, but Yoshida never used polite speech with him. He wasn't arrogant, he was just friendly, and close quarters—like surveillance—tended to breed familiarity. Samejima doubted he spoke to his superiors at a Criminal Investigation Unit meeting with such a low level of speech.

So Araki had to be either a section chief at Public Security or a new face. Either way, he definitely outranked Yoshida.

"Sihai, Zhulian, Niupu. I hear gangsters have no problem joining up with two or three different syndicates," said Araki. Samejima recognized the names of the Taiwanese gangs.

"There might be a warrant out on him. Should we send the video to the International Investigation Unit?" asked Yoshida.

Araki pulled a package of Short Hope cigarettes out of his breast pocket, put one of them in his mouth, and answered, "That won't be necessary." Yoshida didn't have anything to say after that. Araki glanced at his watch. "Why don't you go home, Yoshida?"

"What? Is it that late already? They play mahjong for so long I lose track of the time." He smiled in Samejima's direction, and as Samejima nodded in return, he noticed a stiffness in his smile.

"Me and Samejima'll take care of it for now," said Araki.

"If you're sure..." Yoshida stood up to go. "I'll be back at headquarters napping, so let me know if you need me."

"Get some rest," said Samejima.

"See you this evening," added Araki, glancing up at Yoshida.

After he was gone, it was just the two of them left. Araki's eyes were devoid of enthusiasm as he sat and watched the monitor displaying the apartment door. Samejima picked up the notebook they'd been using. All of the details of the people who had been in and out were duly noted. Dates, times, numbers of people, their characteristics—it was all very specific.

Since they had started surveillance two weeks ago, Samejima counted a total of two hundred people that had visited the apartment. The largest numbers arrived between early Sunday morning and late Sunday night. About twenty of them appeared to be regulars. About half of those were assumed to be Taiwanese hostesses. No Japanese yakuza had been spotted.

"The Taiwanese gangsters hanging out in Shinjuku these days haven't got much going for them," said Araki.

According to the notebook, there were currently about ten people in the apartment, including the bookies, of which there were four. Samejima figured one was the gopher, sent out for cigarettes and food as needed. Two probably played with the customers. One did the accounting; there was usually one who didn't join the tables. This was all just Samejima's educated guess, and the actual situation could be very different.

"Any drugs involved?" asked Samejima.

Lots of gambling operations had uppers at the joint. They offered it to the customers to keep them alert. It was classic. The first dose or two was free. But when the customers began asking for it, it suddenly came with a price tag.

This was one way to recoup if a customer won big. When they had a real addict on their hands, they'd refuse to sell it at all. The customer would become irritated without a fix, lose his concentration, and often lose all his winnings from an entire night of gambling in a single sweep.

The drugs never came out until night wore on and the moon began to set. There would be trouble if the addict knew the goods were in the house and the host was just holding off from selling, so the bookies would tell him that they were just as anxious to get some, but it hadn't been delivered yet. The customer would gamble as he waited, and by the time he got his fix, he'd be up to his neck in debt.

"Who knows?" answered Araki. "They're a lot more careful these days."

Most Japanese gambling operations forbade drugs outright. The bookies didn't use or deal anything, and they discouraged their clientele from bringing drugs or shooting up on the premises.

One of the reasons was that a hallucinating customer could get disruptive and out of hand. Another was that if they ever got caught, gambling alone carried a much lighter sentence than gambling combined with drug use.

Most gambling operations were busted by customers turned informants. They'd go to the police after they'd racked up more debt than they were capable of paying back. This, of course, was a possibly lethal risk to take if the bookies were gang members, but either way, down-on-their-luck customers were on the verge of losing their shirts. Some, armed with an expensive life insurance policy, braced themselves and told the authorities everything they knew.

"Did you get a tip-off about this place?" asked Samejima. He wanted to know how Section One had found out this particular gambling operation.

Araki looked blankly at Samejima, then nodded vaguely. It was obvious that he didn't want to talk about it. He was not proving much fun to work with. Both men fell silent and time passed slowly.

Just before nine, a couple in their forties left the apartment. They argued loudly in Chinese. Samejima got the impression they were blaming each other for gambling losses incurred.

Their voices were loud enough to hear through the closed window. They continued arguing as they walked down the hall, stopping part way to go at it with even more energy. The man was short and stocky, and wore a flashy blazer over a polo shirt. He argued out of pouty lips while flinging his arms around. The woman wore a pink suit over her skinny frame, and clutched her handbag tightly to her breast. She was holding her own, occasionally thrusting her finger accusingly at the man as she shouted.

They must have lost a lot, thought Samejima. She was angry as hell, stamping her feet for emphasis.

"If you keep it up," Araki muttered indifferently, "someone's gonna call the cops."

As if in response to his warning, the door to the apartment flew open. Araki sidled to the camera just as a man in his thirties with an unhealthy complexion leaned out of the door. He wore a white open-necked shirt and shiny greenish gray slacks. His hair was oily, parted on the side and slicked securely in place.

He spoke a few words sharply to the arguing couple, both of whom shut up and turned a sulking glance towards the man. Still holding onto the doorknob, the man looked up and down the walkway.

"Whoops," said Araki as he pulled himself back from the window and hid behind the double curtains.

Samejima kept his eyes glued to the monitor. After a few moments the man, apparently satisfied that the coast was clear, went back inside and closed the door. The couple silently walked down the walkway.

"It's that idiot," Samejima muttered.

Araki shifted and glanced at Samejima. "Do you know him?"

"I've seen him in Kabukicho 2nd Street a few times. He's a manager at a late-night restaurant."

"I guess you deserve your reputation, shark man," said Araki, playing on Samejima's nickname, shark, from *same* in his last name.

Samejima looked at Araki. The edges of his lips were curled up in an ironic smile, and he heaved himself down onto the floor and crossed his legs.

"So, why didn't you quit the force?" Araki started speaking in a much more friendly tone. He pulled out his pack of cigarettes, and put one in his mouth.

Samejima was silent.

"Too personal, eh? Well, my record's nothing to be proud of either." Araki blew out a puff of smoke. Samejima glanced at him curiously.

"I was attached to an embassy. Something happened, I was sent back, and ever since I've been stuck at my current rank."

"You're a superintendent?"

"I'm on loan to Public Security Section One at the moment, but I started out in Investigative Assistance, and these days I'm with International Investigations."

Samejima nodded. They were both "career" cops who had passed the 1st class civil exams. That a detective of Araki's age was still only superintendent meant he'd skidded off the promotion track.

"You're an inspector, right?" Araki didn't wait for an answer. "I know all about what happened to you. None of it makes sense, not my story or yours. We both should have been promoted years ago. Everyone at HQ knows what you can do. It's just that no one wants to get too close to you."

"Is that what you hear?"

"What are you talking about? They're still trembling in their boots over at my unit. You've got Miyamoto's will, right?"

"Whose will?"

"Superintendent Miyamoto, late of Public Safety Section Two. I was in Thailand when it all came down, but I've heard the rumors."

"What sort of rumors?"

"What was it, some kind of infighting at Public Security? He took the fall and killed himself, and they say he wrote down every detail of what happened and who was involved—who drove him to suicide—and sent it to you, his friend in the force. You apparently had gotten into a tangle years earlier with a right-wing assistant inspector from the sticks who attacked you with a Japanese sword and got his head cracked open for his efforts."

Samejima couldn't help but smile. "I wouldn't be sitting here if someone had taken a sword to me. I didn't crack open anyone's skull, either."

"But you shocked them all. It's rare to see a career cop have the guts to get into a pissing contest with a local non-career yokel like that."

Samejima didn't answer.

"And the bad luck never ended. After that, you went back to HQ. All you had to do was keep your nose clean and you would have made superintendent. But, no, you had to rebel again and again. Then you got that letter from the dead guy. It could have been your lucky break."

"Lucky?"

"Sure. You could have used it as leverage. You could have traded it for a step up on the career ladder. Wasn't everyone hounding you for that letter? Seems there was some pretty serious stuff written in it."

"You don't say."

Araki laughed. "You're one stubborn son of a bitch. You were transferred out. Haven't moved up from inspector since you were twenty-five. A dead-end inspector. The brass must have expected you to get sick of the humiliation and quit. But even after you were transferred, you refused to fall into line. There's not a low-life in Shinjuku that wouldn't run for his life barefoot if he heard the

Shinjuku Shark was in the neighborhood."

"And everyone down at HQ believes that bullshit?"

"It's not bullshit." Araki stared at Samejima. Samejima stared back.

Araki was unusually rough and careless. Samejima couldn't be sure if he was born that way or if it was because his career was in the dumps and he simply didn't give a damn anymore.

The career system of the Japanese police was a symbol of its contradictory nature. Every career cop who excelled was very intelligent. But every barrel has a few rotten apples. No matter how blessed they were with intelligence, there were always some who fundamentally lacked the instincts necessary to be a good cop.

Right now, that was how Samejima was feeling about Araki. He and Araki had both lost their footing on the career ladder, but it was for entirely different reasons.

4

It was the third time Nami had seen the club manager beat one of the employees. The first time had been right after she started working there, her second or third day.

The manager was grinding the toe of his pointy shoe into Nan's back as he lay face down on the floor. Nan was the new bar back. He was from Bangladesh and it was his third day on the job at the Fountain of Roses, a Kabukicho club.

He had introduced himself to Nami and the others in halting Japanese, "Call me Nan pees!"

Nami and the others laughed. Nan didn't understand what was so funny.

"It's 'Nan, please,' not 'pees,'" said Kazuki, one of the older girls. Kazuki told customers that she was twenty-eight, but she was actually forty-one, and had two children.

Fountain of Roses was a cabaret club in the Kabukicho 1st Street district. The club had had a menu of set prices that varied depending on whether a customer came in at five, six, seven, or after eight in the evening. The set prices, however, were rarely followed and customers got taken for everything the management could get away with. However, customers rarely complained because Kazuki and the other girls provided them with specific services that were not on the menu.

Recently, because of complaints, anything not included in the set price had to be added as a separate order. For example, a simple order like jelly with a few chocolate sticks cost 5,000 yen. For this, customers had fifteen minutes with a girl and a few wet towels.

Nami had quit her job at Four Hearts in Ikebukuro and started at Fountain of Roses four months ago. She got paid less, but the hours were shorter. There was an early shift and a late shift. On early days she was on duty at four. For the late shift she could mosey in at five-thirty. The club closed at one a.m. At Four Hearts she was sometimes required to come in at eleven-thirty in the morning, and it was hard to be up and about by that time. She was often late.

Like Four Hearts, Fountain of Roses didn't require the girls to have actual sex with the customers, but it had still taken some getting used to. At first, she had gagged just wiping a guy's dick off with a wet towel. She'd learned to rinse her mouth out with disinfectant before each new customer. She was careful about cavities. Gonorrhea and syphilis-causing bacteria could fester in a cavity.

"I'm asking you if you understand, you stupid son of a bitch!" Now the manager was screeching. The four o'clock shift was having a review meeting to discuss manners and attitude, and sales records from the previous month. The manager was scolding Nan for the simple reason of answering too quietly.

Everyone hated Agi, the manager. He was fair-skinned and thin and usually showed only his sickly sweet side. But if something pissed him off, he flew off the handle and there was nothing anyone could do to cool him down.

"He's probably on speed," said An. She was second in seniority to Kazuki. Her last boyfriend had been an addict and she had had a rough time of it. "Once they get mad they completely lose it. It takes superhuman strength to control them," An laughed sadly.

There were thin white scars on her upper thighs. Her ex-boyfriend used to cut her with a razor. "If they cut you all over the place, they can't sew you up. Stitches pull the skin, you see. If they stitched up one side the other cuts pop open. It hurts like hell."

"On your knees, you motherfuckin' son of a bitch!" Agi kicked

Nan in the shoulder as he was trying to pull himself up. Blood dribbled from his nose and one corner of his mouth.

Nobody dared to step in on Nan's behalf. Agi was spiteful and vindictive. He'd hunt down anyone that tried to interrupt his "discipline sessions."

"Answer me!"

"Yes, sir." Nan's voice was small. His eyes were blank and staring, and he had a pitiful expression on his face.

"I can't fuckin' hear you!" Agi made a fist and punched Nan hard in the face. He had a gaudy gem-encrusted ring on his right hand, and they all heard a loud crack as it crunched against Nan's front teeth.

"Yes, sir!" Nan screamed through his swollen lips. He was crying. Dressed in the black pants and white shirt that comprised his uniform, he did his best to sit on his knees on the wooden floor. The club floor was stained with spilled beer and cheap cocktails, and customers' vomit.

"That's enough," someone said in a small voice. It was Kazuki. She, Nami, and Iku were on the early shift today. Iku was a new hire. She was a little slow. She stared expressionlessly at the wall, noisily chewing gum. When Nami ran into her in the locker room, she noticed that she reeked of paint thinner.

There was one other bar back, Yang. He never spoke unless spoken to. Either his Japanese was as poor as Nan's or he just never had anything to say. Nami was nervous around him. She had seen him being disciplined by Agi in the locker room once before.

It had been two weeks ago, right after he had started working there. Nami had been on her way in to get something, but stopped when she heard voices.

"I don't like that look on your face!" Agi had raged. "Can you understand me, fucker?"

"Sorry." Yang just kept apologizing. He was tall for a Chinese and solidly built. Nami didn't know if he was from Taiwan or the mainland, but he was far larger than Agi.

"What were you doing in here, you worthless scum? I told you to sweep the front of the club!" Agi grabbed both of Yang's cheeks and pulled his face towards his own.

"Sorry."

"I'm not askin' for a goddamn apology! I'm askin' what were you doing in here?"

Yang didn't fight back, but didn't speak, either.

"Answer me, you fuck!"

Agi shook his face. Yang's dry hair had grown out. Nami saw a look of agony on his face. Then he muttered something in Mandarin.

"Don't give me that Chinese shit. Speak Japanese!" Agi yelled.

Yang continued on in Mandarin. Agi slapped his face. It was then that Nami got close enough to see that Agi was naked from the waist up. He didn't have an ounce of meat on his bones, and his skin was unnaturally white.

"He's saying he's got a stomachache," Nami spoke without thinking and then immediately regretted it. Agi stopped with his hand in midair and looked in amazement at her.

"What did you say?"

"He's…got a stomachache." Nami's voice dropped to a whisper, and she silently cursed herself. *Stupid, stupid, stupid…*

"So you were taking a little rest because of a tummy ache?" Agi looked at Yang again.

"Sorry." It was all he could say. Agi finally seemed to notice that Yang had gone ashen and was sweating profusely. He was gripping the right side of his abdomen with his left hand.

Agi turned back to Nami. "Sweetheart," he began in a voice that made her skin creep. She knew that he wanted her. He'd been after her ever since she started working there.

The night she'd been hired, he'd taken her out for a dinner of *yakiniku* and almost succeeded in dragging her to a hotel. She told him she was on her period and managed to escape. He had telegraphed his intentions from the very start. The whole time they were eating, he'd taken every opportunity to touch her shoulders, her knees.

She'd often thought it would have been easier for her if she'd slept with him and gotten it over with, but now she was glad she hadn't. She never would have been able to blow him off.

"So, you understand Chinese. That's *so* cool," Agi said in a slithering way.

Nami tried to be nonchalant. "No, he said it in Japanese."

"What?" Agi screwed up his face in what he obviously hoped was a menacing look, and peered into Yang's eyes. "Did you just speak in Japanese?"

Yang looked fleetingly at Nami. His eyes pleaded. "Yes."

"You're lying."

"No, he's not, sir," Nami said, covering for him.

"Oh well, who cares. If your stomach hurts, take something for it. Medicine, got it? No one's going to take care of you."

"Sorry," Yang said again.

"Sweep up in front!" Agi pulled a small bag from a locker and, still half naked, hurried into the toilet.

Yang stood up, still holding his stomach, and slipped past Nami.

"*Xie xie*," he whispered. Nami pretended not to hear.

Agi was looking at Kazuki.

"I know he's new here, Miss Kazuki, but our reputation will go down the toilet unless we teach him how to do things right."

"But the poor thing can't even speak Japanese yet," Kazuki said, exasperated.

"That's what I'm saying. He's got to learn now. He'll thank me for it later."

"There are other ways to learn," Kazuki muttered, unsure whether to keep on.

"What are you mumbling?" Agi prodded until Kazuki finally turned to him defiantly.

"Since when is kicking and punching called teaching? He'll scare off the customers with that bloody, swollen face!" Kazuki said loudly.

"Look who's talking, Kazuki dear. You'd better think of your own problems before you mouth off. The only reason you can pass yourself off as a girl under thirty is 'cause it's so dark in here. Obviously our customers don't care that much about appearance."

Agi had hit Kazuki where it hurt.

After hearing Kazuki speak, Nami couldn't stay silent. "What if he goes to the police? Wouldn't you be in trouble then, boss?"

Agi's eyes flew to Nami. She tried not to blink.

"The police? Now why would someone whose visa expired months ago want to do that? He came on a tourist visa, not working papers. He's the one who'll be in trouble if the police get involved. He can't complain. He wants a job, but who would hire him? We're doing him a favor by letting him work here. He wants to work so he can send money home, but couldn't get a job anywhere. The owner felt sorry for him and scooped him up. You owe us, don't you, sweet little Nan?"

Nan's dark eyes flitted around the room. He had no idea what was being said to him. But what Agi had said was true—he was terrified of losing his job.

"You're picking on him because he can't fight back," Nami said. Her tone changed whenever she had something she felt was important to say.

"Can't fight back?" Agi leered at her, then his expression suddenly changed. "Say that again, bitch!"

Nami heard something behind her. It was Iku. She stared at the ceiling and let out a sigh. Agi thrust his face close to Nami's. His breath stank. "Even if you're a girl, you better watch what you say. You think I'm just a bully?"

Now Nami closed her eyes and waited for Agi to punch her in the face.

"Come right in!" Someone greeted a customer in an extra loud voice in stilted Japanese. It was Yang. Nami opened her eyes.

"Welcome!" Kazuki called out.

Two young men who looked like they had come straight from a construction site walked through the door. They hesitated nervously for a second after seeing Nan prostrate on the floor.

"Hey, boss? Turn down the lights so they won't see my wrinkles!" Kazuki's voice was now positively gay. Agi had the lights on full for the meeting.

Agi stopped mid-rant, took a deep breath and turned around towards the customers.

"Come right in and get comfortable," he smiled and clapped his hands and walked towards the customers. "Today's early girls are lookin' good and ready to make you happy. That will be six thousand yen for the both of you. Come in, come in!"

Yang brushed past with a tray of beers. He wore a headband printed with "Fountain of Roses." Nan turned down the lights. Compared to earlier, the club seemed pitch dark. After he had set the table, Yang slipped back past Nan, who smiled at him, showing a mouthful of white teeth that shone even in the dim light. Yang, however, was expressionless, and Nan let his smile fade away.

"Camin, git confatabo," Nan called out, mimicking Agi's greeting.

Iku crossed in front of Nami on her way to the customer's table. "This is bullshit," she murmured. Nami heard her, but her next words were drowned out by the piped-in rock music blasting at full volume.

5

Sho, fifteen minutes late for their date, was in a terrible mood. She and Samejima were in a coffee shop on the second floor of a building on the west side of Shinjuku. It was close to the precinct, but no one on the force ever went there. The clientele tended to be designers and editors who worked in the area. They were mostly bespectacled older types who renounced neckties. They carried messenger bags and chain-smoked cigarettes.

Sho was dressed in a t-shirt, ripped jeans and a cropped black canvas jacket. She held a bag with the logo of a record company on it. Samejima closed the book he'd been reading as Sho plopped down in the seat across from him. She reached for his glass of water, drank it down, and began noisily crunching the ice cubes.

Sho was just a month away from her twenty-third birthday. She had recently cut her long hair short and removed the colored streaks, and she'd told Samejima she planned to cut it even shorter for the photo shoot of her band's debut album. The short hairstyle made her small features look almost boyish. However, a glance at her t-shirt left no doubts as to her sex. She performed without a bra, letting her ample bosom bounce about freely. Samejima had somewhat unglamorously taken to calling her "rocket tits."

"What's the problem?" asked Samejima as he put the book in the bag. He kept his handcuffs and special nightstick in there, and it was much heavier than it looked. Samejima had arrived at the coffee shop after Saito had relieved him of his surveillance shift at the apartment in Okubo and via a visit to the precinct.

"It's that bastard director," Sho said, glaring at Samejima. When she was angry her eyes glowed like she was a werecat who'd zeroed in on its prey. But the instant she smiled, she had the glow of an innocent schoolgirl. Samejima loved seeing that instantaneous shift.

Sho was frazzled from the busy schedule of recording sessions and meetings leading up to the release of her professional debut album. She was the vocalist for a rock band called Who's Honey. Samejima had met Sho a year and a half ago. Who's Honey was still an indie act then.

"So you got a lecture from him?"

"He's like, 'No drugs, no weed, no coke, no liquor, and stay away from Shinjuku.' Who does he think he's talking to, the little punk!" Sho let it all out and ordered soda water from the waitress who arrived.

Samejima suppressed a laugh. "Little punk?"

Sho glared at him. "Well, he is! He was a band geek in friggin' college. Now the idiot's walking around trying to act cool in his flashy designer clothes."

"I hear they go for that type in Roppongi."

"He says, 'I have to say!' Can you believe it? 'I have to say, my dear Sho, I just don't think you should. This is an important time for us!'" She stuck out her lips as she attempted to mimic the director. "I was ready to ram my coffee cup down his fuckin' throat. But Shu was glaring at me, so I stopped myself."

Shu was the guitarist of Who's Honey. There were four band members aside from Sho—a drummer, a guitarist, a bass player, and one guy on keyboards. It was a simple set-up. They'd all known her much longer than Samejima had, and they all knew she could get out of hand if her temper got the better of her.

"He's just trying to tell you how much he values your music."

"You mean he's trying to prove he's some kinda big shot."

Samejima looked at her. She lost her temper over anyone who walked around acting as though they owned the place. Other than that, she tended to be extraordinarily patient.

"So, why not get the rest of it off your chest, and then we'll get something to eat."

That sent her into a pout. He'd gotten the better of her.

"Forget it," she said.

"What?"

"It's no use talking to you. Ah, you'd think a *cop* would lend an ear to the sorrows of youth!"

"Keep your voice down." Samejima was flustered now, and that seemed to satisfy Sho.

"Feed me," she demanded with a smirk.

Samejima smiled back and they both stood up to go. It had been ten days since they'd last seen each other. That time they'd only had dinner before Samejima had to get back to his stakeout of the Juntoro operation.

This evening they went to an Italian restaurant in a mixed-use building near the west entrance of the Shinjuku station. Sho had an olive and pepperoni pizza, and Samejima got one with anchovies. They also ordered basilico spaghetti, a salad and beers.

Sho had wolfed down her pizza and half of the spaghetti, and was reaching out for a slice of Samejima's pizza.

"So what about tomorrow?" he asked.

"Hang on." She stopped a passing waiter and asked for another mug of draft beer. "I've got another meeting at one."

"You spend more time in those meetings than you do at the studio."

"Who the hell knows why? They say they're working hard to sell our records, but you know they don't really care about our opinions."

"You could always go with some other record company. They're not the only label out there."

Sho drank her beer down in a single, long gulp, and answered.

"Sure, but we don't need to act like spoiled brats. There are lots who do, ya know? There's a time and a place for complaints."

"But it sounds like that director might be taking advantage of you."

"Not really."

"What do you mean?"

Sho twirled some more spaghetti on her fork and shoved it in her mouth. "This is yummy."

"Have it all."

"No, I promised this time. Halvsies."

"All right then. What do you mean 'not really'?"

"It doesn't matter. I don't care what anyone thinks. The important thing is to make sure the people who want to hear our music have the chance to buy our albums. I don't care how the record company handles the details. He's gonna find out how wrong he is if he thinks I'm just another low-grade garage band vocalist. And when *that* happens, I don't care what the hell he has to say to me."

"What about the rest of the band? Do they agree?"

Sho nodded. "Shu said I had the lowest boiling point of all of them, so if I could put up with it, they could, too."

Samejima laughed.

"Be nice," Sho said and put down her mug. She picked up Samejima's and poured half of his beer into her mug. "Hey!" she said, "there's nothing but foam left!"

"Drink the foam then."

As soon as they left the Italian restaurant, Sho put an end to the discussion.

"That's enough about the recording. Let's hit Kabukicho."

"I won't save you if you get into trouble."

"Who's gonna make a play for the Shinjuku Shark's woman?"

The two got onto the elevator and rode down to street level.

"You're a woman?" asked Samejima. Sho kicked him in the butt with her knee. A businessman and a secretary who were riding in the elevator stared in amazement.

Kabukicho was bustling as always. A new school semester had started, so groups of students milled about. Small clusters of students gathered in the vicinity of the Koma Theater. There was shouting and singing, the sound of electronic music from the game arcades, and the occasional verbal explosion from a drunk.

It wasn't the sort of atmosphere most people felt comfortable in, but Sho was different. She'd even peer with interest at a clique of yakuza swaggering down the street.

"Man," she commented, "they're everywhere."

A group of five yakuza with a bald giant of a man in the middle took up the entire street as they walked. Sho watched them walk past the Toa Hall in the direction of the Seibu Shinjuku Station. "Just judging by the ones walking around, there must be more per square foot here than anywhere else in Japan."

"Anywhere else in the world, probably." Samejima stopped to let a group of students, linked arm in arm, walk by. They gave off an odor of liquor, sweat and dirt from a sports ground. They were loudly singing what sounded like a school song.

"And the temperature is always higher here than anywhere else," continued Sho as she bounced along.

She was probably right, thought Samejima. It had to be at least ten percent warmer than the rest of the city. He looked at his watch. It was just past eight. It was bound to get warmer as the night wore on.

"One of the photographers we met with this week said he didn't mind shooting in Roppongi, but he hated shooting in Shinjuku."

58

"Did he have a run-in with a yakuza?"

"No, that's not it. In Roppongi no one pays attention to a flash going off, but here people assume it's a famous person and a crowd forms almost instantly."

"So, people in Roppongi pretend not to care?"

"Right. Famous people don't hang out here because all of the hicks stand and stare."

"Then before long you won't be able to come hang out here."

"Uh-uh!" she objected. "This is where I first hung out and first learned to sing. This is where I'll be."

Samejima laughed uncertainly. He was more than a little concerned about what would happen after she went pro. He worried that they would grow apart. Not that he'd dare mention his concerns and risk her anger. Sho never doubted her own feelings, but Samejima was too old to turn a blind eye to her prospects. A detective with a rock singer. Such a pairing was a miracle in itself. It was the type of affair that could only happen in Shinjuku. Sho was perhaps aware of that, which explained why she wanted to stay here.

"Shinjuku is all I know," she said, wrapping her left arm through Samejima's right. "I don't want to learn about anywhere else."

They passed a gay bar on Kuyakusho Avenue, and then stopped in at a tiny bar, Exhibition, where Sho used to work. It was in a mixed-use building. Like many bars in the area, the only seats were along the counter. Both the walls and the bar countertop were finished with black lacquer. There was a record player at one end, and a rack at the back of the shop that held more than 5000 LPs. Most were rock music from the sixties and seventies.

The bar manager, Taku, had long hair and a long face. He was in a wheelchair. He ran the bar with his sister. The place looked like it would be better suited for the Golden City, which had many similarly tiny bars. Sho had told Samejima that Taku's father owned the entire building.

It was in the elevator of this particular building that Samejima had seen the man who had exited the mahjong joint in Okubo earlier that day. Samejima knew that the owner of the building was Taiwanese, and that most of the tenants were Taiwanese as well, but he didn't tell Sho.

"Well, if it isn't our Sho and Mr. Samejima!" Taku greeted them at the entrance to the bar. "Come on in!"

"Ah, welcome!" said Taku's sister, Emi, as she placed a record on the player. Taku and Emi were both fair with slender faces. They could pass as twins. Taku was in his early thirties and Emi was twenty-seven or eight. They both doted on Sho.

"Yo!" Sho greeted her friends and sat down at the counter. There were two men sitting at the center of the bar. They were dressed smartly but casually, and looked like they might work for some newspaper.

"Good evening," Samejima was more formal. A slow tempo song that fused country and rock came out of the speakers on the wall. Samejima wasn't familiar with the song.

"How are you?" Taku wheeled up opposite Sho and smiled.

"Bored to tears," Sho pouted.

Emi laughed as she got out the bottle of White Label with "Who's Honey" scribbled on it, a bottle of mineral water, and an ice bucket. Taku scooped out a small bowl of nuts from a large can and put it out on the counter. The back of the bar was fitted with a high floor so that Taku could work comfortably behind it.

"Look who's complaining. You're the one who wanted to go pro," said Emi as she fixed their drinks.

"That's what it's like when you do what you want for a living," Taku smiled gently. His hair was parted in the middle and held back by a hair band. It fell just below his shoulders.

Samejima's hair was not quite as long. The back came just over his collar, and Sho had been pushing him to let it grow long enough for a ponytail. The style wouldn't particularly bother him, but would compromise his anonymity on stakeouts. A man with a ponytail was something people were bound to remember.

"I just want to stand on stage and sing. I don't care whether I'm a pro or an amateur," said Sho. "I'm just tired of being cooped up in a goldfish bowl."

"Sho, you should have been a rock singer in the US in the 70s. Don't you think so, Mr. Samejima?" smiled Taku.

"She would have turned into an alcoholic or a druggie," Samejima laughed.

"It wouldn't be so bad to die with Jack Daniels," Emi joined in, her eyes shining. On the wall behind her was a life-size poster of Janis Joplin.

"That means he'd be a hard-ass WASP cop who'd beat me with his nightstick," Sho nodded towards Samejima.

"And you'd stop taking baths, and spend your days indulging in 'free love' and drugs."

"What's that about?" Sho elbowed him.

"That's what I thought rockers were like. I believed that all the way to high school."

Taku smiled in agreement. "Those were the days. We'd skip school to go see 'Woodstock.'"

Samejima nodded. Sho sighed loudly. "Old rockers are bigger slobs than just regular old guys."

"There was a song that went something like that." Samejima tried hard to remember. "Something about some young singer."

"That's what I mean," Sho said rolling her eyes.

"Say, the other day I saw the manager of the restaurant that's upstairs," Samejima mentioned casually.

"You must mean Mr. Go. He hasn't been around much lately," said Emi.

"What's the name of that place?"

"Three Castles. It's a late-night restaurant."

"Has it been around long?"

"Not really. It's only been about four years since Go came to Japan."

"Hey Taku, I want to hear 'Tarkus,'" Sho broke in, and Taku nodded.

"You make fun of old guys who like rock, but you seem to like the rock those old guys listen to," he said.

"It's nice and rough. The music these days is more hard-core, but the sound is colder. In the old days it was more crude, but there was more passion."

"You're a riot!" Taku laughed, winking at Samejima.

"Just don't let him say," Sho said indicating Samejima with her elbow, "that the first time he heard this one was long before I was born."

"You talking about me?" Samejima groaned.

"Exactly. I'm tired of you lording your age over me. Go do that in some sad little jazz bar."

"He's not lecturing you, he's just…reminiscing," suggested Taku, but Sho shook her head.

"No way! I don't want to hear about his life before I was a part of it."

"You're impossible, Sho," said Emi, who was at the other end of the bar with another customer. "You two don't have a clue, do you?"

"What?" Samejima and Taku chimed in together, and Emi and Sho burst out laughing.

"Don't say it, Emi!" cried Sho.

"Why not, hmm?"

"No, no!"

Emi shook her head gently, and smiled as she went and stood in front of Samejima. Since the area behind the counter was raised, he

62

had to look up to address her. Emi didn't wear much make-up, just a dab of rouge on her fair skin. The line from her throat to her jaw was beautiful. Her prominent forehead and wide eyes gave her an air of intelligence.

Sho had told Samejima that Emi had long ago made up her mind to spend the rest of her life with her brother.

Taku had damaged his spine in a motorcycle accident in his twenties. He was the drummer in their amateur band, and Emi was the vocalist. One night, Emi had been visiting a friend in Yokohama. When it had gotten late and she still wasn't home, Taku had begun to worry and gone to pick her up. That was when he'd been in the accident. It turned out that Emi hadn't been with a friend but meeting with the member of a professional band, alone. Plus, they hadn't been in Yokohama, but in a hotel room in the middle of Tokyo.

Taku and Emi had been born and raised in Japan. Their hard-working father hadn't been enthusiastic about them running a bar. In fact, neither of them needed Exhibition to support themselves. Samejima knew their father had an enormous fortune.

He was also sure that there were lots of customers who were interested in Emi. They would never have any luck as long as her ties to her family were so strong.

"You're not going to talk, are you, Emi?" Sho had begun to pout.

"Not if you don't want me to." Emi's eyes sparkled as she looked at Sho.

Samejima looked at the two of them. One was an adult and the other still a girl. Most men would be drawn to the adult, but he was hooked on the child-woman.

"I'm going to the restroom," Sho said resignedly and got off her stool. Taku smiled and shook his head. Samejima watched her go. Emi, both elbows resting on the bar, watched him closely. Her clear gaze was electrifying. It would make any man hope that she was interested in him.

"The reason Sho doesn't want to hear about your past," she began, and Samejima waited for her to continue. All of a sudden, the door to the restroom banged open and Sho flew out.

"Stop! Emi! I don't want you to tell him!"

Emi's checks puffed out in disappointment. Samejima looked back at Sho who was standing brazenly in front of the restroom door. Her face was flushed with child-like humiliation.

"She's impossible," said Taku. Everyone, including the other customers who had been listening in, burst into laughter.

6

"Late-night restaurant" is a term that was first coined years ago. The establishments are similar to the "supper clubs" that existed in Shinjuku and Roppongi since the sixties, the sort of place frequented by hostesses from, for example, clubs in Ginza that closed at midnight. They'd go by themselves or take their customers along, to have dinner or continue drinking. Nowadays they all have karaoke, but there used to be live bands, or a piano or guitar player who would play while telling stories.

The late-night restaurants run by Taiwanese in Kabukicho were a little bit different. While their more traditional counterparts opened at eight or nine in the evening and closed at four or five in the morning, the Taiwanese operations opened at midnight or even one a.m. and closed at nine or so in the morning.

One explanation for this was the clientele, most of whom were hostesses just getting off work at the Taiwanese clubs. They went to their local late-night restaurants to eat and relax after work. Once in a while their Japanese clients accompanied them, but that was rarely the case. And since the restaurants served hostesses, there were usually "hosts" on hand who poured the drinks and sang karaoke with them.

The food they served was made the way the Taiwanese liked it, home-style Taiwanese cuisine. It was unlike the preparations found in regular restaurants that catered to Japanese customers.

There was always karaoke. There were laser-disc sets that kept up a continuous flow, mostly of popular Taiwanese songs. Some of them had subtitles that came up in both Mandarin and Cantonese, since the songs were popular both in Hong Kong and Taiwan. All the karaoke videos were filmed in Taiwan using local actors and locations. Once in a while you'd even hear a folk song or a children's lullaby.

When an especially well-loved folk song was played, both the customers and the employees joined in until the entire place was one enormous chorus. Almost no Japanese was heard in those restaurants.

During the peak years of the Taiwanese clubs, this sort of restaurant popped up all over Shinjuku and they all flourished. Indeed, these were places for the Taiwanese only. They gathered to speak their native language, get the latest news from home and catch up on the latest gossip. It was also where newcomers got advice about how best to get by in a country that was still foreign to them. The late-night restaurants also caught the attention of the Taiwanese yakuza, who would gather there to trade information.

While Shinjuku's Taiwan clubs gave Japanese customers a taste of another country, the late-night restaurants catered specifically to Taiwanese customers. There were so many Taiwanese living in the area that the restaurants had no problem staying in business. At the Taiwan clubs, one would rarely see any Taiwanese men aside from the bartender or the waiter. And since those clubs were so small, there were usually just one or two waiters. However, the late-night restaurants were filled with Taiwanese men. The customers ranged from long-term residents who had put down roots years ago to tourists visiting Tokyo for the first time.

The types of customers varied from one restaurant to the next. Some places attracted upstanding, decent people while others became the haunts of flashy, arrogant Taiwanese gang members who liked to cause a ruckus.

As the Taiwanese hostesses began returning to their homeland and Taiwan clubs declined in popularity many of these late-night restaurants began closing. The restaurants that remained were still popular with the Taiwanese gangsters. One could occasionally catch sight of something exceptional—a group of Japanese regulars. Those regulars were Japanese yakuza who came to talk shop with their Taiwanese counterparts.

Sho and Samejima didn't leave Exhibition until about two a.m., just about the time Three Castles was starting to get busy. If a Japanese owner ran it, it would be possible for a plainclothes cop to walk in, pretending to be a customer. In a place like Three Castles, where everyone was from Taiwan, however, a Japanese walking in by himself would draw unwanted attention.

He probably wouldn't even be let in the door. The only way to do it would be to frequent a Taiwanese club and, after getting close to a hostess, asking to be taken along. Even then, if she figured out he was a cop, she could alert the restaurant staff in Chinese. He could always just walk in and flash his badge and start asking questions, but they could still avoid questioning by pretending they didn't understand Japanese.

Samejima had no intention of checking out Three Castles. He knew that Go, the manager, was involved in running the gambling operation. Any wrong moves right now would give the undercover investigation away. If Go knew he was being watched, he would immediately shut down the gambling joint. No matter how much videotape they had, they still needed hard evidence that gambling was going on.

As for customers, it was almost impossible to get the name and address of anyone not actually caught in the act. If they were lucky, the operation might have a customer list, but if not, they'd never be able to find out the regulars who weren't around when the police raided the place.

Samejima was not technically involved in the Okubo surveillance. He had only gone to help out earlier that day as a substitute. Even so, he would help out with the raid if they needed a hand. However, Araki of HQ and Shinjo of the Shinjuku Precinct's Crime Prevention Unit were handling the case.

Samejima couldn't help but feel intrigued by the whole thing. It was the guy he saw on the monitor that morning. Not Go, but the one who had come out of the gambling place with the two women. He wasn't your run-of-the-mill two-bit gambler. Samejima wasn't the only one who thought he was different from the others. Yoshida, the Public Security veteran, said the same thing, and he had obviously impressed Araki. It would be a rare case if all of their instincts turned out to be incorrect.

If that man had come all the way from Taiwan, he must be there for a purpose. So why had Araki said there was no need to contact the International Investigation Unit for an ID, the very unit that had sent him out to do the surveillance?

The more he thought about it, the stranger it all seemed. Araki had kept his mouth shut until Yoshida had left and the two of them were alone, and then his only topic of conversation had been about Samejima's past. Samejima had a feeling that Araki knew the man. Araki probably sensed his suspicion and chatted about Samejima's past to keep him off the subject. Not only that, but it made no sense otherwise that the International Investigation Unit would be sending one of its own to the local Crime Prevention Unit.

It all came back to Samejima's first question: why, at this late date, was Public Safety going to such great efforts to crush a small-time Taiwanese gambling operation?

Samejima was sure all of this was connected to that one mystery man. Araki and his insomnia—he must have had a premonition that the man would show up.

"No open cabs," moaned Sho. They were in front of the Furin Hall in Kabukicho. There was a line of taxis waiting for customers, but they all had their "reserved" lamps on.

"Let's try a larger street." Samejima turned onto Kuyakusho Avenue, headed for Yasukuni Boulevard. The groups of students and even couples had disappeared. The only people on the streets were women in shiny suits or kimono hurrying home from their jobs at bars, businessmen in suits and ties, and suspicious-looking men in street wear.

"My place?" asked Sho. She lived alone in a rented apartment in Shimo-Kitazawa. Samejima had his own apartment in Nogata in Nakano Ward. When they stayed at her place, Samejima usually went home in the early hours. When Sho visited him, she stayed all night. Samejima visited Sho's place much more often.

"Either is fine," said Samejima and then stopped cold. Sho looked up into his face. He was staring at the first floor of a building diagonally in front of them on the other side of the street. There was a small Taiwanese restaurant there, and a man had just burst through the door.

It was the man from the Okubo mahjong joint. He was wearing a suit of shiny silver-gray material. Samejima recalled his solid build, short legs, and thick neck. The man gripped his belt and pulled his pants up as he looked around. Samejima further confirmed his short hair, deep-set eyes and forceful jaw. It was him. He had appeared just as Samejima had been thinking about him. He was alone. He looked around again, and he began to walk towards Yasukuni Boulevard.

"What is it?" Sho asked in a low voice. She guessed from his expression that it had to do with work.

"Come with me for a bit," said Samejima. He put his arm around Sho's shoulders. She seemed to understand that playing the couple-in-love was part of his camouflage. Only slightly alarmed, she placed her left hand over his right which rested on her shoulders. The two of

69

them crossed the Kuyakusho Avenue, and partway across, they saw another man come out of the Taiwanese restaurant.

He was younger and wore a purple double-breasted suit. He was thin, with prominent cheekbones. He closed the door behind him and looked around. He seemed distracted. Samejima could feel the man's eyes on them, so he began to walk more slowly. He watched as the young man located the mystery man in the silver-gray suit.

The young man's mouth was moving—he was muttering to himself. He used his left hand to hold something in place in the front of his suit jacket and began to walk. His eyes were glued to the back of the older man.

Samejima drew his chin in. Something was about to happen. He wanted to leave Sho behind, but there wasn't time to explain what was happening. They had to follow. The heavy-set man they'd seen at the Okubo gambling operation stopped and looked around as if trying to remember where he wanted to go. He was at the entrance to an alley that connected to Golden City, the "better" part of Shinjuku. There was a game arcade on the left, but it was closed.

The man seemed to have made a decision. He turned left down the alley. The young man followed him, and Samejima trailed them both, one arm still around Sho.

When the Tokyo government offices moved to this part of town, the rent skyrocketed, and a third of the little drinking places along the roads of Golden City had gone out of business. There were fewer customers compared to the heyday. Very few places seemed to be doing well.

The man went past dozens of tiny bars lining the narrow streets of Hanazono Quarter, Golden City. If he kept going, he'd run into the Hanazono Shrine, with the local police station just before.

The young man had begun to catch up to the mystery man in the narrow alleys of Golden City. There were only ten yards between the two. Sho was silent; she seemed to understand what Samejima was

70

doing. Neither man turned around once. The young man especially was so agitated that all of his attention was on the back of the man ahead of him.

The young man slid his right hand into the front of his jacket. Samejima let go of Sho's shoulder and gripped the fastener of the bag he carried in his left hand.

Just then, the door of a bar to the left of the young man opened. Two men in suits, probably businessmen, walked out with their arms around each other's shoulders. They were trying to hold each other up.

"Are you going to be all right?" a woman wearing an apron called from the entrance.

The young man pulled his hand out of his jacket. Samejima watched him opening and closing his fist.

"We'll be arright, ma'am," one of the businessmen slurred.

"Really? Well, the next time you come, don't let it be empty-handed!"

"Yesh, what? Oh." One of the men stopped when he saw Sho.

"C'mon, let's go!" The other one dragged him on.

"Mmm! Where do *you* work, miss?"

"Idiot! 'Scuse me," he apologized to Samejima as his partner stared into Sho's face. The young man in the purple suit glanced back. He didn't seem concerned, though, and continued onward.

The woman in the apron closed the plywood door of the bar. The man in the silver-gray suit had gotten as far as the road in front of the Hanazono Shrine. The police station was directly on his right.

The young man hurried to catch up. Samejima watched the two drunken buddies shuffle off and then whispered to Sho to wait for him in the bar. Sho looked at him silently. He could tell with a glance when the woman came out that there were no other customers inside. That's how small all the bars around there were—you could see the entire place from the front door. From the look of the two drunken friends that came out, Samejima could tell it wasn't the type of bar that overcharged the customers till they went bankrupt.

Sho pouted slightly. "Don't forget to come back for me," she said as she nodded her assent.

"Don't worry," Samejima replied.

Just as he was about to walk off, she grabbed his arm. "Be careful. That guy in the loud suit is carrying something."

Samejima had to admire her powers of observation. He clicked his tongue. "It's fine, I'll yell for a cop if anything bad happens."

"Asshole," Sho said as she turned her back on him and went inside.

Samejima heard the woman in the apron greet Sho as she entered. He glanced at the entrance so he'd remember the name of the place. The sign said "Honeysuckle."

As soon as Sho closed the door, Samejima hurried off. He could see the back of the man in the purple suit at the end of the alley. Samejima followed and saw the man climb the exposed stairs in front of a building. It was right on the edge of the shrine grounds.

The shrine office had closed hours ago. The stairway was dark, and there were so many trees that it seemed even darker. This was a short cut from Kabukicho to Shinjuku 5th Street, but there were always molesters and pickpockets in the area. Punks often gathered to get high on thinner or toluene.

Samejima ran up the stairs. As he approached a large, dark landing he figured the young man would be there to try to attack him. He opened his bag. He could have stopped at the police box to call for backup, but he was afraid of losing too much time. He pulled out his special metal nightstick, and extended it to full length with a flick of his wrist. He'd be out of luck if the young man had a gun, because Samejima was unarmed.

The man entered the grounds of the shrine. Samejima hurried along the path that encircled the shrine.

Samejima heard a scream. He began to run. The young man was standing defiantly on the path that led to the front of the shrine. He was gripping something in his right hand that shone brightly—it looked like a dagger. The man in the silver-gray suit was right in front of him. The young man had cried out to get him to turn around. His expression was not shock or fear so much as it was stupefaction.

The young man screamed something in Chinese, held the dagger in front of his chest and charged towards the older man.

Samejima cursed silently to himself and yelled out, "Hey!"

There weren't more than five yards between the men, and by the way the young man lurched forward, it was clear that he was determined to kill. He was fast. The tip of the dagger was aimed for the center of the older man's chest.

The intended victim let out a fearful roar. In the next instant, he lifted his left elbow and sharply twisted his body to the right in an attempt to avoid the dagger. It was an instinctive defensive move. Instead of his chest, the blade pierced his upper arm.

The young man lowered his head, crouched down, and threw himself into the man's chest. Samejima, running towards them, saw the older man clench his teeth and his eyes bulge wide open. As he straightened his body out, he punched the face of the younger man, his hand flat and strong. There was strength in the blow, and Samejima heard the sound of something crack.

As the younger man fell backward onto his rear from the impact, he managed to pull the dagger from the other's arm. He gripped it firmly in his right hand. Blood spewed out of his nose, but the older man was not done. Breathing hard, he yelled again, pulled in his elbows and kicked out with his right foot, dealing a nasty blow to the jaw of his attacker. He held his own injured body up by just his left leg, which was perfectly straight.

The younger man flew backwards from the powerful blow, his arms flailing as he fell. He landed on the back of his head, while his legs seemed to float momentarily in mid-air. The other man pulled back and took what Samejima believed to be a defensive stance, but the young man was motionless.

"Stop right there!" shouted Samejima. He couldn't tell if the man was using karate or kenpo, but it was obvious he had mastered his moves. The man pulled in his raised right knee and lowered it. When he turned to Samejima, he kept all his weight on his left leg, ready to let the right one fly at any time. He looked intensely at Samejima, keeping his guard up. The left sleeve of his suit was ripped and drenched in blood, but he did not appear to be in pain.

His eyes were terrifyingly sharp. Even though Samejima didn't think it was safe to break his gaze away, he looked down for a moment at the younger man. His face was bright red and he was out cold. The dagger had fallen out of his hand. When he looked back at the other man, he saw his gaze fall on Samejima's nightstick. He used his left hand to collapse it back down.

"Don't call the police," the man said abruptly. "I didn't do anything. He just suddenly stabbed me."

"I know. He was following you." The man blinked. Samejima knelt next to the younger man and felt for his pulse. He was still alive.

"I didn't do anything. I was just heading home. He's the one at fault."

"Why was he after you?"

"I don't know. Is he a thief?"

"He said something before he stabbed you. Seems like he knows you."

The man shook his head. "I didn't understand him. I don't remember. He hurt me."

"I can see that. It looks bad. You'd better go to the hospital."

"I'm fine. It only hurts a little. I'll be better soon."

"Are you sure? It looks pretty deep."

"Who are you?" asked the man cautiously.

"I apologize. My name is Samejima. I'm from the Shinjuku Precinct."

"Police?"

Samejima nodded and showed him his badge. The man seemed to relax and soften up enough to balance his weight on both legs.

"Have you been here the whole time?"

"No, this guy looked suspicious, so I followed him. Do you mind if I ask where you are from?"

"Taiwan."

"Do you have your passport or some other form of identification?"

The man twisted his face into what looked like a smile. "Identification?"

"That's right."

The man pulled a black leather case out of the front of his jacket and handed it to Samejima.

"Thanks." Samejima accepted the case with a nod and opened it. Inside was a gold badge embossed with a bird. A number was engraved on it. On the other side was a photograph of the man affixed to an ID card. He looked at the Chinese characters written over the badge and then back at the man, who was almost smiling.

Samejima breathed a sigh of relief.

The man was named Rongmin Guo. He was a detective from the Criminal Investigation Division of the Taipei City Police Department.

7

Nami first realized that Yang was acting strangely right before closing time, around eleven-thirty. There hadn't been many customers that evening. It really only got crowded on the weekends or at the end of the month. Nami had just followed her fourth group of customers to the door and bid them goodnight. She figured that they would be the last for the evening. Occasionally, customers would show up right before closing, but they were usually too drunk to stand.

Yang was sitting in the dark behind the cash register on a small stool that was usually reserved for Agi. Agi had been agitated, walking around yelling and talking nonsense. He might have been trying to liven up the atmosphere but only succeeded in irritating the rest of them, before he finally left the room.

Yang looked like he was deep in thought. He held his face in both palms with his elbows resting on his knees. Nami saw her customer out and then peeked into the back. The cash register area was shaped like a box, about a three feet square. A small lamp was perched on the edge so the cashier could work in the dark club. The light was currently shut off.

"Tired?" Nami asked. She wanted Yang to be ready to happily welcome any last-minute stragglers. If Agi came back and found Yang sitting around without greeting customers, he was sure to beat him. If no one greeted guests at the door, they were sure to turn around and leave.

Yang lifted his head, looking stunned, as if he had been caught daydreaming. Nami peered at him. Yang stared wordlessly back.

He looks so gloomy, she thought. Looking more closely, she saw that he was quite handsome. His nose was slightly flat, but he had high cheekbones. His eyes were expressionless and clouded, so it was difficult to figure out what he was thinking. If you ignored his dry, rumpled hair, he had a very masculine appearance. His hands and feet were large.

"I'm fine," said Yang without a change in expression, and looked out at the club.

Iku and two other girls on the late shift were with customers. Iku was the closest to Yang. She was naked except for a negligee draped over her shoulders. She sat on her customer's lap and spoke saccharin nothings. The customer seats were like those in a movie theater, all facing in the same direction towards the back of the club. The girls sat opposite them, facing the entrance. Iku mewed like a cat. Their hands reached across towards each other, both moving rhythmically up and down.

Iku glanced toward Nami, her eyes cold and jaded. She lowered her head and it disappeared between the knees of her customer. His hand hung limp over the seat and the back of his head rocked back and forth.

The seats further away were clouded in cigarette smoke, and Nami couldn't see much of anything. She looked back at Yang.

"Are you sure you're not sick?"

Yang shook his head.

"Do you need some medicine?"

"I'm fine."

Nami nodded slightly and began to move away from the register, but Yang spoke again in a low tone. "Do you come from the mainland?"

Nami froze. He spoke in Mandarin. Iku's head was moving up and down. Her customer's face was strained—it wouldn't be long until he came. Nami turned back and spoke quickly in a whisper.

"I came when I was thirteen. Don't speak Chinese here!"

Yang looked at Nami, and nodded slightly. Nami hurried away. The front door opened, and Agi walked in.

Nami remembered well the first time she came to Japan. She arrived at Narita Airport. It was summer and everyone was dressed in paper-thin garments. It had surprised her.

She was born in Heilongjiang. Her father was a teacher and her mother worked in a cotton mill. Nami was ten when she first learned her mother was Japanese. Nami's mother's parents had left her behind in China after World War II, and she had been raised by Nami's other grandparents.

One time Nami heard her parents talking late at night. She hadn't known what was happening then, but she remembered it three months later when they told her they would be moving to Japan. Her mother longed to move there.

"You'll be able to wear beautiful clothes in Japan, and you'll make lots of new friends," her mother said. Nami hadn't wanted to leave her friends in Heilongjiang. However, her parents continued to talk, night after night, and she gradually resigned herself to the fact that they were going to move to Japan.

It seemed her father had been against the idea, but her mother eventually talked him into it. Nami had known since her youngest years that her mother was stronger than her father. It didn't surprise her that her mother was getting her way again this time.

Nami and her brother, who was seven years younger, were left with an uncle in the neighborhood. Her parents left for Japan first. They sent for Nami six months later, and her brother followed six months after that.

Her parents lived in public housing in Chiba. Soon after Nami arrived, she was enrolled in a local junior high school.

Thus began the most difficult time of her life.

Nami spoke almost no Japanese. She learned the basics when she arrived, but it wasn't enough for her to chat with her classmates. Her mother worked in a nearby food processing plant, and her father commuted an hour by bus and train to a lumber mill.

Nami was lonely. Until her brother arrived, she went straight home after school and watched TV. It was her only friend, even though she had no idea what it said. She was just grateful that she never had to say anything back. Communicating in Japanese was torture. At first, whether out of friendliness or mere curiosity, her classmates had made attempts at conversation. Their teacher had apparently encouraged them to be friendly towards her, and Nami felt pressured to respond. She felt she had to say something even if she didn't know what the question was. If she stayed silent, she thought everyone would hate her. Even so, there were some students who obviously disliked her from the start.

When her brother finally arrived in Japan, they took on Japanese names to apply for Japanese citizenship. Nami's name—Qing Na Dai—was changed to Kiyomi Taguchi. Before their move, she hated having to look after her brother, but now she was eager to see him. If her brother was there, she could have someone to speak Chinese with.

Once he arrived in Japan, she'd race home to see him. Her brother's new name was Tatsuo. Nami never got used to their new Japanese names. When they were alone, she continued to call him by his Chinese name.

The joy of their time together, though, was short-lived. While she was away at school, Tatsuo quickly made friends with the other children in the public housing project, and his Japanese improved in leaps and bounds. By the time he started first grade, he blended seamlessly with the other children.

Once again, Nami was alone. Right after her brother started

school, their father was injured at the lumber mill and became unable to work. The family fell on hard times. Even though her father was at home all the time, he became bitter, and rarely answered when she spoke to him. He spent his tiny monthly disability pay at the game parlor and on liquor.

Her parents fought often. At night, Nami dreamed of returning to China. In her dreams she was back with her friends in Heilongjiang. Everyone spoke Chinese as they chatted and laughed and played. Then she'd wake to the voices of her parents quarreling. Her mother's voice was shrill and her father's was slurred from too much liquor.

Nami covered her ears and tried to go back to sleep so she could dream again. It was always the same, night after night.

When she was in ninth grade, Nami's father was hit by a train and died. They never knew if it was an accident or suicide. Nami was suddenly filled with hatred for her mother, and she ran away from home just before graduating from junior high.

She stayed with a boy, the first real friend she had made. He had quit high school and was working at a gas station. He was a member of a local gang, but he was always nice to Nami. In fact, it was the gang members who taught her Japanese. He was a "squad leader," and the others treated her with the respect owed a ranking member's girlfriend.

In the spring of her second year away from home, Nami had her first abortion. She became depressed, and decided she needed to get out more. Lying about her age, she got a part-time job at a pub. There she made friends with a customer, a twenty-two year old salesman who one day proposed marriage to her. However, the boy she lived with found out about it, and he and his pals laid in wait for the man as he left work one day and beat him to within an inch of his life. He was bedridden for three months.

The police caught up with the gang members, and Nami fled Chiba for Tokyo. She knew a girl there who was the head of the ladies auxiliary of a gang. She worked in a cabaret club in Shinjuku. When her friend's lover moved in with them, though, Nami became an unwelcome third wheel. A few weeks later she rented a place of her own. She was nineteen.

To pay the rent, she got a job at a so-called health club—basically a brothel—in Shibuya. They lent her the deposit for her apartment with the condition she work at least six months. The manager of the club signed as her guarantor. She stayed at the club for eight months, and then moved to the club in Ikebukuro, which was looking to hire younger girls.

Nami worked there for a year and a half before getting a job at Fountain of Roses. She moved to a nicer place, a studio apartment in Shin-Okubo.

While she worked in Ikebukuro she had had three boyfriends. The first was yet another gang member. They broke up when he was forced to return to his hometown after breaking his leg in a serious traffic accident.

The second one worked in a Shinjuku disco. Nami had never liked discos. There were a few in China, but social dancing was more popular. While she lived at her uncle's, a girl eight years her senior had taught her how to dance. She could waltz, tango, and even do the jitterbug. She wondered if she had forgotten all the dance steps she learned. All she knew was that she liked those dances better than disco. She broke up with her second boyfriend after two months when it became apparent that he was after Nami's paycheck.

After a while, she became involved with a regular customer, a businessman of twenty-four. He didn't pressure her for spending money, but Nami had more money to spare than he did, and she was usually the one who paid when they went out. Her new lover was married to a woman three years his senior, who was pregnant. About the time the baby was born, six months after he began seeing Nami, he left her.

She didn't lose much sleep over it. By then she knew she could take care of herself. She could speak Japanese and she could even read comic books. She had only told her first Tokyo boyfriend, the gang member, that she had come to Japan from China when she was thirteen. After that, she had never told anyone. She knew that if she did, people would ask nosy questions. Plus, she wanted to avoid people making fun of the fact that she was Chinese.

In truth, she didn't know what to think of her heritage anymore. She only knew she didn't want to spend the rest of her life in Tokyo. If she was going to stay in Japan, she wanted to be in the countryside. Chiba was out, though. She was never going back there.

She dreamed of making a lot of money and going back to China, building a splendid house and living there with her old friends. Nami was almost twenty-two, but when she thought of her friends, they were still twelve and thirteen.

"Later!" Iku came out of the locker room wearing a mini skirt. At the club, she wore almost no make-up, but she always applied it after work. They all knew she'd be stopping somewhere on the way home.

Nami changed into jeans. She could still make the last train on the Yamanote Line. Kazuki had already left, obviously in a hurry, and the other two girls on the late shift were talking about stopping somewhere for a drink. These days they were really into host clubs.

Yang and Nan were out front cleaning up. Agi was probably counting the evening's receipts.

"See you!" Nami called out as she left the locker room. She ran smack dab into Agi who had apparently been laying in wait in the dark for her.

"You surprised me!" she cried out, looking up into Agi's leering eyes. He had changed out of his uniform and into a cheap, dark-blue suit. It looked like the suit was cut for a woman's figure.

"Nami, honey."

"Yes?" Nami tried to maintain a cool demeanor. She was terrified of Agi.

"I went a little too far this evening, don't you think?" He had a smarmy grin glued on. He was so thin that when he smiled his face shriveled up in wrinkles.

"No, not at all."

"I should apologize." Agi spoke in a strangely flat, high-pitched voice. He sounded like a bad actor reading lines. "So we're friends again?" He put out a moist right hand. Nami suppressed her distaste and took it.

"Let's go drinking then." This had obviously been his intention all along. Agi gazed at her with glassy eyes. Chills went up her spine. "There's this really nice place I know," he continued. "It's quiet. Almost like the bar in a hotel."

The word "hotel" set Nami's teeth on edge.

"You really don't have to do anything for me—"

"But I'm not. I just want to get a drink. Come with me!" Agi pursed his lips playfully.

Nami just wanted to go home, but she was afraid of his wrath if she turned him down.

"Don't you live in Shin-Okubo?" he purred. "I'll escort you home."

Nami went stiff, terrified of the idea of sleeping with him. She looked away. Nan was mopping the floor, and Yang was heading out back, carrying a large bag of trash with both hands.

"I'm meeting someone."

"Who?"

"A friend."

"Male or female?"

None of your business! She wanted to scream. She knew that if she said she was seeing a girlfriend he'd beg to come along.

"A…a guy."

"Hmm." Agi clearly didn't believe her. Nan and Yang were hard at work. Nami watched them to avoid Agi's eyes.

"Are you going drinking with Yang?" he suddenly asked. He must have mistaken the way she had been looking at them.

"What?"

"Are you going out with Yang?" Agi repeated.

Yang, carrying a case of empty beer bottles, stopped for a second and looked over at them. Nami noted absently that he was carrying two cases, and they looked totally weightless in his arms.

"Um, no…"

Agi twirled around. "Yang!"

"Yes?"

"Are going out drinking with Nami?"

Yang stared at Agi, his expression unchanged.

"I'm asking if you're going out with her!"

Now Yang looked at Nami, trying to figure out what was going on.

"No," Nami hastily answered for him, "I'm not going anywhere with Yang."

"Really," Agi answered without turning back around. "Yang, stay after the others leave."

"Yes," Yang replied, nodding ever so slightly.

Now Nami was worried. What would Yang tell Agi about her? It would just make him bother her more. She'd have to find another place to work.

"Go on home, then, good night," said Agi, turning back to look at her. She didn't like the overly pleasant tone of his voice. She was more worried than ever. He was bound to take out his frustration at being turned down on Yang. But what could she do? If she called the police, it would mean trouble for Yang and Nan. Agi knew he could get away with beating both of them.

84

"Don't wanna leave?" Agi asked, staring at her.

"See you tomorrow," Nami said, bobbed her head, turned and quickly left. As she went she heard the voices of Agi, Yang, and Nan, returning the greeting, each in their own peculiar accent. Nami slipped under the partially closed shutter and breathed a sigh of relief.

She sped through Kabukicho and crossed Yasukuni Boulevard. About the time she reached Studio Alta, she felt her legs grow heavy.

It has nothing to do with me! She tried to tell herself. But by the time she was in front of Shinjuku Station, she had to admit she was worried about Yang. She knew she couldn't help him. All she could do would be to watch as Agi beat him. She slowed her pace, and unconsciously pulled her shoulder bag closer to her chest. If she had gone out with Agi, Yang would have been spared a beating. Yang had helped her out that evening, and now she had left him to face Agi's wrath.

Up to now she hadn't felt anything for Yang. Indeed, she had done her best to avoid him since the incident in the locker room.

Things had changed. He had never forgotten how she helped him by translating for him the fact that he had a stomachache. He was dark and silent, but he wasn't a bad person. She was the one who was bad.

Nami felt a wave of harsh emotion heaving inside her. She opened her mouth and gasped desperately for breath. She didn't know what to do, but she knew she couldn't just go home and pretend nothing had happened. She couldn't ride the train, enter her apartment, shower, crawl into bed, read the last few pages of her comic book or watch TV like nothing had changed.

She turned and began to run back the way she had come. She had to help Yang.

8

The Hanazono Shrine was just outside the Shinjuku Precinct's jurisdiction. It was part of the Yotsuya jurisdiction. Samejima went back to the police box in front of the shrine and got the patrolman on duty to call an ambulance. The younger man was loaded in, and Rongmin Guo was taken to the hospital in a patrol car. Samejima explained to the patrolman that he had seen everything that had happened, and Guo had only acted in defense. He also asked if they would turn over the incident to him. The main suspect was unconscious, and both the attacker and the victim were foreigners.

The patrolman was quick to give his consent: "If that's what you'd like, Inspector, I'll leave it to you."

Samejima was finally able to head back to Honeysuckle, the little bar in Golden City where he had left Sho. She was sitting at the counter, and she flew to the door as soon as she heard it open.

"It's all taken care of."

"What happened?"

"Nothing exciting, but I'll have to head back to the precinct."

Sho laughed, but it was a sad sort of laugh. "I figured you'd say that."

"I'm sorry," Samejima apologized as he paid Sho's tab. The woman charged twelve hundred yen for one bottle of beer.

He put his arm around Sho's shoulders and walked her out. "I'll make it up to you."

"You liar," Sho sulked as she put both of her arms around his neck and pulled his head towards her. "I had hoped for some action tonight," she whispered and then bit down hard on his ear.

"Ouch!"

"Serves you right. Call me!" Sho raised her arm to flag down a taxi and ran towards it.

"I'll call tomorrow," Samejima yelled in her direction.

"You better," she yelled back, "or I'll start hanging out in Roppongi."

Samejima cracked a smile. The taxi door slammed shut, and Sho was gone. He headed back to the police station. It had been a long day that had begun at six-thirty the morning before. It was already four a.m., and he still wasn't done. He looked up which hospital Guo and the other man had been taken to.

When he got to the hospital, both of the men had already been patched up. The young man had a broken nose and jaw, and had suffered a concussion. Guo had a gash in his left arm that would take a month to heal. The doctor told him his muscles had kept the dagger from going in any further, and that his bones were unharmed.

"Amazing muscles. Like steel. He must have terrific reflexes, clenching his muscles just before the dagger went in," the doctor said.

The younger man had been given painkillers and was heavily sedated. The passport in his jacket identified him as Huan Xu, twenty-three years old, a citizen of Taiwan. He had been in Japan for about six months on a tourist visa, which he had renewed once. Samejima asked the International Investigation Unit at HQ to look into both Guo and Xu.

As soon as he had been bandaged, Guo had asked to be discharged even though the doctors recommended he stay for a full week.

"I'd like to talk to him," said Samejima. Both of the men were in private rooms with police guards posted outside. Samejima knocked on the door of Guo's room and walked in. He was sitting on the bed, and he looked over at Samejima as he entered the room.

The left arm of his shirt had been cut off, and he had a sling around his neck holding his damaged arm up. Guo's gaze was as sharp as ever, and Samejima caught no hint of either agitation or unease. If he was really a cop, he thought, he had to be a veteran who had seen more than his share of carnage.

"Does it hurt?" he asked.

Guo shook his head. "I'm fine. I want to go back to my hotel."

"Which hotel?"

"Sanko Hotel, Shinjuku 5th Street."

Samejima recognized the name of the no-frills business hotel just off Meiji Boulevard. He must have been on his way back there when he took the short cut through the Hanazono Shrine.

"What about the other man?" Guo asked.

"Broken bones in his nose and jaw. You might be charged with unjustifiable self-defense."

"Unjus—what…?"

Samejima took out his notebook and wrote it down in kanji characters, which are based on Chinese characters, and Guo seemed to understand.

"You mean I'm too strong?"

"That's right." Samejima smiled and sat down on a metal folding chair next to the bed. "He's sedated. We'll bring in an interpreter tomorrow to interrogate him."

"Are you in charge?"

"Yes. I'm Inspector Samejima, Crime Prevention Unit of the Shinjuku Precinct."

"Inspector." The muscles in Guo's face began to relax. His complexion was rough with the scars from bad acne in his youth.

"I thought you were younger. But you have a high rank."

"Almost thirty-six."

"I'm thirty-eight."

"Would you mind showing me your ID again?"

"It's in there." Guo indicated his jacket hung next to the bed. The left arm was torn and thick with blood. Samejima walked over to the bed and pulled a leather case from the right pocket of the jacket.

"Take a business card, please."

Samejima nodded his thanks and took one out of the case. Guo's home phone number was printed on the back. He inserted a business card of his own in return.

"What's the name of your unit?"

"You call them Marubo."

"So you're in the Organized Crime unit of the Taipei Police?"

"Yes, my rank is a little lower than yours." He appeared to be an assistant inspector. He was not a "career" cop.

"So you're here in Japan on a tourist visa?"

"Yes," Guo smiled vaguely.

"Are you alone?"

"Yes."

"When did you arrive?"

"Four days ago."

"And how long do you plan to stay?"

"About ten more days."

"So, two weeks in all. That's a long vacation for a cop. I wish I could get a vacation that long."

Guo was silent.

"So, do you plan to visit anywhere else? Kyoto?"

"I don't know."

"Your Japanese is excellent."

Guo smiled thinly. "Taiwan used to be a Japanese colony. Old people all speak Japanese. They all know the emperor's name. My aunt married a Japanese. They lived near me, so I learned Japanese. But I have forgot so much."

"You speak it very well. What is your native language?"

"Mandarin. Old people speak Taiwanese, too. It's based on the Fujian dialect."

"Where do you live in Taiwan?"

"Are you going to check my background?"

"Yes, it's part of our procedure. Would you mind writing your address here, please?" Samejima held out his notebook and a pen. Guo hesitated, but took them and began to write. He lived in Taipei. Samejima needed the address to make sure he was a bonafide detective.

He took the notebook back, thanking him. Next, he turned the page to show him Huan Xu's name and passport number. "This is the name of the man who attacked you. Is it familiar?" Guo gave it the briefest of glances and nodded.

"Xu. The whole family is…" Guo didn't know the Japanese for the next word, and he motioned for Samejima to lend him his notebook.

"What does it mean?" Samejima asked, reading the characters.

"Like yakuza. Thugs. They rob banks and jewelry stores."

"Gangsters? Mafia members?"

Guo licked his lips and looked at the ceiling, trying to figure out how to describe it. "Do you know Taiwan gangs?"

"You mean like Sihai and Zhulian?

"Those are big gangs. But there are many small groups, too. They commit crimes, but are not part of syndicates. Lots of guns. Pistols, carbines, submachine guns."

"That's a lot of weaponry."

"All comes from the mainland. Hundreds. Thousands. All smuggled. Black Star, Red Star. All the numbers are connected."

"You mean the smuggled guns all have serial numbers that are consecutive?"

"Yes," he said, then gave an ironic smile. "On the mainland, there are military men who like to make money. Maybe it comes from the government."

Samejima was inclined to believe him. He knew that Black Star and Red Star were the names of guns produced for the Chinese government. The Chinese bought licenses to make Soviet automatic weapons like the Tokarev and Makarov. Their nicknames came from the star emblems on the grips. HQ was well aware that attempts had been made by gangs to smuggle the weapons into Japan, and it was a matter of great concern among the police ranks.

It was the first Samejima had heard, however, that the weapons were flowing into Taiwan with consecutive serial numbers. In other words, they were coming straight off the production line in the hundreds and thousands. It would be no surprise if military suppliers were directly involved.

"The mainland government loves to hear that crime in Taiwan is going up." Guo was insinuating that the guns were part of a strategy to destabilize Taiwan, which would imply that the Chinese government was squarely in the middle of the situation.

Samejima shook his head. This was something America and the USSR were infamous for doing. They offered weapons and know-how to Third World countries in the midst of a civil war. Such practices had been factors behind the prolonged wars in Vietnam and Afghanistan. There were similar arms deal situations in Central America and the Middle East. It was a widespread criminal web that the laws of no single country could control. It would be close to impossible for a single detective from the Criminal Investigation Unit at HQ to take on the arms smuggling activities of an entire nation.

However, it seemed that was what Guo was trying to do.

"So, are you saying Huan Xu belongs to a small gang?"

"They're called the Xu Brothers. There were five of them. The second oldest and youngest are the only two still alive. The older one is in jail. The youngest is Huan Xu. He was still a child when it all happened."

"What happened to the other three?"

"One had a fight with another gang member. The two others were in a shoot-out with police. Huan Xu was too young to convict and too young to get killed," Guo explained. "Huan thinks I killed his brothers."

Samejima waited for him to continue.

"I looked for them, but they were killed by…" he wrote down some more characters in Samejima's notebook.

"I see, the SWAT team. So Huan Xu is getting revenge for the death of his brothers."

"Yes, he disappeared after the shoot-out. Must have come to Japan recently, and then he saw me tonight. He must have thought it was a good chance to get back for his brothers' deaths."

"Is that what he told you?"

"Yes. I forgot his face. The shoot-out was four years ago. He was nineteen. Now he's twenty-three. A man's face really changes."

"But he hadn't forgotten you."

Guo nodded gravely.

"Did you realize he was following you?"

"After a while."

"Weren't you afraid?"

Guo shook his head, his eyes never leaving Samejima's face. Samejima decided to change the subject.

"You obviously are skilled in the martial arts. A normal man could never have taken a knife like that. Was that kenpo?"

Guo let a small smile creep up before suppressing it. He was silent.

"A normal guy could never do that. You must have trained a long time. Are all Taiwanese cops that good?" Samejima pressed.

"All Taiwanese men have to join military. We learn how to use guns, how to fight. Everyone knows how, both criminals and police." Such was Guo's reply, but Samejima didn't believe for a minute that

92

all soldiers were as skilled as he. He waited for Guo to go on, but that was all he had to say.

"I see. Are you planning on staying at the Sanko Hotel for a while longer?"

Guo nodded.

"Well, then stay here in the hospital for the night. The doctor recommends you stay for a week, but..."

"I'll go back to the hotel. I can change bandages and treat the wound by myself."

"What about the stitches?"

"I'll get them out back in Taiwan."

"At least, stay for tonight."

Guo laughed. "Okay. I will stay. Sorry for the trouble."

"And let me know if you change hotels. I'll come back to see you tomorrow."

Guo got up from his bed and bowed. Samejima returned the gesture and left the room.

9

Nami found Nan walking down Yasukuni Boulevard, his hands in his pockets, his head down. He was walking on the other side of the broad intersection heading in the opposite direction, towards the station. His long, thin body was bent forward. He walked quickly, never taking his eyes off the ground in front of him.

That meant Yang was alone with Agi. Agi was probably just getting down to business. Nami felt a pain of anxiety shoot through her chest. Yang was probably on his knees, and Agi was circling around him like a wolf, slapping and kicking him. Agi would take issue with Yang's poor Japanese, asking him the same question over and over again, kicking him each time.

Nami felt like the wave of people heading the opposite way was pushing her back, towards the station. It seemed as though each one of them was trying to keep her away from Fountain of Roses.

She took her wristwatch off her left hand. It had been a gift from her last boyfriend, the businessman. It wasn't expensive, but she treasured it. She shoved it deep down inside her bag. She'd tell Agi she had forgotten it. It would be her excuse for coming back to the club.

Then what? She'd ask Agi to go out for a drink. But then he'd want to sleep with her. She couldn't bear to do that. But somehow she had to get Yang out of there. She'd tell him a friend of hers from Taiwan worked at a nice bar that she wanted to take Yang to. That would do.

94

But Agi might ask to go, too. Nami slowed her pace. She needed to get back there quickly, but she had to think of a way to avoid raising Agi's suspicions. She'd heard rumors that he had the yakuza's protection. She wasn't sure if he was actually a member, but most of his friends were gangsters.

Since he used speed, he must be buying it from some gang. That evening he had been irritated. He had finally left the club for a while, probably looking to buy a fix. Thinking about that made her more reticent than ever. She'd heard lots of stories about junkies who injured and killed people while in a drug-induced rage. Once, in Ikebukuro, she had seen a boy who worked at a neighboring cabaret club fly into a frenzy. He was blue in the face and totally wild. It took a group of policemen to get him under control. She found out later from the manager of her old club that the man was a speed addict. She was terrified by the way he had looked. He had drool running down his chin, and he screamed unintelligible words. He was stripped to the waist, running around, smashing everything in sight. His eyes bulged out of his head. Nami could hardly believe it was the same guy she had seen so many times before.

What if Agi was in the same state?

Maybe she had better not go back. She stopped walking. She was back at the entrance to Kabukicho. Crowds were walking out of it and towards the station, brushing past her.

"What's wrong, babe?" A bespectacled man in his thirties stinking of liquor walked up to her. "Did you get jilted?"

Nami looked the other way, but felt the man's hand on her shoulder. She threw it off. "Get your hands off me, fucker!"

The man pulled back in surprise. "What're you sayin'? I was just tryin' to be nice." Nami ignored him and walked off. The man stood rooted to the spot mumbling to himself.

Nami lifted her head and took a deep breath. She told herself that she had to go back to the club. She decided she'd call the cops if she found Agi ranting and raving like a madman. It would be bad for Yang, but at least he wouldn't be murdered. Anyway, she didn't know for sure that he was an illegal alien.

I guess I really am Chinese, she suddenly thought to herself.

She wondered if she was this worried about him only because he was Chinese. They both spoke the same language. She wondered if she would be heading back to the club if it had been Nan who was in trouble. She wasn't sure.

Nami turned right across from a curry stand. She was almost back at Fountain of Roses. She kept telling herself there was nothing to be afraid of. This was nothing compared to the terror she felt in her first years in Japan when she was still in school with her classmates talking at her even though she could barely respond.

The shutter at Fountain of Roses was still half open. Everything else in the neighborhood was closed and dark, even the strip clubs, soaplands and other late-night places. She stood in front of the shutter, her heart pounding. She waited to hear the sound of flesh being beaten, screams of pain, deranged ranting. But there was nothing.

Now she was more worried than ever. Had Agi beaten Yang so badly he couldn't even cry out? She slipped under the shutter and walked into the darkened club. On the other side of the blackness, with its smell of liquor and stale cigarette smoke, she saw light flowing in from the locker room door. She stood and listened a few moments longer. It was silent.

Had they already left? Looking around, she spotted Agi's bag next to the cash register. He was still here.

"Hello?" she called out in a small voice. Nothing. She tried again, in a slightly louder voice.

"Hello?"

The locker room door opened, and a tall man stood in the doorway, the light shining from behind him.

"Yang!" She called out in relief. Yang was expressionless as usual.

He was wearing a long-sleeved polo shirt and a pair of jeans. He must have been getting ready to go home. He had a wet towel in one hand. Nami walked up to him. "Where's the boss?"

Yang looked at Nami intently, but didn't say a word. She couldn't see any bruises from blows to his face.

"In back?"

Yang nodded slightly.

"Hello?" She called out sweetly. She smiled and looked behind Yang into the locker room. There was Agi, out cold. He was propped up against the lockers, with both of his arms gone limp and his legs splayed out on the floor. His face was white. He seemed to be staring down at his knees.

"Boss?" she called to him again, sensing that something was wrong. She noticed that his eyes were open, but he wasn't blinking at all. His neck was at an odd angle, and his jaw drooped onto his shoulder.

Nami felt weak as she spun around again. Yang was still standing wordlessly at the door.

"He's dead?" she asked in Mandarin.

Yang nodded in a barely perceptible manner.

"Did you do it?" she continued on in her mother tongue.

"Yes," Yang answered in kind, still looking into her face.

"You've got to escape!" she said without thinking. "He's a yakuza, he has friends all over the place. You've got to get out of here!"

The look in Yang's eyes puzzled her, and she wasn't sure what it meant. It reflected unease but also keen interest in the situation he had got himself into.

"Let's go!" she insisted, "Hurry!" Nami's knees were beginning to shake. She was sure that Yang had only been defending himself, and accidentally hit a weak spot that was lethal. Surely Yang hadn't meant to do it.

"You want me to run away with you?" Yang said.

"Well..." Nami started to speak and then stared into Yang's face. She saw in it someone quite different from the silent, helpless man she had seen before. *He's strong. He's stronger than I ever imagined.* Yet strangely, she wasn't afraid of him. Yang seemed to sense this.

"Wait for me," he said. Then, as she watched, he began wiping down all the surfaces he had touched with the wet towel. The countertops, his locker, the cash register.

At first, Nami didn't understand what he was doing, but then she spoke. "It's no good. Your fingerprints must be everywhere."

Yang turned around as he wiped the doorknob. "No, I know exactly what I've touched. Every night during clean-up, I wipe down everything."

Nami was incredulous. Who would do such a thing? Keep track of what they had touched and then wipe the fingerprints away each and every night?

Yang continued to work, calmly cleaning up with a corpse on the floor behind him. "Okay, I'm done." He tossed the rag into a big paper bag he had pulled out of his locker. The bag also contained his uniform. "Let's go," he said casually. He was totally calm.

One would expect someone who had just committed a murder to be more panicked and wired. Nami was flustered, but her fears were eased by his calmness.

Maybe Agi was really still alive. Maybe that was why Yang was so collected. No, she couldn't imagine them playing practical jokes on her like that. Nami looked at Agi again. She hadn't noticed before the tiny trickle of blood coming out of his nose. His complexion was gradually turning blue.

He was unmistakably dead.

Yang left Nami and headed for the entrance. "What's the matter?" he asked. Nami just shook her head. She felt like she was having a nightmare. Yang had got as far as the cash register. He picked up Agi's bag and shoved it into the bottom of his paper bag. Then he poked his head under the shutter and looked around. "Hurry!" he whispered.

All of a sudden, Nami was afraid. She started to run after she crept under the shutter. As she did, Yang grabbed her by the arm.

"Don't run. Just walk normally." With another cloth in his hand, he pulled the shutter all the way down until it clicked into place. Then he began to walk, his hand still clutching Nami's arm.

She was still scared, but she had no choice but to follow his instructions. Yang wasn't holding on very tightly, so she could easily shrug it off and escape. But for some reason she didn't want to. She was frightened because a man had just died. She wasn't afraid of Yang, the murderer. She felt a little sorry for Agi. But there was nothing heart-wrenching about his death. To be honest, she was relieved that he was gone.

They reached the street that led to the station, and Yang finally let go of her. The crowd on the street wrapped around them.

"What are you going to do?" she asked. Yang was silent. She knew he wasn't going to turn himself into the police. If he did, there would have been no reason to wipe off all his fingerprints.

"Where do you live?" Yang asked.

"Shin-Okubo, it's only one stop away. What about you?"

Once again he was silent, and Nami realized that she had never heard Yang chatting with anyone. She didn't know where he was from, where he lived, or even how old he was. Agi was the only one at work who would have known anything about him.

Yang had shown up at Fountain of Roses after seeing a "help wanted" sign on the shutter. Agi probably hired him without checking his background. Agi was the one who paid Yang and Nan their salaries, although she was sure they hadn't been paid in the few weeks they had worked there. Nami was almost certain they wouldn't get as much as he had promised when he interviewed them. Agi probably pocketed the difference. He knew they'd never complain because he could threaten to turn them over to Immigration Services.

Yang and Nami stood waiting for the signal to change before crossing Yasukuni Boulevard.

"You don't have anywhere to go, do you?" she asked him. Yang remained silent, his eyes facing straight ahead. Nami's chest suddenly felt tight. "You can stay with me, just for one night."

Yang turned his head slowly to look at her.

"You'll help me?"

"Help?"

The traffic signal changed. The people around them began to walk, and Nami and Yang were pushed along with them. Yang took long strides, and Nami had to hurry to keep up.

"What kind of help do you need?" she asked.

Yang stopped suddenly, and Nami almost ran into him. Yang took her arm again, and this time he held on tightly.

"Let's go to your place," he said.

10

At the precinct the next day, Samejima spent the morning reporting to Momoi, his direct superior, about the Hanazono Shrine incident. He had put in a request with the International Investigation Unit at Headquarters to confirm that Rongmin Guo was in fact a Taiwanese policeman.

The main issue was that Guo was a victim of one crime and a possible perpetrator of another. Samejima had seen him at the gambling joint under surveillance in Okubo. If he was a real policeman, what had he been doing there?

He couldn't ask Guo about it yet because it would give away the surveillance activities. It was a joint operation between Public Security Section One and the Crime Prevention Unit of the Shinjuku Precinct and Samejima wasn't officially involved. If he made a false move he would end up compromising four of his co-workers, including Assistant Inspector Shinjo.

That's what Samejima wanted to talk to Momoi about. He didn't want Section One walking in to give Momoi a hard time about anything Samejima had done.

"So you think Huan Xu might be connected to the bookies who run that gambling operation?" Momoi asked. There were detectives doing deskwork in the Crime Prevention Unit room, but none of them were part of the surveillance team and they didn't participate in the conversation. During the investigation of a serial cop killer, Samejima had been designated as an independent roving inspector, and he retained that status ever since.

"You can find that out by checking the records of the surveillance unit."

"I'll have Shinjo and Kawada and the others on duty look him up. If Huan is involved, it's possible that his beef was gambling-related and he wasn't trying to avenge anybody."

"Which would mean Guo was lying to me."

Momoi nodded. "So what do you think of this Guo, personally?"

"I believe he's a genuine detective, and a veteran at that."

"Do you think he's clean?"

"Hard to tell. But he's probably the type who'll do anything to solve a case."

The fact that Guo was a detective who investigated organized crime made it difficult to judge whether or not he kept his hands clean. Whether they wanted to or not, detectives with such units inevitably got to know the gang bosses. If there was a gang office within their jurisdiction, it would be impossible not to pay a visit there at least once. It was an occupational risk. They learned the names, facial features and characteristics of bosses and high-ranking members, which meant they were always at least nodding acquaintances. Interviewing gangsters was a normal part of the detectives' lives. They had tea together, they ate together, and they went drinking together.

The crime bosses paid for themselves and their members, considering it an entertainment expense. The police, however, had to pay for themselves. A cup of coffee was no problem, but what about the restaurant, bars, and clubs the bosses preferred? It could get expensive. The police department would only reimburse a small amount for job-related information gathering, so the cops ended up paying the rest out of their own pockets.

And they were not very well paid to start out with. In the real world, if a regular Joe hung out with a rich guy, you'd expect the rich guy to treat his pal to a night of drinking worth 10,000 yen, and have the favor returned for a cup of coffee for just 1,000 yen. As friends, they'd have no trouble calling it even. However, this wasn't the way police and yakuza dealt with each other. In an extreme example, a gangster might treat a cop to a few drinks and the cop might return the favor the next day by serving the gangster with an arrest warrant. It was complicated.

It wasn't just a matter of money. If the cops got information about a crime in progress from yakuza informants, then they would have to confirm the tip by heading to the scene. It didn't necessarily mean arrests could be made on the spot. The police might arrive to find a completely unrelated crime in process.

Take, for example, a detective conducting surveillance of illegal amphetamine sales. He gets word of drug deals being made at a mahjong parlor and visits pretending to be a customer. When he gets there, he finds that illegal gambling is going on, and the cop is forced to participate or blow his cover.

This sort of undercover work is not something regular policemen usually enjoy. Some exceptions might be narcotics agents who, despite their position in law enforcement, conduct investigations in a manner completely different from normal police. Narcotics agents fell under the jurisdiction of the Ministry of Health and Welfare rather than the Ministry of Justice.

It was on record that Guo had been to the gambling operation in Okubo. Momoi looked as if he was trying to figure out why. Guo certainly had no authority to conduct an investigation in Japan. Even if he had come to Japan from Taiwan looking for a fugitive criminal, he was not authorized to take action. If a criminal had fled Taiwan for Japan, he was under the jurisdiction of the Japanese police. If Guo was after such a fugitive, then he should have made a request through the International Criminal Police Organization (ICPO). Basically, an ongoing investigation in a foreign country was no excuse for him to be visiting an illegal gambling operation.

If he was caught gambling, it would be a prosecutable offense.

"He might have been taking a break," Momoi suggested.

"Right. Or he really could be in Japan on vacation, and he just happened to run into his friendly neighborhood gangster and ask him where he might find some action."

"You said you saw him with a hostess."

"There were two, and they both appeared to be Taiwanese."

"Last night he was alone?"

"Yes. Do you plan to search the place?" asked Samejima.

"It's too early for that, but HQ might be itching to make a move."

"It could be more trouble for us."

Momoi, expressionless as always, shook his head. "It's their call. We're assisting at their request."

"I plan to see Guo again today. Should I avoid the Okubo case?"

Momoi nodded. "Do you think he's here to track someone?"

Samejima thought for a moment. "He might be. He gives me the impression that once he's caught a scent, he won't give up until he's got his prey."

"Sounds like someone else we all know."

Samejima had to laugh at Momoi's comment. "He's worse than me. You should have seen the way he ripped into Huan Xu."

"It could be dangerous if a loose cannon like that is hanging out in Shinjuku. We could haul him away, but I'd hate to do that to a fellow cop," Momoi said.

"I agree. I'll talk to him again and see what I can—"

Momoi's phone rang in the middle of Samejima's response. Momoi picked up the receiver.

"Crime Prevention Unit. Yes, yes, he's right here. It's for

you," he said, handing Samejima the receiver. "It's International Investigation."

Samejima took the phone. "Samejima speaking."

"Good work yesterday." Samejima recognized the rough voice. "Araki here. I'm calling about your request."

"When did you get back to International?" Samejima asked, surprised.

"I'm not officially back," Araki began and then paused. "Look, I need to see you. We've got to talk. It's about what happened yesterday."

"Anything you say. Where should I meet you?"

"Well, I can't really have you come here, and I'm not too keen on going to your precinct. I'll head over in your direction and meet you for coffee."

Samejima looked at his watch. It was one twenty. He thought it might be better if he went to see Guo first. Araki might be planning to keep him away.

It was as if Araki was reading his mind. "You're planning to see that Taiwanese guy you've been asking about, aren't you?"

"Yes."

"I want to talk to you first." Araki was sharp.

"I see," Samejima replied.

"I'm leaving right now."

"Fine."

"How about meeting at just past two in a hotel coffee shop. I'd like to avoid seeing anyone else in your precinct."

Samejima agreed and suggested a place in West Shinjuku.

"All right, see you soon."

Momoi watched him replace the receiver. "What do you know about a superintendent named Araki?" Samejima asked him.

Momoi shook his head. "I don't know much, but he seems a little strange."

"He said he'd fallen off the career track."

Momoi leaned back in his chair and spoke slowly. "I have heard rumors. But they were just rumors, so I'd rather not pass them on. But he's very sharp."

Samejima nodded. He knew he was being warned to keep his guard up.

Araki showed up at the coffee shop a few minutes after two. He wore a brown plaid jacket without a tie. It was a disheveled-yet-fashionable look. He sat down across from Samejima and ordered ice coffee. Then he took out a cigarette, put it in his mouth and began to talk, the unlit tip of the cigarette bouncing up and down as he spoke.

"We've confirmed the identities of both of them. Rongmin Guo is a plainclothes detective for the Taipei Police Department. Huan Xu has a police record going back to when he was thirteen."

"I heard he was a member of a gang called the Xu Brothers."

"The youngest of five. A mass arrest of gangsters turned into a shoot-out, and two of them were shot and killed. The second eldest is in prison for life. Another was stabbed to death. During the round up, Huan Xu was still a minor, and he hadn't really played a major role in the gang's activities, so he never had to do time. He disappeared for a while and ended up here in Japan."

Samejima nodded. It all jibed with what Guo had told him. Araki went on. "I don't know what he did here. He might have been a host in a late-night restaurant in order to make some spending money."

"What about the gambling operation in Okubo?"

"Yoshida came to check the record this morning, but he said he'd never seen him before."

"I see."

"Will you be doing the interrogation?"

"I'll be needing an interpreter." Samejima knew that even if Xu spoke Japanese, he'd probably claim he did not.

Araki nodded vaguely and asked another question. "Are you going to charge him with anything?"

"It's a case of bodily harm that could easily be tagged as attempted murder."

Araki blew out a puff of cigarette smoke.

"If the Okubo surveillance is going to be compromised, I can wait," Samejima offered. Araki seemed to be deep in thought.

Huan Xu had injured Guo in Japan, which meant he would be tried and might serve time here. The same would go for Guo if he were found guilty of unjustifiable self-defense.

"Don't you want to know about Guo?" Araki finally asked.

"Of course."

"He's a veteran of the Taipei police force. He's known for his dedication to his investigations. He'll go to any length to get his man. He's been threatened with lawsuits several times because he comes close to crossing the line on torture during interrogations."

Samejima was surprised that the Taiwan side had given out so much info for a single request from the International Investigation Unit.

"He's an equivalent of an assistant inspector. They say he would have moved up in rank if he didn't use such extreme methods."

"Is that what the Taiwan police told you?"

Araki shook his head and grinned cunningly. "That's what I heard from a chief superintendent. What's funny is that the characters they use for his rank are the exact same ones we use for 'gang boss.'"

"This chief superintendent is a good friend of yours?"

Araki's smile disappeared as he shook his head again. "No, we're just casual acquaintances. But he owed me a favor. There was trouble with some Taiwanese gangs. We intercepted some of them and held them at Haneda until the Taiwanese police could come pick them up. That's how I got the information so quickly."

"Did you tell them Guo had been seen at that gambling operation?"

"No. But I asked if they thought it was likely that he would hang out with yakuza over here. They said it was impossible. It sounds like he's after Japanese gangs who have business in Taiwan. He wants them out of the country."

"Got to admire the guy."

"Sounds like he might be your long-lost brother," said Araki and then added, "You know I'm not making fun of you."

"Don't worry. My boss said the same thing."

"Your boss was a good cop. If he hadn't been through that all those years ago, he'd be right up there at HQ. He's helped you out before, hasn't he?"

Samejima nodded. Momoi had shot dead a violent criminal suspect to save him. It was a burden the two of them would have to bear for the rest of their lives, but Momoi had never mentioned it since the incident.

"Do you think Guo's really here on vacation?"

"Not a clue," replied Samejima.

"What does your gut say?"

"How would that help anything?"

Araki laughed at his failure to get anything out of Samejima. "If he came here looking for someone, then he's overstepping his boundaries in a big way. There's bound to be trouble."

"Is that your theory on Guo?"

Araki was silent as he sipped his iced coffee. They were each trying to size the other up, thought Samejima. Araki put down his glass. Condensed water dripped off it and onto the paper coaster.

"Let's just say for argument's sake that Guo had chased a major criminal suspect to Japan. We all know that once that suspect steps onto Japanese soil, he should be left to the Japanese authorities to take care of. All Guo has to do is put in a request with the ICPO.

Let's imagine that Guo is certain the Japanese police will never catch this guy because he won't commit any crimes in Japan. Plus, the police are too busy with the criminals who are committing crimes in their own jurisdiction. It's the same everywhere.

"Guo knows the Japanese police would never spare the manpower and he knows the guy is too smart to get caught. He decides to take some time off from his regular duties and take a trip to Japan, perfectly aware that anything he does here will be way out of line."

"That could only be the case under certain conditions," said Samejima.

"What, for instance?"

"First of all, why can't Guo let this guy go? A veteran gang specialist should have enough to do to keep himself busy without looking for random fugitives. Guo told me he planned to be here for two weeks. What sort of cop on the organized crime squad would spend two weeks of vacation time chasing a single criminal? You'd think he'd want to avoid even seeing a gangster on his precious vacation time.

"And another problem: where did he get information that the suspect was in Japan? As you must know, Taiwanese gangs have spread out to Hong Kong and the US, not just Japan."

"How do you know so much? Have you been reading up on foreign thugs?" asked Araki.

"A little." Despite having only taken a nap in the early hours, Samejima had stopped in at the Shinjuku Library before reporting to Momoi. There he did some research and came to the conclusion that the Taiwanese gangs were the largest system of organized crime in the world.

Chinese syndicates or "The Chinese Mafia" had spread to North and South America and Europe, not to mention their connections in Hong Kong, Taiwan and Thailand. The core of their operations, what kept everything glued together, was their drug network.

They were quick to make local connections, but they were also constantly ready to relocate. At the first sign of danger, gangsters would leave their current country for another one; especially by moving back and forth between the American continents and Eurasia, they knew how to stay on their toes to avoid getting caught.

In other words, while individual Taiwanese gangs might not be at the center of it all, Chinese organized crime as a whole, with its lateral network, spanned the globe. It lacked any central command. The sprawling nature of the organization meant a thug from Taiwan could be a member of several different gangs if he wanted to. This would be unthinkable with Japanese yakuza, who were much more tightly organized. The Taiwanese gangs were much more tumultuous, with juniors often challenging their seniors.

"You're right about the fact that a normal cop would never bother coming all the way to Japan for a criminal."

"So you do have proof that Guo is here to catch someone?" Araki had avoided saying this, so Samejima finally asked outright.

"What do you want me to do?" Araki laughed. "You know I'm in no position to tell you anything."

Samejima responded with a strained smile. He took out a cigarette and lit it. "So you've heard about it off the record."

"That's right. The Taiwanese chief superintendent I mentioned told me everything I know. He didn't ask us for cooperation. Actually, he probably can't ask."

"He talked to you directly?"

"Yeah, and I thought about it. If I were worried about covering my own ass, I would have asked my boss first for permission to follow a lead. Guo's boss would never allow him to leave the country and do whatever he pleased."

"But Guo didn't ask his boss."

"No…"

"Why?"

"He's following a drug and gun route. He's after a top guy in a Taiwanese gang. If Guo makes a fuss, the Japanese yakuza will get involved. Taiwanese gangsters in Japan are not the low-lifes they used to be. They're all more like exchange students sent over by the bosses. I've heard that the Taiwanese are better at hauling ass when something happens. The young Japanese gangsters pull out their abacus and figure out how much jail time they'll have to do for their 'work.' The Taiwanese are gone as soon as they get the order to go."

"So you think the man Guo is after is connected to a Japanese yakuza group?"

"Or he's dealing with one."

"He might be under yakuza protection?"

Araki nodded. "That makes more sense. The suspect is probably staying with a Japanese boss who he's dealing drugs and guns with. Guo got wind of that fact and came here on his own to find him."

"What's he planning to do without a warrant? He can't just slap this guy around and drag him home."

"That's what I'd like to know."

"No information on the alleged suspect?"

Araki thought before he spoke. He looked a little torn. "The Taiwanese chief superintendent didn't want to tell me about that. He obviously didn't want to blab to me and then have the Japanese police getting in Guo's way. If he's to tell me about the suspect, he needs me to guarantee our cooperation with the Taiwanese police. If we aren't going to, then he's taking the official line that Guo is here strictly on vacation."

"I see." It sounded as though Guo's boss was trying to get Araki to help him out. However, he refused to talk about Guo's target until he knew he could count on Araki's support.

"To be honest, what I'm interested in is the smuggling route from Taiwan to Japan, and that's what I got a whiff of when Guo went wild like that. It'll look good for me if I can get something on it. I might even get reinstated. The only reason I'm telling you about this is that you've had some of the same problems as me. But, look, I understand. In your case, you don't have any ambition to get your career back on track." Araki said all this quickly before Samejima could open his mouth.

Samejima had to laugh. There was something about Araki he couldn't hate. Solving crimes was just a way for him to climb the career ladder, but he didn't make any bones about it.

"So you didn't promise him anything?"

"No. I may be a failure, but no one can accuse me of irresponsible behavior. I don't want to be one of those sniveling bureaucrats who make a promise and then renege on it, bungling the whole thing."

Samejima had to agree that there were people like that. Araki was no different from them in his desire to get ahead, but at least he had principles. He's an odd one, Samejima thought.

"So you don't know who or what Guo is really after?"

"Exactly, and that's what I want to find out."

"Why don't you just ask him?"

"I don't think he'll talk. And if he knows anyone here is onto him, he'll go underground in a flash and we'll lose him. I say we toss him back into the pond and watch him swim."

"What if he's after someone totally unconnected to Japanese yakuza?"

"I don't think that's possible. That would be like getting the end of a round of mahjong without a single winning move."

"So what do we do?"

"There's nothing we can do. Not unless Guo breaks a law. And as far as you're concerned, this conversation never happened."

"What if you're caught?"

"By the powers above?"

Samejima nodded.

"Well," Araki shrugged, "they can't hurt me more than they already have."

112

Samejima looked at Araki, finally realizing what had been going on. "You're the one who got Section One to set up surveillance. You've been after Guo from the start."

"And don't think it wasn't tough trying to keep the truth a secret."

"When did you first know he was here?"

"From day one. I've got friends in Immigration, and I asked them to keep a lookout. They also let me know where Guo would be staying. The only problem is that I can't follow him around. I can't just walk into a crime scene like you. It's impossible for me to watch him without him catching on."

"I hope Guo's unarmed?" It would be much more dangerous if he had a gun.

"I don't know. I don't think he is. He can't be that stupid."

Samejima exhaled. "You want me to just keep an eye on Guo, is that what you're saying? You'd like to see him walk on this one?"

"In a nutshell, yes."

Samejima looked at Araki, and Araki averted his eyes. "Obviously, there's not much in it for you," he admitted. "But the reason I'm telling you all this is that I know you're not the type to take that sort of thing into consideration. The other reason is that if Guo hurts any Japanese yakuza, they're bound to be ones Shinjuku has put away before. For drugs and guns."

Samejima was silent.

"I'm sure you must think I've got some nerve," added Araki.

"What happened in Thailand?" asked Samejima, recalling the incident Araki had mentioned while they were holed up together in the Okubo apartment.

Araki drew back in surprise, narrowed his eyes and looked Samejima up and down. Finally he spoke.

"A visa. I arranged for a visa to bring a woman over from Thailand. Not that it's an excuse, but it had nothing to do with yakuza. It was

113

a madam I met there. She wanted to come work in Japan and send money back to her destitute family to give them a better life. I was moved by her story. Of course, there was collateral."

Samejima nodded. Araki continued. "It's still the same. The gap between rich and poor is huge. When I was there, there were bastards who would go into the countryside to buy babies. They put out their eyes, cut off their arms and legs and put them on a street corner to beg. Damaged kids get more money." Araki shook his head. "When I first heard about it, I wanted to track those bastards down and kill them. But they were just trying to survive. Some of those kids would have been culled for other things. I saw so many of them on the streets of Bangkok."

Samejima let out a long breath. "Well, I don't know if I can take care of everything the way you'd like me to, but I'll wait to see how Guo plays out. Just as long as he doesn't go around torturing every Taiwanese gangster hiding out in Shinjuku."

"Thanks."

"Of course, all bets are off if Guo catches on to me."

"I'll bet he'll try to contact you if he thinks he can trust you."

"If that's the case, I'll have to weigh my options—you versus him."

"All I want is the smuggling route the yakuza use. You can keep Guo for yourself."

"Are you going to raid the place in Okubo?"

"That'd be the bonus. I'll take care of it when we're done with Guo."

Samejima grinned. "You like gambling, don't you?"

Araki took out another cigarette and lit up. "Investigations are gambles. The judges are our bookies." Then he wiped the grin off his face, and spoke seriously.

"I appreciate your help."

11

Guo was released from the hospital and he returned to his room at the Sanko Hotel. Samejima went to pay him a visit. He called from the phone at the front desk.

"This is Samejima. I'm here in the lobby."

There was a pause before Guo replied. "Come up. I've been waiting for you."

Business hotels usually frowned upon people other than customers entering the rooms, but the Sanko Hotel was different. Samejima saw guests coming and going. Many of them were foreign, mostly Asian.

Guo had a single room on the fifth floor. Samejima bought two cans of coffee at a vending machine and rode up the elevator. He knocked on the door and Guo opened it from inside. He was wearing the cotton kimono the hotel provided as sleepwear. The room was so small it felt claustrophobic. The single bed and tiny desk took up all of the space. In the closet next to the bed, a number of suits were hung neatly on hangers, including the one Guo had been wearing the day before. Below them was his Samsonite suitcase.

The window was open and they could hear the rush-hour sounds from the street. The room was tiny, but the view was fair. Samejima put the two cans on the desk.

"Help yourself."

"Thanks," said Guo, his face blank. "Sit, please," he said and sat on the bed. An envelope from a pharmacy sat on top of the blanket.

"Were you about to change your bandage?" Samejima asked.

"No, already finished."

Samejima glanced at the ashtray. It was clean of ashes.

"I don't mind smoke. Go ahead," Guo said, quickly noticing Samejima's glance.

"Do you smoke?"

"Only sometimes."

"Like one now?" Samejima held his pack out.

"Thanks." Guo took out a cigarette. Samejima put one into his own mouth, and held out his lighter. Guo continued looking into Samejima's eyes as he took it.

"Did you look me up?"

"Yes, you and Huan Xu both. It matched everything you told me."

"That was fast."

"It's going to be a while until we can interrogate Huan, what with his jaw broken like that."

"Will you arrest me?"

"No."

"But I might go back to Taiwan."

"You said you were staying longer."

Guo blew smoke out his nose.

"And I can't imagine you going very far in the shape you're in."

"I'm fine."

"So, where have you been so far?"

"Just Shinjuku. It is the most interesting place in Tokyo." Guo looked out the window.

"There must be places like this in your own country."

"Wanhua."

"Wanhua?" Samejima passed him the memo pad on the desk, and Guo wrote down characters that read "ten thousand flowers."

"I see. It sounds like a happening place."

"Lots of crimes happen there." Guo smiled slightly.

"Is it like Shinjuku?"

"A little bit. Some parts are very different. There are many gangsters."

"Japanese yakuza?"

"Not many. They aren't out in the open. You only see them in hotels, restaurants, night clubs, cars."

"Do Japanese yakuza go to Taiwan regularly?"

"Some. They pay to open shops in Taipei. The gangs have become like businesses. They are advisors or presidents of big companies, always driving in Mercedes or BMWs."

"Corporatization."

"It's the same for all big organizations. Businessmen at the top. If there is any trouble, the ones at the bottom go to war. Only the ones at the bottom get arrested."

"It's the same everywhere."

"Japan too?"

"The ones at the top hide behind their suits. They almost never get caught, unless something big happens. They hire lawyers to tell them how to do things in a way that will keep them out of trouble."

Guo nodded. "Very smart. Taiwanese gangsters are learning from Japanese yakuza."

"But they're all doomed. Maybe not in our lifetimes, but they will be taken down."

"You believe that?"

"I do. Thugs who make money illegally, use violence to bend people to their wills, throw their weight around and try to live high on the hog will eventually get what's coming to them."

Guo smiled. "You are a good policeman."

"I don't know. A good cop is probably a little different from me.

"How?"

"Patriots. Guys who are committed to protecting the government.

The main reason why countries have police forces is to protect their political power. Anti-government forces are of far more interest to the police than your run-of-the-mill burglar."

"But you do not think that way?"

"I'm not worried about a revolution happening here. Nor do I think anti-government activities are going to destabilize the political situation. There aren't any groups that have enough support from the general population. There is some terrorism, but those are almost a form of advertising. It may emphasize the presence of some group or other, but it won't increase their following."

"What about sabotage from another country? Japanese need to pay better attention. You forget both good things and bad things so quickly, what you did and what was done to you."

"You're right. That is the Japanese mindset. Like you said, I don't think there's much chance of a coup d'état from within the country, but outside pressure could cause one to happen. But such a move would still have to be supported by many Japanese citizens. That would take a long time to happen. If a foreign country was going to invade Japan, it would be the army's responsibility, not the police."

"Things are very different in Taiwan."

"Japan is different from other developed nations in Asia. We have no political tension. Taiwan has the problem of mainland China. South Korea always has North Korea in its shadow. Japan has no military threats."

"Lucky."

"Lots of older people in Japan try to warn the younger ones who have never experienced a state of war. They tell us that we need to be prepared."

"Same thing in Taiwan. Older Taiwanese, especially the ones who came from the mainland after the war, say there is only one Chinese government. Taiwan has the only true Chinese government. They say the mainland government is a false one. Younger people don't care.

They are fine with it being two countries. One is Communist China. The other is the Republic of China. But Taiwan leaders refuse to give up. We have to enforce this view."

"Well, I'm not in a position to criticize you."

"Me, I don't care. I want to catch gangsters, killers, thieves. If they get weapons from a foreigner, I want to catch that foreigner, too. That's why I don't divide gangsters up, local and foreign, like you do."

Samejima nodded.

"Are there many police like you in Japan?" Guo asked.

"No, probably not. We don't really talk about this sort of thing."

"Worried what the boss might say?" Guo's face had an ironic expression.

"Some of that, I guess."

"Why did you become a policeman?"

Samejima thought for a moment. "I thought I was different from others. It might be hard to understand, but I knew I wasn't suited to work a regular job. I didn't think I'd be able to graduate school, get a job somewhere, follow the rules and be happy there until I retired. Now I know that there are lots of different jobs in different kinds of companies; not all of them are nine-to-five and not all of them are restrictive and boring. Besides, police have to obey all kinds of rules—they bind us, hand and foot. But as a cop, at least you always know your work is helping society. You can see it with your own eyes. It's different from serving the country as a patriot. I probably do it for my own sake. To me, it's all a matter of whether or not I believe in what I'm doing. It's not as easy as it sounds because the police are such a large organization."

"Do you like policemen?" Guo asked.

"They're a pain sometimes, but yes, I usually like them. Of course I do hate some of them."

"What kind?"

"The kind that are reckless and swagger about. And the kind that always talk about 'national interests.' I never trust that type. The most important thing is people, not the system or the organization. Police have more power than regular people. But that's so we can protect them, not make them follow rules. Some people do bad things and come to police to apologize. 'I'm sorry Mr. Policeman,' 'Please let this one go, Mr. Policeman.' To them, the police are like judges. They think we're the law in uniform. But I believe they are wrong. It's one thing to break a law. It's another issue entirely to *apologize* to us the police.

"You can't see the law with your own eyes. To me, police are like a fence. If you try to climb over that fence, you'll hurt yourself and maybe hurt others. So, if you can see the fence, just stay on the right side of it and everything will be fine. I'd be glad if the role of police was to make people think like that.

"But there are always the types who want to live outside the fence. They think it's a shortcut. Everyone knows it, but regular people usually don't go that way. They just take the more roundabout, law-abiding path. When someone speaks up about the ones getting away with cutting corners, the people outside the fence make threats to get the tattle-tales off their back. If the cheaters get away with it, the others see their own lifestyle and eventually feel like idiots for doing things the right-but-hard way. It's inequalities like that that I can't abide. There's a lot about life that's unfair, but there are some things I can't let go."

Samejima talked on, not really sure that Guo understood it all. It seemed stupid to talk to a fellow policeman about subjects like this. However, he felt that a lonely cop in a foreign country who had come so far to carry out his own agenda might understand.

Guo smiled at him. "Another cigarette, please?" Samejima gladly held out his pack. He'd never been able to speak so honestly before, even to colleagues in his own country.

Guo lit his cigarette and looked at Samejima. "You know why I'm here. You know I'm not here on a pleasure trip."

"That's true," Samejima quietly admitted and returned his gaze.

"I was in the military before I became a policeman. Army. I was recruited. I was a good swimmer and also very strong, so I trained for the Special Forces. I was assigned to the island of Jinmen Dao." On the memo pad Guo wrote two names, Jinmen Dao and Mazu Dao. "These islands belong to Taiwan. But mainland guns can reach it. If the mainland attacks Taiwan, they will start here. That's why Special Forces training is so hard. If attacked, we would have to dive into the sea and fight the enemy. In Taiwan, we are called *shuiguizai*."

"*Shuiguizai?*"

"Frogmen, an elite corps. We can all shoot well and are excellent at hand-to-hand combat. Yesterday I used Korean Tae kwon do. All frogmen can do it. We were taught by a Korean master. All the techniques are meant to kill. Frogmen are very loyal to each other. We would die for each other."

Samejima was quiet as Guo went on. "When I was twenty-nine, my father got sick. I couldn't be with my father if I stayed in the Special Forces. I asked for the help of my leader. He helped me transfer to the police. My father was in Taipei, Jinmen Dao was so far away. I was sad to leave my comrades, but I had to do it."

Samejima nodded.

"After a while, I became a detective. 'Operation Cleansweep' began. We were cleaning out the so-called 'Black Society' of gangsters. We planned to catch gang members and put them in jail. All the bad ones escaped to Hong Kong, Japan, Bolivia. Taiwan became a little safer. But then, in 1987, Taiwan and mainland China opened their doors to each other. And what came in? Black Stars, Red Stars, all kinds of guns. When people have guns, they form gangs because guns make them feel strong. Gangs sprouted up all over.

"Big gangs learned from 'Cleansweep' and attached themselves to companies in order to do business. Small gangs rob banks, rob jewelry stores, kidnap rich people. The Xu Brothers are a small gang. Big gangs do not get involved with small ones. They leave the dirty work to subordinates and pros."

"Pros?" asked Samejima, and Guo wrote something down on the memo pad. Samejima recognized the Chinese. "The first time I ever heard the expression was in a Hong Kong movie."

"Professional killers, hit men. Small-time thugs all use this fancy name to make their work sound important. They can use it to brag about what they do to others. Idiots."

"So there weren't actually any professional killers?"

"There are really only a few. But they stay hidden. Only the major gangs can hire them. Pros only talk to major gang bosses who order the hits. All of them have different day jobs. Shopkeepers, taxi drivers. Police do not suspect them. They are too smart to say they are gangsters."

"How do they go about their work, these pros?"

"An example: a gang wants to link up with a company. A big bank, or a real estate developer. The boss goes to the head of the company. He offers to become the company advisor. He tells them he'll take care of any trouble, but it's really just a racket for 'protection money.' The company president disagrees, but the vice-president says 'okay.' So, the gang boss calls a pro. It might take a week, a month, six months. The pro studies the company president—his house, what time he gets up in the morning, how he goes to work, favorite restaurants, night clubs, golf courses. Does he have a driver? Bodyguard? Then one day, 'bang!' The hit man uses a bomb or a rifle to make the kill. Police move quickly, but they can't pin it on the gang boss if they cannot catch the pro."

"I see."

"We have caught some pros and by those arrests we caught some bosses. But there is one pro we can't catch, no matter what we do. I think he is a former military man. He can use guns and bombs, but always kills by using a *nerio chagi*, a Tae kwon do kick. The kick I used yesterday was a twisting kick, *bituro chagi*. This pro uses an axe kick to crush the skull of his target. He moves as lightly as a monkey swinging from tree to tree. And he always leaves a wooden figurine of monkeys next to the body. The 'see no evil, hear no evil, say no evil' monkeys."

"So you've got that in Taiwan, too?"

"There's lots of Japanese culture still in Taiwan. This figurine is like a warning. It means nobody sees, hears or talks about him. It's his calling card. We think he does the sculpting himself. Newspapers have taken pictures of it and gave the pro a nickname: Du Yuan."

Guo picked up his pen and wrote down the characters for "poison ape." "I am after Du Yuan. I heard rumors that he was betrayed by a gangster." He wrote down some more characters. "I don't know how you say this in Japanese. I heard about it from a man I arrested."

"An informant," explained Samejima.

"Right. All detectives have informants. Mine checked it out for me. Wei Ye, a boss of the Sihai gang, betrayed Du Yuan. He used Du Yuan to kill people who made problems for Sihai, but he never got caught because Du Yuan always escaped. But last year Wei Ye himself was kidnapped by gangsters."

It was unthinkable in Japan, but in Taiwan, small gangs who did bank robberies and kidnapping also kidnapped top men in major syndicates and held them for ransom. The victims probably assumed wrongly that they were much too well protected for it to ever happen to them. Small-time gangsters would lay in wait until their target had no more than a few bodyguards around him. Then they came out with rifles and submachine guns, grabbed the target and whisked him away in a getaway car in a matter of seconds.

The culprits always wore masks to hide their identity. They demanded ransom from the victim's families, and when they got it, they took their hostages and dumped them out in the countryside. That was the pattern.

Men who were kidnapped were not inclined to go public about it. If it got out that men of their stature had pleaded for their lives, weeping and snot-nosed, finally forcing their families to pay the ransom, it would make them laughingstocks. Not to mention the bad example it would set for those under their command.

Wei Ye was kidnapped by Baiyin, a syndicate comprised of eighteen gangs. It was named after its leader, Wen Baiyin. Wei Ye was snatched from the home of his mistress in Taipei. The mistress and three bodyguards were shot and killed on the spot. Three days later, Ye's family paid a ransom of 500,000 Taiwan dollars, and he was released. Once free, a mortified Ye hired Du Yuan to avenge himself and, above all, to keep the matter a secret. Du Yuan discovered that Baiyin had been behind the kidnapping, and got right to work.

After Du Yuan killed the first three Baiyin members, Ye fled to America. He wanted to avoid both the Taiwan police and subsequent revenge of the Baiyin syndicate.

Du Yuan kept up the Baiyin slaughter. Knowing they were being stalked, the members tried scattering; they tried staying together; no matter what they did, Du Yuan managed to get to them.

In one month, Baiyin lost five members. One shot, one beaten to death, three killed at the same time by a bomb in their apartment. They all knew Du Yuan was after them, but they were helpless. Nobody knew his real name or his address.

On the orders of Wei Ye, Wen Baiyin, the leader, was the last to go. Rumor had it that he ordered Du Yuan to deliver Baiyin's eyeballs to him. When there were only two members left alive, Wen Baiyin took a gamble. He left Taiwan and went to Los Angeles to kidnap Ye again. Taken completely by surprise, Ye yielded to Wen Baiyin, and promised to withdraw Du Yuan's orders.

Baiyin, however, wasn't satisfied. Among the gang members murdered were two of his brothers. He demanded that in exchange for Ye's life, he tell him Du Yuan's real name so he could track him down and kill him.

"So was Du Yuan murdered?" asked Samejima.

"No, he was suspicious as soon as Wei Ye contacted him and told him to spare the lives of the last two Baiyin members, and so he went into hiding."

As soon as Wen Baiyin got back to Taipei, he tracked down Du Yuan's home, but he was gone. There was a woman in the house, and they murdered her in cold blood. They pumped her full of drugs, raped her repeatedly and then shot her.

It was believed that this woman was Du Yuan's lover. They didn't live together, but that day she had come in to sort through mail and clean the place up.

"Wen Baiyin and his fellow gangster never had a prayer after that. Three months later, they were found dead in the Wanhua area of Taipei."

"What happened to Wei Ye?" Samejima asked.

"He had to leave the US because the Chinese and Vietnamese mafia in Los Angeles were at war. But he couldn't go back to Taiwan. Du Yuan was waiting for him. So he came here, to Japan."

"Does he have people here to protect him?"

"Yes. Do you know Takezo Ishiwa?"

Samejima nodded. He was the boss of the Ishiwa gang, which was part of a wide-ranging syndicate that had been designated for attention by Headquarters. The Ishiwa gang was known for its violent tendencies.

"Ishiwa owns coffee shops, arcades, and video shops in Taipei. The puppet heads of the companies are Taiwanese, all relatives of

Wei Ye. The video shop stocks Japanese movies and TV programs. Pirated copies. They make Ishiwa a lot of money. I borrowed videos from their shop before I came here, so I could work on my Japanese." He mentioned the names of popular dramas and detective series.

"When did Ye arrive in Japan?" asked Samejima.

"One month ago. Probably using a Bolivian passport. He must be living in fear. He knows he can't escape from Du Yuan."

"Do you know Du Yuan's real name?"

Guo shook his head. "His apartment in Taipei was rented under a false name. But I have an idea."

Samejima looked at Guo. Guo stood up. He pulled his Samsonite suitcase from the closet with his good hand. He opened the combination lock and pulled out a black-and-white photograph from the inside pocket. Samejima took it.

A group of men in wet suits were standing on a speedboat, their arms around each other's shoulders. There were six of them, all equipped with knives and underwater guns, aqualungs at their feet. A sailor with an M16 stood next to them. In the bright sunlight, their tanned skin offered a contrast to their wet masks. Guo was second from the left. He pointed to a tall man standing next to him. Then he wrote on the memo pad as he spoke.

"I believe his name is Zhensheng Liu. He is the same age as me. He was also a frogman. But three years after I left, he was involved in a major incident and quit the military. He was a very quiet man, but skilled at Tae kwon do. He was the strongest of us all. He mastered the *nerio chagi*, the kick that can crush a man's skull."

Samejima took a good look at Liu's face. His eyes were lowered; he was obviously camera shy. He looked much younger than Guo did.

"Why do you believe Du Yuan is Liu?"

"His family was very poor. Long ago his sister got sick, but no doctor would come out to see her, so she died. Liu always carried

126

her picture with him. I lost track of him after he quit the military. I looked for him because I wanted to talk. I went to his family home and met his mother and another sister and brother. His father died a long time ago. His mother was ill. This was right after he quit the military. His brother said he called and told them he would take care of things. Every month he sent them lots of money, but his letters never had a return address.

"One more thing. Wei Ye has many friends in the military. He knows frogmen are the army elite. When frogmen had vacations, Ye invited them to his restaurants and hotels. He invited us to work for him after we left the army. This began about the time I quit in 1987."

"So you've suspected all along he was Du Yuan?"

"I thought it was a possibility. Liu was always good with his hands. When he had time, he used a knife to carve wood. He made toys called, what do you call them? *Taketombo*, bamboo propellers. But I never saw him make the three monkeys. I wanted to find out for sure. Liu was my best friend in the army. If he is Du Yuan, then I am the only one who can catch him. If a SWAT team ever surrounds him, they will shoot him. I don't want that. I want to make sure it is Liu. But I can't do it in Taiwan. He can hide and wait for days or months. He always had the most patience of anyone in our troop. But right now, I am sure he is in Japan. He is going to kill Wei Ye. He can't forgive the man who betrayed him and had his lover killed."

Samejima breathed in deeply. If everything Guo said was true, Shinjuku was harboring a live bomb. A hit man named Du Yuan—the Poison Ape—might be in Japan hunting down a boss of the Taiwanese mafia. In the process, he might get Japanese yakuza embroiled in a war.

"Do you have positive proof that Du Yuan is in Japan?"

Guo shook his head. "No, it is impossible to read Du Yuan's movements. I have visited every Taiwan bar in Tokyo that Taiwanese

127

gangsters frequent looking for information about Wei Ye, about Du Yuan. But Du Yuan is clever, so maybe he won't go to Taiwan bars. Maybe he's not here yet."

"Do you think Ye might be with the Ishiwa gang?"

"I checked. Some of them go to Taiwan bars. But not Ye. He is probably hiding."

There were two Ishiwa offices in the jurisdiction of the Shinjuku Precinct. One was called "headquarters," and the other was known as "the dorm." But Samejima doubted Ye was at either of them.

"I believe you are a great cop," said Guo. "Please keep the business about Du Yuan a secret."

Samejima looked at Guo. If Du Yuan was about to attack the Ishiwa gang, it could mean war. If Du Yuan made a move, young yakuza might think it was an attack from another gang, and they would fight back. That would spoil what both Guo and Araki were trying to accomplish. Shinjuku would be in a state of alarm, either forcing Du Yuan out into the open or further underground. Samejima wouldn't be able to keep any secrets if there was a chance of a gang war threatening ordinary citizens.

"Tell me one thing," Samejima said seriously, "that's important for me to know."

"Yes?"

"Has Du Yuan ever killed anyone unconnected to his targets? Either to gain information or as collateral damage from bombs?"

"No. Du Yuan is a professional. He only kills the people he is hired to kill."

"What do you think might happen this time? Would he kill any members of the Ishiwa gang, or the leader, Takezo Ishiwa?"

Guo bit his lip as sweat broke out on his forehead. "I can't say. Maybe if they are bodyguards for Wei Ye."

"Would he torture Ishiwa gangsters to get them to tell him where Ye is?"

"Probably not. If Liu is Du Yuan, then he can't speak Japanese. He can't ask anyone anything about where Ye is."

"He would need someone to interpret for him."

"But who? I have talked to many Taiwanese in Shinjuku to ask about that. But I haven't found out anything yet."

"Just so you know," Samejima spoke slowly, "if Du Yuan makes one wrong step, we could have a gang war on our hands. I understand how you feel, but my first priority is to prevent that from happening. I can only help you until Du Yuan hurts or kills someone. If that happens, I'll report everything we've said here to my superiors. It would mean watching the Ishiwa gang, closing in on them, and ordering Takezo Ishiwa to turn over Wei Ye."

Guo's expression went blank. He finally spoke in low tones. "There is nothing I can do about that. I would do the same if I was in your place. This is your country."

"That's right. But you trusted me by telling me about Du Yuan. I want to be worthy of that trust. Two nights ago you were at an illegal mahjong gambling operation in Okubo."

Guo looked stunned, but managed to respond, "I remember! It felt like someone was watching me."

"I was on a surveillance team that was staking out the place," Samejima nodded slowly. "I saw you. I knew you were unusual just by looking at you."

"What about last night?"

"That was a coincidence. I saw you, recognized you, and followed. I wanted to know who you were."

"Where did you see me?"

"I saw you come out of a Taiwanese restaurant on Kuyakusho Avenue."

Guo nodded. "I went to a Taiwan club before that. A place Ishiwa gang members use. But there was no one there last night."

Samejima was dumbfounded by Guo's skill. He had only been in

129

Shinjuku a few days and had already found the spots where Ishiwa might meet with Taiwanese gangsters. He looked at his watch. It was already getting dark outside.

"I'm on my way back to the precinct. Like I told you, it will take a while longer to settle this business with Huan Xu. Do what you like until then."

Guo bowed his head. "Thank you."

"I'll contact you if I learn anything."

"Okay."

"Will you be going back to Kabukicho tonight?"

Guo nodded, his eyes glistening. "Yes, I'll go back. I'll go back again and again until I find Zhensheng Liu."

12

Nami was terrified. She was on the late shift. Yang had instructed her to go to work and act as if she knew nothing. She had not slept a wink. Yang had been satisfied to sleep on the floor of her studio apartment, with only a single blanket to cover him.

When they had first arrived at her apartment, she had asked what she could do to help him. But no matter how many times she tried, Yang had been silent. He seemed to be thinking about something. Finally, he spoke.

"I'll leave in the morning. I'll call you if I need your help again, either here or at the club."

"I can't go back to the club."

"You have to. Show up for work as if nothing had happened. Otherwise the police will be suspicious about you."

"But what about you?"

"I can't go back. Nan knows I was the last one with Agi. I'll be a suspect no matter what I do. I'll go out in the morning to get my things. Then I'll come back here, if things look safe. If you don't mind."

Nami felt the inside of her mouth go dry, but she was not afraid of Yang even though she was alone with him.

"I don't mind. What should I do if the police come?"

"Here?"

Nami nodded. Yang looked around the room. She hung her undergarments to dry inside to hide the fact that she was a woman

131

living alone. He stopped when he saw them.

"Hang those out on the balcony if anything goes wrong." Her apartment building was on the right-hand side of a one-way street leading north to Okubo Avenue. There was a convenience store on the ground floor, and she lived on the fourth. Anyone who arrived would have to come up the stairs, but the balcony was visible from the street.

"What should I say to them?"

"Give them the time you originally left the club. Say you went straight home. Just don't let them know you went back." Yang paused for a moment to look at Nami. "Why *did* you come back?"

Nami just shook her head. Now that she knew what sort of man he was, she couldn't tell him what she used to think of him. As the sun was coming up, Nami, half asleep, saw Yang get ready to leave. He looked down at her in the half-light and whispered in Chinese, "Many thanks," and went quietly out the door.

All alone, Nami began to get more nervous as the time to leave for work drew near. Had Agi's body been discovered? She turned on the TV and flipped through the channels looking for the news. She usually didn't watch news programs. There was no mention of a dead body found at a Shinjuku nightclub. It made sense, really, since neither Agi, Nan nor Yang was due to report for duty until three-thirty or so. They would have been the first to enter the club.

Nami had a sudden thought. Agi always stopped in at the head office of the company that owned the club and turned over the receipts from the night before. Yasui Enterprises owned Fountain of Roses and also ran a high-interest loan business. Yasui, the company president, might come looking for Agi and find him before anyone else.

Nami had only met Yasui a couple of times, but she could tell at a glance that he was yakuza. He was much more of a gentleman, though, than Agi ever was.

It was possible that Yasui, wondering why Agi didn't show up, would head over to the club. The only other possibility was that Nan would find Agi. She felt sorry for him. He would be in a tough spot if the police arrived.

Nami got ready to go at four-thirty, preparing to leave as usual.

Would the police be there? Would the interrogation be frightening? Would it be like a TV drama where suspects were taken into a room one by one for questioning?

If that happened, she wasn't sure if she'd be able to keep her mouth shut. They'd be sure to guess when the color drained from her face. She tried to remind herself that no cop could be as scary as the mean girls she went to junior high school with. Plus, she couldn't suppress the relief she felt now that Fountain of Roses was free of Agi and his tyranny.

She went down the stairs of her apartment building, her knees shaking badly, and headed towards the station. Riding the train, she tried to calm herself with a series of deep breaths. She felt as though everyone was looking at her. The one-stop ride had never seemed so long. As she tried to walk through Shinjuku Station, her legs could barely hold her up. She grabbed onto the handrail of the crowded stairwell and leaned heavily on it as she walked down.

She stopped in at a restroom just before the turnstile to check her complexion. She didn't know what she would do if she had gone pale. She had applied her make-up more heavily than usual, and her reflection in the mirror looked about normal to her.

The expression on her oval face was not particularly cheerful. She kept her hair tied back because the ends were damaged. The only part of her face she really liked was her white teeth. Her eyes were small and her eyelids didn't fold. Her face looked fleshy, her nose was nothing special and her lips were too thin.

She knew her appearance was dismal, but it improved slightly when she managed to smile. She had never known what Agi liked about her. At any rate, she was satisfied that she looked the same as usual.

She went through the turnstile and climbed the stairs up to the street level. Sometimes she continued through the underground walkway for a distance. It depended on her mood. She was afraid that if she stayed underground too long and came up to find policemen, she'd be startled and it would make her look suspicious.

The area in front of Studio Alta on Shinjuku Avenue was as crowded as ever. Her heart began to pound as she stood waiting at a traffic light. She kept telling herself, *I'm not guilty! I didn't kill him!*

She walked straight ahead until she got to Yasukuni Boulevard. As she waited for the walk signal, she noticed that nothing seemed any different than usual. There were neither patrol cars nor policemen about. She gulped several times, and then walked across Yasukuni Boulevard. She felt her expression go as stiff as a Noh mask. She checked her watch; it was four fifty-six.

She entered Kabukicho, but there didn't seem to be as many people there as usual. No hawkers stood on the street calling customers into the clubs. Why were there so few people at the game arcade?

She saw the curry stand on her left, and saw a few young people run by, turning down the street she was about to take. She turned the corner, holding on tightly to her purse.

Then she saw them. There was a dark mountain of people, with camera flashes going off wildly. Police cars blocked the road, their red lights shining in the windows of the shops on the street. Policemen swarmed the area.

Nami wanted to turn around and go home, but she set her feet in the direction of the crowd and kept on walking.

13

Samejima learned the next day about the Special Murder Investigation Headquarters set up at the precinct. It was the same day he had been debriefed about the stabbing of Saji, the Hongo gang member, in front of the Shinjuku Station coin lockers. Samejima was questioned by Momoi, other section chiefs from Shinjuku and an official from HQ.

Having a suspect killed while surrounded by the police was a case that was not handled lightly. The purpose of the inquiry was to decide whether there had been any mistakes during the procedure while they collected the evidence, kept the suspect in custody and held the crowd at arm's length.

Samejima had been the superior officer on the scene, and he took full responsibility. He reported that he had been unable to predict that the man who killed Saji would make such a move at that point, and insisted that the uniformed officers who backed him up were not at fault.

The members of the inquiry informed him that he would be notified of any formal reprimand at a later date. Happily, there was relatively no media awareness of the incident. There had been a pile-up on an expressway in Kansai, the western region of Japan, on the same day. Newspapers and news programs did not make a fuss over the loss of a yakuza member. In this case, newscasters and viewers had more sympathy for the murderer.

If the media had put the blame on the way the incident had

135

been handled, Samejima's treatment would have been much harsher. Fortunately, punishment rarely meant being removed from fieldwork. And any attempts to transfer Samejima would have been impossible, since no other section or precinct would touch him.

The upper ranks at HQ certainly considered stripping him of his badge, but they knew that Samejima would fight back with everything he had. He assumed they would rather let sleeping dogs lie. Plus, if he was dismissed over this kind of case it would be fodder for the tabloids. They would figure out that Samejima irritated the brass to the point that they were constantly on the lookout for any easy excuse to fire him.

The more Samejima strove to excel, the more opportunities they would have to dispose of him, but it didn't keep him from putting his all into his work. Samejima believed that people have the right to live their lives in a way that allows them to justify their own existence. His job as a detective and his relationship with Sho were the most precious things in his life, and losing either of them would be like losing his life.

The inquiry ended in the morning, and at noon Samejima visited the cafeteria for lunch. He almost never sat with anyone unless it was Momoi or Yabu, from Criminal Identification. That day, Yabu came into the cafeteria a few minutes after him. He was a singularly unattractive man, with a large face and a big, bald head. He apparently put no thought into what he wore or what he ate.

Yabu was known for his skills in ballistic testing, and HQ's Criminal Investigations and even the special forensics unit had invited him on a number of occasions to work for them, but he never agreed. Within the precinct he was as notorious as Momoi for being an eccentric, and he used his reputation to stay in a position that let him do work he was good at in a place he felt comfortable.

As soon as he spotted Samejima, he wandered over to say hello.

His hands still in his coat pockets, he plopped himself down in the chair across from him.

"Raked over the coals again?" he asked perfunctorily.

"Not too badly," Samejima replied. Noting that Yabu had nothing to eat, he pointed absently at his own lunch. "The special is edible today."

"Really? You don't say." Yabu reached over and pulled Samejima's tray to his side of the table. He took a bite, and as Samejima watched, started shoving most of the main dish into his mouth. "You're right," he nodded and unapologetically polished off the entire meal.

Samejima stood up and went to get another lunch, returning to the table as Yabu put down an empty rice bowl. He looked at the new tray, and with his mouth still full, growled, "I can't eat all of that!"

"What're you talking about?" Samejima growled back. "That was *my* lunch you just ate!"

"Oh." Yabu didn't seem to be excessively burdened with guilt, and he casually reached out for a pickle on Samejima's new tray, which he popped in his mouth and crunched on noisily. Now thirsty, he picked up Samejima's teacup. Samejima went to get a new one, filled it with tea and set it out for his friend.

"Take this."

"Thanks," Yabu mumbled as he took a sip. As Samejima finally got back to his own meal, Yabu started on a different topic. "So there's a new case."

"Yeah, that's what I hear, but I don't suppose you'll be involved," said Samejima, implying that there had been no guns.

"I went to the scene yesterday, but the cause of death was blunt force. It was as if the victim had been bludgeoned from directly overhead. The top of his skull was split, and there were pieces of it in his brain. It was a single blow. The perp must be tall with long arms. He would have had to swing something hard over his head—assuming the victim had been standing." Yabu's eyes followed

Samejima's chopsticks as he demonstrated the crime.

"So who was the victim?" Samejima asked, wanting to change the subject.

"Some nightclub manager. He was a drug addict, had tracks all up his side. They found him yesterday evening. The owner called the police. You ever heard of Yasui Enterprises?"

"Kabukicho 1st Street, right?"

"Right. The president's Mr. Yasui. He runs the place. Probably yakuza."

Samejima nodded, put down his chopsticks and picked up his teacup. He knew that Yasui was part of the same crime syndicate as the Ishiwa gang.

"Was the victim a gang member?"

"Not officially."

"Who is the suspect?"

"One of the bar backs who works there went missing."

"Did he leave any evidence behind?"

"Nothing. Not even a fingerprint."

"No fingerprints? The guy worked there. There had to be something."

"Everything was clean and neat. There were plenty of other fingerprints of customers and other employees, but everything this guy touched—his locker, trays, ashtrays—all of them had been wiped clean."

"But you haven't figured out who all those prints belong to, have you?"

"How long do you think I've been at this? The guy left no prints. Everything he touched was clean."

"Strange," Samejima said.

"Why?"

"If you were afraid of leaving prints, wouldn't you just wipe everything? This guy just wiped the things he had touched. It would

138

be one thing if it was a place he'd never been before, but he worked there."

"Been there two weeks, they said."

"After two weeks, how could he have known what he'd touched?"

"Yeah, it's strange."

"What does HQ say?"

"Anyone who needed to wipe off prints must have a record."

"Do they know his name or address?"

"Records are pretty sloppy. Yasui couldn't tell us anything because he didn't keep employees' resumes. The victim was the one that hired him."

"No photos?"

"Nope, they're considering putting together a composite. They think he's foreign."

"Foreign?"

"There was one illegal worker from Bangladesh. The victim always hired illegals he didn't have to pay much."

"Where was he from?"

"Somewhere in Asia. At the club, he told them his name was Yang."

Samejima nodded. "They'll catch up with him before long."

"The cash register was empty. They're looking at Chinese with burglary records. We'll get the other employees to identify him if we show them photos."

"What's the name of the place?"

"Fountain of Roses. Used to be a catch bar." A catch bar was a now-illegal type of club that used pimps and hostesses to drag customers in off the street and then charge them exorbitant prices. "They probably shut it down, changed the name and re-opened."

"I'm sure. Horn-dogs don't care what the place is called as long as they can get one off."

Araki called that afternoon, and he and Samejima met once again. They went to the coffee shop in the same hotel as before, and Samejima told Araki what he had learned from Guo.

"A pro hit-man?" Araki was surprised.

"I'm just worried about what'll happen if any of the Ishiwa gang get in the way. We'd have to stop all hell from breaking loose."

"Do you think he's really here in Japan? Someone as deadly as that?"

"Guo said Sihai gangsters got in on Bolivian passports. You want to check?"

"It wouldn't work. Immigration doesn't note ethnic Chinese Bolivians separately. Columbia and Bolivia are on their list of watched countries, but they couldn't pick out gangsters unless they had tried to bring something illegal into the country."

"I know it's a long shot, but would you mind checking?"

Araki nodded his assent and continued. "So what are you going to do?"

"Just watch for a while. Guo is doing his best to find Du Yuan. It's someone he has a connection to."

"Can you really do kicks like that in Tae kwon do?"

"It's a martial art. It just depends how good you are at it. If Du Yuan is stronger than Guo, then he's a walking lethal weapon. Think about it. Guo crushed Huan Xu's nose with just his hand. He broke his jaw with a kick. Just those two moves, I saw them with my own eyes. It was instantaneous. If there's someone better than he is, an average thug won't have a chance against him."

"If Ishiwa gets involved, they are going to use arms."

"Of course they will, but Du Yuan won't be stupid enough to come at them head-on."

"Will he be armed, too?"

"I can't say, but from what I've heard, Taiwanese can be armed to the teeth."

"How do you mean?"

"Automatic guns and hand grenades."

Araki bit his lip. "We would have a mess on our hands if they really have all that."

"It could mean the annihilation of the Ishiwa gang," added Samejima.

"Impossible. I don't care how strong you say he is, he's just one guy, right?" asked Araki.

"According to Guo, we shouldn't make light of him. He believes Du Yuan won't rest until he finds Wei Ye. We need to find him, too."

"But if we're not careful, Wei Ye will go underground. If that happens we won't have any excuses for crushing Ishiwa."

"Right. As I see it, we have two alternatives. One is to work Ishiwa into a corner so they have to give up Wei Ye. The other is to keep a close eye on them and wait for something to happen."

"The first way would require a major operation. We'd have to call in SWAT teams and surround the boss's home and all of their offices. And even if we find Ye, we don't have a justified reason to interrogate him."

"And if we do it like that, Du Yuan will just wait for us to bring Ye out in the open."

Araki sighed and looked at the ceiling. "Surveillance on Ishiwa…"

"It'll be tough without the help of Section Four. There's not much chance Ye will be in the first place we look for him."

"And no matter how scared he is, he probably won't be holed up in some sort of fortress. I'll bet he goes out to eat and drink once every few days."

"I agree," said Samejima. "He's a gangster. It's not in his nature to lay low for long."

"So I guess we'll just have to wait for Du Yuan to smoke him out," sighed Araki.

"Du Yuan isn't wanted for anything in Japan. He's free to move around."

"And if we catch Du Yuan first, we'll lose our chance to link Ishiwa to Taiwan."

Samejima nodded. "All we can do now is wait."

14

Fountain of Roses closed. What other alternative was there? The manager was dead and the two bar backs had quit. After the police finished questioning them all, Nami and the other hostesses were called into the Yasui Enterprises offices.

Yasui had discovered Agi's corpse and called the police, but he didn't seem particularly upset about the matter. Nami figured yakuza must be used to this sort of thing.

"The club will be closed for a while. If you're worried about making ends meet, feel free to quit, and I'll pay you the day rate you're owed. It'll take a few days to do the paperwork, but raise your hands if you need me to pay you."

The others all raised their hands, and Nami followed suit.

"I see," said Yasui. He was accompanied by a young man he called his chauffeur, but it was clear that he was actually a low-ranking gangster.

"What's the matter with you greedy bitches," the chauffeur snarled, "after everything the boss has done for you?"

"Stop it." Yasui put a hand on the man's shoulder to call him off. Nami noted the enormous diamond ring he was wearing. It was much larger and looked far more expensive than the one Agi wore. "The girls have to make a living, too."

"When can we expect to be paid?" Kazuki spoke up. The young man glared at her and spit. She ignored him.

"The end of next week, or the beginning of the next."

There was a moan of disappointment among the girls.

"Either that or you can do without," Yasui calmly stated. "I've got to give Agi a funeral and I lost everything in the cash register. It's not easy for me either."

"Do any of ya know where Yang is?" the young thug spoke up again. Nami realized that not only the police, but the gang members also knew who was suspected of the murder. "Well?" The chauffeur glared at each girl in turn.

Iku suddenly spoke out. "Nami was friends with him."

Nami's breath caught in her throat, but she managed to keep a blank look on her face. Yasui looked at her.

"You're Nami, aren't you?"

"Do ya know where he is?" The thug stuck his face up to hers, his breathing ragged.

"Come now," Yasui said in a placating manner as he walked over to her. "Do you know? Tell me if you do. If I don't cooperate with the police there'll be trouble."

"I don't know where he is," said Nami, glaring at Iku. Iku ignored her and continued to loudly snap her gum.

"Are you sure?" Yasui urged. "I won't bother you. There's nothing to be afraid of. Just tell me anything you know."

"I don't know anything."

Yasui stood there for a few moments, silently staring at her, then nodded slightly. He pulled a business card out of his pocket and put it in Nami's hand. "The bag Yang took has an important business card in it. Some guy I lent money to. I just want that card back. I won't do anything to you. If Yang contacts you, call this number. Even if I'm not there, whoever answers will ring my mobile phone or pager."

Nami was silent.

"I'd consider it a favor." Yasui patted Nami on the shoulder. "All right then, you can all go home now."

144

All the girls started filing out of the office. On the way down the stairs, Nami watched Iku from behind. Kazuki berated her.

"How could you say something like that? That was an awful thing to do to Nami."

"Right! You'd better apologize," An joined in.

"Whatever," grumbled Iku.

"Don't give me that attitude," Kazuki snapped.

"It's all right." Nami spoke up.

"What do you mean? You ought to be pissed off! She's such a bitch! He was about to threaten you!" An was having trouble keeping her temper under control. Iku just shrugged her off.

When they got outside, Iku swung her head back and forth as she looked up at the sky before turning her attention back to Nami.

"I hate the Chinese," she said.

"What are you talking about?" asked An.

"Her." Iku indicated Nami with her chin.

"What do you mean? Nami is…"

"In junior high there was a girl from a family left in China after the war. She really pissed me off. She looked a lot like her." Iku spoke defiantly. "That weird accent, her crappy way of talking. I never liked it."

Nami felt herself go cold. Her face stiffened.

Iku kept talking. "I saw her speaking Chinese to Yang!"

"So what?" Kazuki said. "It doesn't matter where she came from. You should be ashamed of yourself!"

"Fuck you!" Iku growled and spit the gum she was chewing at Nami's feet. "Go to hell," she said in a low voice and then skipped on ahead of the others.

"Nami…" Kazuki said.

"I'm fine!" Nami shouted, startling Kazuki.

Nami turned around and looked towards Kazuki and An who were walking behind her, and bowed her head.

"I appreciate the time we've spent together. Take care of yourselves!" She smiled as broadly as she could, then turned back around and ran off.

15

That night, Sho came to Samejima's apartment after a recording session. Just minutes after Samejima got home at eight, Sho called.

"Have you eaten?" she asked right away.

"Dinner, but no midnight snacks yet," laughed Samejima.

"I'm starving. What would you do for a fledgling rock star on the brink of starving to death?"

"I'd think about feeding her if her days on the stage are truly numbered."

"Then you better feed me quick. I'm on my way!"

Samejima met Sho at a family restaurant along Route 7. She was famished. She polished off her orders of hamburger steak and spaghetti soon after they were set on the table. As Samejima watched with a glass of beer in his hand, she drank down her own water and reached out for his.

"Ah, much better!" She glowed with satisfaction.

"You remember this night when you're rich and famous and insist on steaks from just one restaurant and only go to a certain high-end sushi place," Samejima teased her.

Sho finally laughed. "You can bet I won't be hanging out with a cop if I'm that rich and famous. I'll switch to some CEO with a Porsche."

"I bet."

"But if I don't become famous, I'll settle for a civil servant who can keep me fed."

Samejima swung at her from across the table, but Sho ignored him and stood up.

"Where are you going?"

"To the penniless cop's apartment. Now that my belly's full I'm tired. I didn't sleep at all yesterday or the day before."

When they got back to his apartment, she crawled into Samejima's bed fully clothed.

"You're really going to sleep?"

"Yup!" she declared without hesitation. She pulled the blanket up to her chin and rustled around underneath. Then her jeans, socks, and sweatshirt fell out from under the covers. She fluffed up the pillow, then draped her arm over Samejima. He was sitting on a cushion next to the bed watching TV.

"Turn it down."

Samejima clucked his tongue and turned down the volume. Sho yawned in pleasure and rubbed Samejima's shoulder softly. Her face was towards him and her eyes were closed. Within ten minutes she was breathing deeply and slowly. She was asleep.

Samejima smiled resignedly, got up, turned on a small reading lamp and switched off the ceiling light. He watched TV for two hours, but she showed no signs of waking. He gently put Sho's arm under the covers, stood up and went to take a shower. Afterwards he put on his pajamas and headed for bed. Sho opened one eye.

"Don't think you're going to get any just because you're all nice and clean."

"So I feed you and you expect to sleep for free?"

"My taxes pay your salary."

Samejima picked up the extra pillow and silently shoved it in Sho's face. She laughed and screamed at the same time.

"I think there's either a murder or some other violent crime going on here," Samejima said without letting up. Sho wrestled with him until she got the pillow off her face. She was bright red and gasping.

"You'll pay for this! I'll sue you!"

"Let's see your evidence then. How did the suspect hurt you?"

Sho's tank top had shifted and one of her large breasts was exposed.

"Did the perp do this, right here?"

"S-Stop it!"

"How about here, like this?"

"Ah—hold on!"

"And finally, did he do this right here?"

Samejima got both her tank top and panties off. He held down both of her arms with his left one, and put his right hand on her upper thigh.

"Is that all you got?" Sho's breathing became more even and her eyes began to sparkle.

"So what happened next?" asked Samejima.

"He kissed me. Hard," she managed to get out.

"Hard?"

"Yeah, he used his tongue, the bastard."

Samejima kissed Sho and let her arms go. He pulled his lips away.

"And then?"

"Then he climbed up on the roof and howled like a dog."

"That's all?"

"That's all."

"A false accusation will get you nowhere."

"Heh, heh, heh," Sho laughed as she clicked off the reading lamp.

16

Nami spent the entire next day in her room, eating prepared food from the convenience store on the ground floor. She kept the TV on for news at seven, nine, ten, and eleven-thirty. There was nothing about Agi's murder. She didn't know whether or not police had caught Yang. While in the convenience store, she bought a magazine of wanted ads for women. She had to find somewhere new to work, and soon. But she couldn't bring herself to read the listings.

At twelve-thirty the phone rang. Nami jumped, it was the first time it had rung all day.

"Hello?"

"Are you alone?" It was Chinese.

"Yes."

"I want to go to your apartment."

"That's fine."

The caller hung up. The doorbell rang five minutes later. Nami stood up and opened it to find a man she had never seen before. His hair was carefully combed, and he wore glasses and an expensive gray suit. When she looked closer, she saw it was Yang. In his hand was a metal attaché case. He walked in silently, and quickly scanned the small apartment with his sharp eyes.

Nami was stunned. "Wow, you look like a rich guy."

Yang didn't respond. He slid the attaché under her bed, and sat down. "What did the police say?"

"They didn't suspect me, but..." Nami tried to speak, but she was still amazed by Yang's transformation.

"But?"

"They're looking for you."

Yang nodded slightly.

"The owner is looking for you, too."

"Owner?"

Nami showed him the card Yasui had given her. Yang looked at it as Nami told him what had taken place at Yasui Enterprises. However, she didn't tell him what Iku had said to her outside the office.

She felt something strange in her chest. As usual, she was unafraid of Yang. In fact, this new version of Yang piqued her curiosity.

"This man told you to call?"

"Yes."

"If you called, do you think he'd see you?"

"I don't know. Probably."

Yang thought for a few moments. Nami was worried about what he might do, so she asked him what he was thinking. Yang looked at her with vacant eyes.

"I'm looking for someone. He's with a Japanese named Ishiwa. I want to know about this Ishiwa."

Nami shook her head. She'd never heard of anyone by that name.

"He's the head of a gang, the Ishiwa gang."

"I don't know him."

"Yasui is yakuza. He must know Ishiwa."

"Why do you think that?"

Yang pulled his attaché case out from under the bed and opened it. He was careful not to show the contents to Nami, quickly pulling out a plastic bag. In it was Agi's bag, the one Yang had taken from the club. He opened it. There was a wallet, some receipts and business cards. There was something that looked like a leather pen case.

Yang opened the case. There was a slim disposable hypodermic needle and four tiny packets that looked like the desiccant put in snack foods to keep them from going stale.

"This is what he wants." They were packets of amphetamines. "If the police find this, they'll ask more questions. That's what Yasui is afraid of."

Nami watched as Yang picked up one of the packets, pulled off the corner and poured it into his hand. Nami was amazed at how beautiful it was. It was white and it sparkled. Yang held his hand up to the fluorescent ceiling light. Then he lowered his hand and put a tiny amount on the tip of his tongue. Nami couldn't take her eyes off of him.

"It's been mixed," Yang finally said, "but it's from Taiwan." He spit into a piece of tissue paper, and frowned.

"Does it taste bad?"

"It's very bitter."

"Do you use it?"

Yang shook his head. "Only idiots use this stuff." He stood up, went to the sink and poured the contents of all the packets down the drain, then washed his hands thoroughly.

Nami handed him a can of cola from the refrigerator. Yang nodded in thanks, pulled the tab and took a drink.

"I want you to call him," he said.

"Why?"

"Tell him you know where I am."

Nami's eyes opened wide.

"Tell him you want to see him somewhere where no one will disturb us."

"Where?"

Yang thought for a few moments.

"Shinjuku Gyoen Park. It's quiet there."

"It's closed at night."

"I know."

"Have you been there?"

Yang nodded.

"There's a building called the Taiwan Pavilion. That's where we'll meet."

"When should I call?"

"Tomorrow morning before it opens."

"He won't come that early."

"He will. Tell him about the leather case."

"What time?"

"Five a.m."

"There won't be anyone in the office to answer the phone."

Yang held out the card. "Don't worry. Someone will definitely be there."

Nami wondered what made him so sure, but she agreed to do as he said. Then to her surprise, Yang stood up to go.

"Where are you going?"

"Back to my place."

"Already? You have a place to stay?"

Yang was silent. Just then, the phone rang. Yang looked alarmed. Nami looked at Yang as if asking for instructions. He nodded for her to answer.

"Hello?"

"Nami, right?" It was a man's voice.

"Yes."

"This is Yasui. I met you yesterday." His voice sounded husky. Nami kept her eyes on Yang.

"Yes?"

"Are you alone?"

"Uh, yes."

"Do you mind if I pop in? I won't be long."

"I was just about to go to bed."

"I'll just be there a second. I want to talk to you about something."

"No, I'm sorry."

"See you in a few minutes." The caller hung up.

"Yasui is on his way! What should we do?" she said.

"Turn out all the lights," Yang directed. Nami jumped up and turned off the fluorescent overhead light. Yang walked quickly over to the window. There was a thin lace curtain covering it. He pulled it back, opened the window, and climbed out onto the balcony.

"What are you doing?"

"Be quiet." Yang hunched down and looked down at the street from under the handrail. He glanced over at the apartments on either side. Most of the other residents worked late in bars and clubs, too, and wouldn't be home from work yet. Yang came back in and closed the window.

"What is it?"

"Yasui has men watching the building. He suspects you."

"What should I do?"

"It's all right. He doesn't know I'm here. He wants to check out a man they saw come in the building."

"But…"

"I'm going to hide on the balcony next door. If he threatens you, say you'll call the cops. Don't tell them anything about me."

Yang picked up his shoes from the entrance and attaché case and went back out on the balcony. He hunched down again, looking down under the railing, possibly trying to find the lookout. Then he suddenly sprang up and climbed onto the handrail and pulled himself over the panel separating Nami's balcony from that of her neighbor. The handrail was only a few inches wide, but he stepped up as lightly and confidently as if he were simply walking across the floor. He jumped down onto the balcony next door.

"Close the window and turn on the light!" Nami heard a voice from the other side of the panel.

She did as she was told, closed the window and the curtains and looked around the room, her heart pounding.

The doorbell rang.

He's here already! Yasui must have called from downstairs. So he really did have someone working as a lookout. The bell rang again. Nami opened the door slightly, keeping the chain fastened. Yasui stood there with two other men. He had on a cream-colored jacket and plaid shirt and, somewhat oddly, a pair of sunglasses.

"Yes?" Nami inquired.

"I know this is sudden, but I'd like to have a word with you." His tone was gentle, but his expression indicated that he wouldn't take no for an answer.

"What about?"

"Why don't you open the door so we can speak more comfortably. It's not something I want to talk about standing here like this. Plus, I'd hate to disturb the neighbors." The two thugs kept a wary eye on the doors on either side.

"But I'm a woman living alone…"

"I promise I won't be long. You don't need to serve me tea. I'll make sure these two stay out here."

"Promise?"

"Of course, I promise. If I break it, you can call the police or whoever else you like."

Nami closed the door to remove the chain. As promised, Yasui came in alone.

"Thanks," he said. He checked the entryway for shoes, and craned his neck to look around before stepping in. Nami noticed that he kept the front door open a crack in case he needed to call in his thugs.

"You can't say much for the men we hire, but the women we keep careful track of. Your address was on file at the office," said Yasui as

155

he removed his shoes. "Nice place. How much is the rent?" he asked as he entered the room. "Mind if I use your bathroom?"

He opened the door to the toilet, washed his hands and came out, wiping his hands on a handkerchief he pulled out of his jacket pocket. He pulled open the curtains and peered out at the balcony, and then sat down cross-legged in the middle of the floor. When he pulled a pack of Larks out of his breast pocket, Nami gave up and sat down on the bed. She rested both hands on her knees and waited.

"I'll leave after I've had one of these. Let me use this cola can as an ashtray."

Nami heard him flip his metal lighter on. Yasui noisily exhaled cigarette smoke, and then spoke again.

"So did you hear from him?"

Nami looked up questioningly.

"You know, that bar back who disappeared. Yang."

Nami shook her head. Yang was not three yards behind her beyond the wall. Her back felt hot.

"I see." Yasui tapped the cigarette ashes into the can. Nami heard it sizzle as it hit the liquid left inside. "Are you from China?"

Nami looked up for a second.

"One of the other girls said you were from one of those families left in China after the war."

"My mother was."

"Were you born and raised in Japan?"

"I came when I was thirteen."

"So you can speak Chinese."

Nami nodded.

"I hear that Yang didn't speak much Japanese."

"I really don't know."

"Did you ever translate for him? Like when he spoke to Agi?"

She shook her head.

"Did you talk to him often?"

"No."

"Look at me. Let me see your face."

Nami looked up.

"You're very pretty. Yang must have had a thing for you."

"I don't think so."

"How can you say that if you never talked to him?"

"I just know."

"Did Yang ever give you the name of any of his friends?"

"No."

"He told Agi that friends were letting him stay with them. You never heard about that?"

"No."

Yasui was silent for a few moments. "A man came into this building not long ago. But there are only two apartments with lights on. No other lights went on after he walked in. Which means he's got to be in one room or the other.

"How can you know that?"

"I've got one of my men stationed out in front. He's been watching this building since yesterday."

"Why? You're not the police."

"I've got my reasons, and I'm sure it's a lot of trouble for you, too. I understand how you must feel. And that's why I just want me to tell you what you know."

Nami took a deep breath. "I don't know anything."

"I don't think that's true. You haven't had any calls? You must have gotten at least one."

"Nobody has called."

"Really." Yasui dropped the half-smoked cigarette stub into the can. "You can play hard-to-get. I'll be back again."

"I'll call the police."

"Do whatever you like. I haven't done anything wrong. The cops'll thank me for helping them out with their investigation."

157

"Liar."

"I don't think so. Yang is a killer. Law-abiding citizens have a duty to catch criminals like that."

Nami suddenly wanted to laugh in his face. Yang may be a murderer, but he was not nearly as scary as Yasui. Yasui was hardly a law-abiding citizen.

He sat for a while longer without saying a word, and the unnatural silence was frightening. "Well, all right then. You'll let me know if you hear from Yang. Day or night, call the number on that card I gave you. Somebody will be there to answer."

Nami nodded. Yang had been right. Yasui finally stood up to leave and walked slowly towards the front door. He put on his shoes and, as if remembering something, turned around and pulled an envelope out of his breast pocket.

"Thanks for letting me use your toilet," he said, handing Nami a ten-thousand-yen bill.

"I don't want your money," she insisted.

"Just take it. It doesn't mean anything. And I'll make sure you get your pay from the club right away." Yasui opened the front door. The two thugs quickly dropped the cigarettes they were smoking, stomped them out, and lowered their heads.

"Let's go," Yasui said irritably. He nodded to Nami. "See you later." Yasui yanked up his pants, and walked in long strides down the hallway. His two bodyguards ran after him.

Nami closed the door and locked it. She had barely enough energy left to put the chain on, nearly slumping to the floor in exhaustion. She turned around and gasped to find Yang in the room.

"Oh, you scared me," she said quietly. Then she noticed that something was amiss. He had his hand on his right side, and he sat down on the bed.

"What's wrong?" Nami whispered. Yang shook his head silently. His face was deathly pale. He slid out his attaché case, opened it and pulled out a red capsule, which he quickly gulped down.

"Are you sick?"

"It's all right. I took my medicine."

"Does your stomach hurt?"

"It's appendicitis. It's become chronic. I'm fine. I'll have it taken out some time."

Nami remembered the time Agi and Yang had been together in the locker room. Yang must have been in there waiting for his medication to start working.

"Do you need a doctor…" she started, but realized that it would be impossible, since he probably didn't have any insurance. "Are you sure you're all right?"

"I'll feel better in a half hour or so."

"Lie down. You won't be going anywhere right away."

Yang nodded and lay down on the bed. Nami sat at the foot of it. Yang took off his glasses and put them in the breast pocket of his suit jacket. Then he propped himself up and tried to take off his jacket. Nami helped him.

Yang put his attaché case under his head and closed his eyes. There was sweat on his forehead. Nami went into the kitchen, ran a towel under the tap and wrung it out. She put it on Yang's forehead. He spoke without opening his eyes.

"Call him in the morning. Don't forget."

"What are you going to do?"

"Talk to him."

"But they'll catch you."

"No, they won't." He spoke without a shred of doubt in his voice. "Nami," he began again and she looked over at him. "After tomorrow, forget about me."

She nodded. "Nami is the name I use for work. My real name is Qing Na. Qing Na Dai."

"Qing Na. Where were you born?"

"Heilongjiang. What about you?"

"Taiwan. Do you know anything about Taiwan?"

Nami shook her head. "Tell me about it."

"It's very warm. A lot warmer than Tokyo."

"Are there as many people there?"

"In Taipei and Gaoxiong, yes. I was born in the country in the central eastern area, close to the sea. I used to dive for fish. I've always been a good swimmer. What about you?"

"No, I can't even put my face in water. My friends all swam in the river, but not me."

"It's easy. I can still stay underwater for three minutes."

"Did you fish for a living?"

"No, I just did it as a child. We were poor, so we ate what I caught."

"I'm a good dancer."

"Dancer?"

"A nice lady taught me. She was my cousin." Nami stood up. "I can do the jitterbug, the tango, waltz…" She began to show him her steps in the tiny space of her room. "I've never had anywhere to dance in Japan. I thought I had forgotten how," she laughed.

Yang smiled. Nami was pleased to see he was enjoying himself, so she showed him all the moves she could remember. "Better than disco, huh? The Japanese don't dance enough."

"People like to dance in Taiwan, too."

"Can you?"

Yang looked flustered. "A long time ago, when I was in the army, I used to go out dancing when I had time off."

"You were in the army?"

"In Taiwan, everyone has to serve." He didn't seem to want to talk about it, so Nami changed the subject.

"Do you like to drink?"

"Just a little."

"What about travel? Where have you been?"

"All over, but this is the first time I've been to Japan."

"How about America?"

"Sure," he said, but didn't offer any other details.

"Do you have family? Are you married?"

"No one," he said casually.

"So you don't like girls? No! There is no such man!"

Yang nodded. "I don't hate girls."

"Do you like Japanese girls?"

Yang shook his head. His eyes were closed.

"Do you want to sleep?"

"I can't sleep with you talking."

"Oh, sorry, I'll be quiet then," Nami laughed, pressing her hand over her mouth.

"Aren't you going to sleep?" Yang asked.

"I'm not tired yet."

"Because I'm here?"

Nami shook her head. "Do you hate girls like me?"

"Why do you ask?"

"Well, I mean, all the things I did at the club."

"I've already forgotten."

"Well…" Nami began and then stopped.

"What?" Yang's eyes were open now.

"I want to lie beside you."

Yang looked at Nami for a long moment, and then silently shifted over to one side of the bed. Fully clothed, Nami lay down next to him. She turned on the lamp on her nightstand and turned off the ceiling light. She stared at the halo of light the lamp made on the ceiling.

"Does it still hurt?" Nami asked after a while.

"It's better now. The medicine helps."

Nami nodded, and Yang, lying on his back, closed his eyes. Nami reached out to touch his stomach. Yang started, but then was still. Nami ran her hand over his stomach. It was hard. His muscles were like rope. Yang was silent.

Nami stroked his stomach for about ten minutes, and then her hand moved down a little further. Yang still didn't move. She rubbed him on the soft spot she found and waited for it to react. Yang's eyes opened—there it was.

"Don't move," she whispered as she unzipped his pants.

Nami woke to a gentle shaking. Yang was dressed in his suit. He stood by her bed. It was four a.m.

Startled, she asked, "Wasn't I supposed to call at five?" She was still terribly sleepy.

"That's right, but you're not calling from here."

Nami pulled herself into a sitting position.

"Where?"

"Anywhere but here." Yang picked up his attaché case. "We have to split up. Wait for ten minutes after I leave. Then go wherever you like and call from a pay phone. Tell them that you got a call from me and that I told you I had no place to go so I was sleeping at the park. Tell them I asked you for money and that I was waiting for you."

"Nowhere to stay, slept in the park, waiting for me to lend you money," Nami repeated. Yang nodded. His face was tense and stern.

"But the park is closed."

"All you have to do is climb the fence. It's easy to get in on the Sendagaya side. Tell them I told you that. I'll be at the Taiwan Pavilion, near the pond in the back."

"Taiwan Pavilion. But what if they call the police?"

"Them? They won't call the police. They'll try to capture me and take me somewhere."

Now Nami was frightened. "What should I do?"

"Do anything you like, just don't come back here."

162

"No, I want to go with you to the park."

"It's too dangerous."

"How are you going to talk to them? You don't speak Japanese well enough."

Yang looked at her long and hard.

"They'll think I'm in it with you anyway after I call them."

Yang still said nothing.

"Please, take me with you. I'm not afraid."

Yang's eyes went hollow. "You'll see something you've never seen before, and it's going to make you sick."

"I don't care. I can take it."

"You'll be terrified of me."

"Never. I'll never feel that way. The most terrifying thing is the thought of losing you," she blurted out.

Yang nodded. "Okay, we can leave together. Don't wear a skirt."

"I'll change into jeans. What about Yasui's lookout?"

"They're gone. I guess they gave up."

Nami jumped out of bed and quickly dressed.

"You'd better plan to be away for a few days."

Nami pulled out a cloth bag and crammed some underwear and a dress into it.

"I'm ready."

"Let's go."

Nami grabbed Yang's arm as he headed for the front door. He turned around to look at her.

"Don't you dare try to leave me behind," she said, staring into his eyes.

"I won't," he said in a low voice.

The sky was taking on a bluish tinge. The two walked silently, and hailed a taxi driving by.

"Sendagaya," Nami told the driver.

Apparently Yang had been to Shinjuku Gyoen Park numerous

times. As soon as they reached the Sendagaya 5th Street neighborhood, he nudged Nami with his elbow.

"This is far enough," Nami said to the driver. Nami paid and the two got out. Yang turned left down a road that led away from Meiji Boulevard, where the taxi had stopped. Nami had to run to catch up. It was a mixed residential and commercial district, and all of the shutters were still down. The only people on the street were a few elderly people walking dogs.

Yang pointed to a phone booth on the left-hand side of the street. Nami went in, put her bag down on the ground and picked up the receiver. Yang got inside the booth with her.

Nami pulled out Yasui's business card, put a phone card in the slot and punched in the number. After it rang a few times, the other end picked up.

"Yasui Enterprises." It was the voice of a young man.

"Mr. Yasui, please."

"Who is this?"

"My name is Nami."

"The boss isn't here yet."

"It's urgent. I got a call from Yang."

"Just a minute." The phone went on hold and began playing soft music until someone else came on the line.

"Hello, what can I do for you?" The man must have been awakened from a sound sleep.

"I have a message for Mr. Yasui," Nami told him.

"Go ahead."

"I got a call from Yang. He said he doesn't have anywhere to go, so he's sleeping in Shinjuku Gyoen Park. He wants me to lend him money, and he's waiting for me by the Taiwan Pavilion."

"The Taiwan Pavilion at Shinjuku Gyoen Park? Where are you now?"

"At the Shin-Okubo station," she lied automatically.

"Wait right there. Don't hang up." The music started playing again. Nami put her hand over the receiver and told Yang what was happening. Yang nodded and then pushed the lever for the receiver. The line was cut, the phone beeped and ejected the telephone card. She stared at him.

"Don't worry," he told her, "they'll come."

They left the phone booth and began to walk again. They walked down a street heading northeast. They finally came to a high iron fence. It was painted black and the tips at the top were sharp. They went down a narrow road along the fence with buildings lining the other side of it. Part way down the street was a string of old, deserted houses.

Yang went around to the back of one of the houses. In that area the fence changed from iron to a thin concrete wall that was badly worn and cracked in some places. It was dark and quiet. Yang held out the attaché case and Nami took it.

She got a strong whiff of the deep green smell of the park. She watched Yang grab the top of the concrete wall and hoist himself astride it as if it were a horse. Nami held out the attaché case and her own bag. Yang took them and dropped them on the other side of the wall. Then she raised both of her arms. She felt as though someone was watching, but there was no sound or voice from the windows of the houses. Yang grabbed her arms and swung her up onto the wall. When she was sitting securely on it, he jumped down the other side. He held out his arms for her as she swung both her feet around and jumped. Yang caught her around her hips to break her fall.

Nami looked around, and saw that they were in a grove of trees and bushes. Just beyond that was a gravel path. It was her second trip to this park. Her first had been last spring with her boyfriend when they came to see the cherry blossoms.

Yang set off walking. The park was so thickly overgrown that it felt much darker than the rest of the city. Once in a while, birds flew overheard making a squawking racket. Other than that it was quiet, and as they walked on the gravel path, their footsteps sounded abnormally loud. Nami felt chilly. She couldn't help but wonder why Yang was able to walk so confidently through such an enormous park.

Before long, she could see a pond that was oblong in shape, with some spots narrower in width than others. It didn't seem very deep. Turning onto a path that led to a place where the pond narrowed, Yang looked to the left. A wooden pavilion stood amidst a thicket of trees. The numerous peaks in the stylized oriental roof seemed to reach for the sky. The windows in the white walls were large and round.

"That's the Taiwan Pavilion," said Yang in a low voice as he continued walking towards it. As they walked around, she could see that it was on the edge of the pond.

Nami stood looking at it. She hadn't even noticed the pavilion when she was here before. It looked like it was perched on a pedestal of dark green with the sky as a backdrop. The grass at the edge of the pond was neatly cropped, and the path followed it like a finely sewn seam. At its front was a dense grove of trees, and above them Nami could see the skyscrapers of Shinjuku.

The grass looked like it belonged in a formal Japanese garden, but Nami was drawn to the mysterious shape of the Taiwan Pavilion, rather than the grounds around it. Before she knew it, Yang was far along the path, heading into the dark grove. The branches overhead blocked out the brightening sky.

Nami thought she would certainly have gotten lost if she had been alone. It was like an enormous maze. With all the large trees, she could see no more than a few feet ahead.

She had the feeling, however, that they were headed in the direction of Shinjuku. All of a sudden there was a clearing, and right in front of them was a pond with concrete walls. Irises grew out of the marsh-like water. There was a stairway to their right, and a concrete building beyond that.

Yang was heading towards the building, and Nami followed. The pavestones near the pond were cracked and broken here and there. In the middle of the staircase was a slide that dipped into the pond. It wasn't a pond, Nami realized, but a swimming pool. Then she noticed the drinking fountains and a public restroom to the left.

The roof of the building was supported by large, square, concrete columns. At one end was a room with windows, but there was no evidence that anyone was there. In front of the building were three round tree stumps about three feet high and a foot and a half in diameter, which looked like they may have been used as picnic tables. Their roots were covered with overgrown weeds.

Yang went up to one of the stumps, set his attaché case down and moved the stump. It looked quite heavy. Then he began to dig in the ground beneath it.

Nami watched from a short distance away, puzzled. Eventually something black was uncovered, and Yang pulled it out. It was a black trash bag. Inside was a bundle. Yang opened it to reveal a duffle bag. He set it down and began to take off his clothes. When he was down to his underwear, he began to undo the string tied around the opening of the duffle bag.

First he pulled out a rope that was wrapped in a tight ring. Next he pulled out something about a foot and a half in length, wrapped in a paper bag. Finally, he pulled out a black sweat suit and boots with rubber soles. Yang quickly pulled on the sweat suit and boots. He pulled the hood of the sweatshirt over his head and tied the string under his chin.

Nami watched him as she folded up his suit and set it on top of the attaché case. Now she was thoroughly confused. Why on earth would he have clothes and other things hidden in a place like this?

Yang moved quickly and efficiently, not wasting a moment.

Finally, he pulled out a knife in a sheath out of the paper bag. He secured it to his right calf using the two attached straps. He looked at his watch, and Nami, almost in a trance, looked down at her own.

It was seven minutes to five.

Yang put the duffel bag back in its hole and replaced the tree stump. "Over here," he directed her.

There were two small huts next to the pool, pump rooms that were no longer in use. One of the huts was built slightly below ground level and almost completely covered with overgrown weeds.

"Stay here." Yang told her. "No matter what, don't come out until I come back for you." He looked just like a ninja in a TV program. But this ninja spoke Mandarin Chinese. Nami nodded as Yang fixed her with a fierce stare and then, in the blink of an eye, turned his back to her. He ran quickly back in the direction they had come.

As soon as he disappeared back into the woods, Nami pulled his attaché case over and sat down on it. She perched her own bag on her knees and clutched his suit to her breast, wrapping herself into a ball. She stared down at the damp floor—she was sure it was covered with bugs.

She was uneasy. Not for herself, but for what lay ahead for Yang. She sat there unmoving. Before long, she heard people talking. They were drawing closer. Nami crossed her arms and held Yang's clothes as tightly as she could and closed her eyes. She felt dizzy from the scent of the forest around her.

17

It had been three days since the Shinjuku Precinct set up the Special Investigation Headquarters for the murder of the Kabukicho cabaret club manager. Contrary to their original projections, they had not yet managed to find any suspects. Samejima was visiting the ballistics expert Yabu about a separate issue, and got an update from him.

"They're beginning to panic. They thought it was going to be open and shut, but they can't find their main suspect, the Chinese guy. He's gone."

The bit about the suspect being Chinese gave Samejima pause, and he inquired further.

"The one who didn't leave any fingerprints," said Yabu. "We spoke to the other hostesses, but they didn't recognize the photos of the people we had arrest records for. The address he gave was false, and there are no photos of him. He can't even speak Japanese and we still can't find him. He must be laying low at the home of some friend or other."

"Do they have proof that he's the perp?"

"No, but the victim was an addict, so we're following that line of investigation. But it's strange…"

"What's strange?"

"The victim's boss, Yasui. You must know him. He's the one who discovered the body, and now he's missing, too."

"You mean he's a fugitive?" asked Samejima.

"No, he went off yesterday morning with three of his thugs, and that's the last anyone has heard of them."

"What could that mean?"

"An investigator went to see the hostesses and Yasui himself to try to put together a composite of the suspect. They couldn't get hold of him, and the Yasui Enterprises office was in a state of upheaval. Something's wrong."

"So there was some kind of unplanned behavior."

"Yeah, he got a call at his office early yesterday morning. Someone called him out. Yasui was at home, but they called him from the office. He went off somewhere with his driver, the guy who took the call and another henchman. Four of them in all."

"What time was it?"

"Four or five o'clock in the morning."

The only time yakuza were out at a time like that was when they had a job to do or when they got a call from the boss of the syndicate. It's the time of day when most people are the least able to either think or move. Yakuza know that, and that's why they choose to burst in on their prey early in the morning to get them to sign contracts to pay back loans or hand over their property.

As far as the police could tell, the syndicate headquarters was not involved in any conflict. That must mean they had received information about someone they had been watching. Yasui ran a high-interest loan racket. If his underlings had reported that one of their hapless "customers" that owed a lot of money had shown up, Yasui might be out doing business at a time like that.

"Yesterday morning, huh…" Samejima mumbled, and Yabu nodded.

"And none of them has heard a word for an entire day. It's very odd for them."

"And they're not just leading the police on?"

"They wouldn't have any reason to do that unless Yasui or one of his men was the murderer. But the MO is not theirs."

"You said the victim was hit on the head, right?"

"With something hard and round. A stone, or maybe an ashtray."

"Have you found the weapon?"

Yabu shook his head. "There was nothing at the scene."

"Is there a possibility that the weapon was a part of the human body?"

"You mean was it done empty-handed?"

Samejima nodded. "How about a foot?"

Yabu frowned in thought. "Crushing the cranium without a weapon? Well, karate experts break boards and blocks as a show of strength, so I guess it's not impossible. But wouldn't a blow to the stomach do the trick?"

"That's a typical karate move," Samejima agreed.

"If it were a foot, the attacker kicked the victim after he fell," Yabu continued. "But the only injury on this guy was the lethal blow to his head. If he hadn't been kicked while sitting or lying down..."

"How tall was the victim?" asked Samejima.

"About five foot six. He wasn't big, but it would be difficult to kick the top of his head like that if he was standing up. There weren't any chairs or anything like that near the body."

"Was the blow from the front or the back?"

"It's hard to tell since we don't know the shape of the weapon, but based on how he fell, we're thinking it was from the front."

If a man of that height was standing and someone wanted to crush his skull, the first thing you'd suspect was something long like a baseball bat being swung straight downward, like a kendo sword move. It would be swung from the front at a diagonal angle onto the head. Samejima wasn't sure exactly what a *nerio chagi* was, the Tae kwon do kick that Guo had told him about. All he remembered was that the blow was made with the heel of the foot.

"Could the blow have been made with the heel?"

"The heel?" Yabu was surprised. "How could anyone crush some-one's skull with their heel?"

"I don't know the answer to that, but would it match the shape of the weapon?"

"It would, but it would mean the perp had legs as long as a ballet dancer." Yabu smiled at the image. "Should I let them know they should be on the look out for a vicious-looking ballerina?"

Samejima shook his head.

That night Samejima was awakened by the phone. He looked at the clock. It was one-thirty. He had crawled into bed just before one and turned out the light, so he must have just fallen asleep.

"Hello?"

"Is that you, Samejima?" asked the caller.

Samejima recognized Guo's accent and sat up. "Yes. Guo, right?"

"Sorry to wake you."

"Don't worry. What's the matter?"

"I want to take you somewhere that will interest you. I'm in Shinjuku. Can you come?"

"I'll be there. Did you find Du Yuan?" Suddenly Samejima was on edge.

"Not yet. But please come."

"Where should I meet you?"

Guo directed him to a place in Kabukicho on Kuyakusho Avenue. "I'm calling from a pay phone."

"I'll be there in fifteen minutes."

"I'll be waiting."

Samejima hung up and flew out of bed. His apartment was near Route 7. He should be able to flag down a vacant taxi and make it through the empty streets toward the center of Tokyo in a matter of

172

minutes. Or he could take his own car if there were no cabs.

He quickly dressed in slacks and a shirt, made sure he had his nightstick and handcuffs attached to his belt, and put on his coat. He knew that if they ran up against Du Yuan his nightstick wouldn't do much good, but there wasn't time to stop at the precinct for a gun.

Samejima got out of the taxi near the place on Kuyakusho Avenue at just after two. He ran along the street and saw Guo sitting on a guardrail waiting for him. His left arm hung in a sling underneath his jacket.

"Sorry to keep you waiting."

"Did you bring your badge?" Guo asked.

"You mean my police badge?"

"Yes."

"I've got it."

Guo gave a lopsided grin. "You might need it."

"Why?"

"You'll find out soon." Guo set off towards Kabukicho 2nd Street. He turned right at a large intersection near Furin Hall. There were three Mercedes parked with their hazard lights on. Several gangsters squatted down or stood around smoking. They must have been lower-rank drivers waiting for their bosses. They were all scowling, and they glared at Guo like a pack of wolves as he came into view. However, one of them recognized Samejima and his expression changed.

"Good evening," he called out. He was a thug from the Ishiwa gang. As soon as they heard the code word, the rest of them froze. Samejima ignored them, but became uneasy as he surveyed the scene. This many thugs outside must mean that most of the top gang members—probably including Ishiwa himself—were in the vicinity.

Guo and Samejima passed through the center of the group. Guo turned left at the first corner, his expression cool.

"Let's go the back way," Guo said and headed behind the building where the Mercedes were parked. "The third floor."

Samejima looked up. There was a neon sign that said "Arisan." He realized it was a late-night restaurant.

"Let's go." Guo led the way up the emergency exit stairs past boxes of restaurant supplies. Samejima followed. There was no lookout following them. On the wooden door of Arisan was a plate that said "Members Only."

"If anyone asks you any questions, just say we'll only have one drink and leave," Guo instructed as he pushed open the door a crack. They could smell Chinese food and heard a Chinese voice coming from a karaoke machine. Clapping and cheering accompanied the singing. It sounded like a lively place.

The instant Guo pushed opened the door, a man in a white silk shirt came running from the back. Guo began speaking in Chinese before the man could get out a word. The man answered and tried to push the door closed. It was clear that he was refusing them entry.

Guo refused to give up and continued to argue. Samejima could see inside over the man's shoulder. There was a central aisle dividing the restaurant in half. Next to each side of the aisle were two large televisions in front of two square seating areas. A handrail ran down the aisle, and the kitchen was in the back on the left. There were no customers in the area on the left. There seemed to be customers on the right, but the man against the door blocked his view.

Guo indicated Samejima as he spoke, and the color of the man's face changed.

"Shinjuku Precinct?" he asked. Samejima nodded and pulled out his badge. "We're rented out tonight," he continued, but Guo started speaking over him again. The man's face fell. Samejima didn't know what he was saying but he understood that he was trying to get inside. The man finally let go of the door and stepped back to let them in, but seemed to be asking him not to cause trouble.

Guo made a casual response, pushed past the man's shoulder and walked into the restaurant. Samejima followed.

174

There was a group of fifteen or sixteen in the area on the right. A spotlight shone on them. Two women and four men sat at the table in the center, and groups of two and four men respectively sat at the tables on either side. The two tables on the sides each had a woman on duty. The singing was coming from the table on the right, the one with two men. One of them was standing with a microphone in his hands.

Samejima knew three of the four men at the center table. There was Takezo Ishiwa and his top henchmen, Takakawa and Hata. Ishiwa wore a silver-gray suit and dark-rimmed glasses. He was short and heavyset, and he had a crew-cut hairstyle. He was in his early fifties.

Takakawa was a handsome man, and wore his hair slicked back. He was tall, with a long chin and sharp eyes. He wore a green double-breasted suit. Hata was next to him. In contrast to Takakawa, his hair had a tightly curled perm, and his square face was covered in acne scars. He wore a black suit with a loud tie.

Between Ishiwa and Takakawa sat a thin man with silver hair. His complexion was dark, giving the impression that his health was failing. The two women sat across from him.

Guo quickly took a seat in the area on the left side of the aisle. Samejima sat across from him. They were in the shadow of the TV. On the TV, a young man and woman were walking in front of a fountain in a park. Chinese lyrics scrolled across the bottom of the screen.

The man in the white silk shirt came over to Samejima and Guo and spoke in an urgent whisper.

"No fighting!"

"Don't worry," Samejima assured him.

"Something to drink?" he asked, his tone distrustful.

Samejima glanced over at Guo. "We'll have beer," he said, and Guo nodded in agreement. Suddenly Samejima grabbed the man's silk-sleeved arm. "Don't tell anyone we're here, understand?"

There was terror in the man's eyes.

The song ended and there was applause in the other area. Just then, the four men seated to the left of Ishiwa's table stood up. They stood at the edge of the spotlight, staring over at Samejima and Guo. The air in the restaurant turned thick with tension. Samejima noticed two young men in brightly colored suits standing frozen in the kitchen doorway staring in his direction.

"Where's the manager?" a husky voice shouted out from the other side of the aisle.

"Coming!" The man in the silk shirt stood up. The husky voice was that of Hata.

"We've rented the place for the night. Get rid of them!" The four men who were standing were Ishiwa members, bodyguards for Ishiwa, Takakawa, and Hata.

The place went silent. The man in the silk shirt looked down at Guo and Samejima. His eyes were blinking rapidly and he licked his lips in distress.

"Get rid of them, or we'll do it for you!" Just then the introduction to the next karaoke song began. The hostesses and the two men at the table on the right-hand side began clapping in time to the beat.

The microphone was passed to the silver haired man next to Ishiwa, but Hata stood up before he began singing.

"Go!" he said, directing the bodyguards towards Samejima and Guo with a thrust of his chin.

The silver-haired man began to sing. His voice was hoarse as he sang a song in Chinese. The four men walked over to Samejima's table. Samejima looked down, lit a cigarette and sighed, wondering at the trouble Guo had gotten them into.

"Wei Ye."

The singing stopped. The two men at the right-hand table stood up and moved closer to the man with the silver hair. The other four made a move to grab Guo.

"Stop," Samejima lifted his head and spoke.

"Wha—" One of the men recognized Samejima, and stopped mid-word. The four of them froze in place.

There was no doubt that the man with Ishiwa was Wei Ye. Guo had somehow managed to sniff him out and follow him here. The yakuza were on edge because they were guarding Ye's life. They were all undoubtedly armed. That's why they all froze as soon as they recognized Samejima—a quick body search would send them to jail for possession of firearms.

"Son of a bitch!" Hata stood up and put his arm over his head to keep the light out of his eyes. "Turn out the light!"

Both the karaoke and the spotlight instantly went out. Guo began to speak in Chinese. He sounded forceful. He began to walk around. Wei Ye pushed out from behind his bodyguards. His face was tense. The four bodyguards now turned their attention to Guo. Hata glared at them, furious that they weren't reacting.

"Don't move, I know you're armed," said Samejima in a low voice. His face was still hidden in the shadow of the karaoke screen. Hata couldn't see him.

"What do you assholes think you're doing?" Hata screamed at the bodyguards. Guo continued to move forward towards the table where Ye sat with Ishiwa, Hata and Takakawa.

This was a reckless move. None of them knew he was a detective from Taiwan and there was no telling what they might try.

Samejima stood up and moved into the light. He knew that if Hata made a move for him, Guo would retaliate. That would probably cause a bloodbath. Hata shifted his glare from Guo to Samejima, and the recognition was instantaneous.

"You bastard…" he began, and then fell silent.

Guo stopped in front of the center table. Ye appeared to recognize him, and the two Taiwanese at the table to the right grimaced in fearful recognition. Guo turned slowly to Hata and Ishiwa.

"I won't do anything. I want to talk. Talk to Wei Ye, the important boss from Taiwan."

"Who the hell are you?" Ishiwa said. He seemed terribly uncomfortable.

Guo bowed. The action was filled with irony. "I'm Rongmin Guo, a policeman from Taiwan. He is a Japanese policeman," he said indicating Samejima with his right hand. There was a loud clunk as Ye's younger bodyguard came to attention. Guo whipped his head around to glare at him, and spoke in a low voice. Ye put his hand on the young man's shoulder, and he reluctantly lowered himself back onto his chair.

"Excuse me. I'm with Japanese friends," said Ye in Japanese, and Guo nodded.

"Okay, we'll speak Japanese. We have the same friend. Have you seen him yet? Probably not. If you had, you would not be here."

Ye was expressionless as Guo continued.

"You know him best. Du Yuan. He always catches and kills his target. You are the one who taught me this."

"Get rid of him!" Ishiwa spat, glaring at Samejima.

"We'll leave before long," said Samejima.

"You're from Shinjuku Precinct, aren't you?"

"Yes, I am. It would be wise to remember my face. My name is Samejima. I'm with the Crime Prevention Unit."

"Oh, Officer Samejima, why did you come here to trouble us? We're just having fun and having a few drinks."

"We're not here to trouble you. This guy is just here to speak with an old friend."

Ishiwa's expression darkened. "That's what people usually call trouble."

"Is that true?" said Samejima as he stepped over the handrail. He went to stand next to the four Ishiwa thugs who were rooted to the spot. "Causing trouble would mean questioning these young men after stripping off their clothes to see what they're hiding underneath."

"Bastard!" yelled Hata.

"Come, come, Mr. Hata." Takakawa spoke for the first time. He was obviously nervous. He was a rare intellectual type among the hot-blooded Ishiwa gang, which was infamous for armed conflict. Samejima recalled that Takakawa and the missing Yasui were like brothers.

Guo began speaking again in Japanese. "Ye, I'm staying in the Sanko Hotel. It's close by. Come to me if you need help. I'm the only one who can save you from Du Yuan. If you confess everything, I can help you."

"What the hell is he talkin' about?" Ishiwa glared at Samejima. Samejima glared back at him and said quietly, "Don't know. Obviously something only they understand."

"Fuck off, you little ass-kisser!" roared Ishiwa.

Samejima kept his eyes fixed on Ishiwa's face. He was terrifying, but it was too late to back off. "Mr. Ishiwa, do you know what they call me? I don't kiss anyone. I bite."

Ishiwa sharply drew in his breath, his face turning white. Takakawa noticed and he paled as well. He stood up and yelled out in a flustered tone of voice, "That's enough. It's time to leave, shark!" He realized that Ishiwa was preparing to take on Samejima single-handedly.

Samejima looked over at Guo, who nodded in response. He reached out for a handful of food on the plate in front of Ye. It was a dish of meat, vegetables and cashews. He picked up a piece, popped it in his mouth and then wiped his hand slowly on Ye's jacket. He never took his eyes off of the other man's face.

"Yummy," he said. Ye stood with his back arched, but didn't attempt to move at all.

"See you later," he whispered, staring into Ye's face. Guo walked slowly for the door, and Samejima followed behind. Sweat streamed down his back. He reached back to pull the door shut, and the next instant they heard the sound of breaking glass from inside. Someone had flipped over a table.

Guo and Samejima went back down the stairs the way they had come. Once they were on the street, Samejima breathed a deep sigh of relief. Guo, walking ahead, turned back and grinned at him.

"Did I scare you?"

"You're a piece of work. If you'd tried anything else, we would have been killed."

"If this were Taiwan, Ye would not have let me go. But this is Japan, and Ye will not go back to Taiwan again."

"Why?"

"Du Yuan."

"You mean he'll kill Wei Ye?"

"Definitely. Du Yuan will get him. No matter what it takes."

Samejima shook his head. Guo sounded positively charmed by this Du Yuan.

"By the way," he said, "what sort of kick was that *nerio chagi* you said he was good at?"

Guo gave Samejima a puzzled look. "Why?"

"A guy was murdered four days ago. His skull was crushed."

Guo's eyes narrowed. "How?"

Samejima shook his head. "I wasn't in charge of the case. I know it was a blunt object. Do you understand what I mean?"

"Something like a stone? Not pointed?"

"That's right. He was hit in the head by something round. From the front."

"Show me this corpse." Guo was serious.

"I can't do that just yet, I'm afraid."

"I see. Well, with the *nerio chagi*, he comes around to his opponent's front, and does this." Guo suddenly stopped, pulled back his left arm, put his right arm out slightly, and quickly lifted his right foot bringing his right knee sharply to his chest. Then he lifted his right foreleg until his shin reached his forehead. From there he turned his foot to an angle and brought his heel straight down.

His foot was easily as high as Samejima's forehead. A number of drunks passing by stopped to watch the display.

"That's *nerio chagi*. The Japanese name is *nohten kakato otoshi*, heel skull drop. It crushes the head or this bone." Guo pointed to his collarbone.

Samejima watched in mute astonishment. It was a powerful move. If it were made by a tall man there would be no way to avoid it. Even if you guarded your head, it would easily crush your shoulder.

"Could it kill someone instantly?"

Guo looked at Samejima. "It depends on who is doing it. It wouldn't be easy to kill someone at once. But Du Yuan could do it. He did it in Taiwan. When we saw the corpse, everyone thought it was done with a stone. Thrown like this."

Guo made a gesture of holding something in both hands over his head and flinging it straight down.

"But we were wrong. Du Yuan crushed the skull with his heel. It's a terrifying move. The victim probably never knew what hit him." Then Guo's expression went dark. "If this murder in Tokyo was by Du Yuan, there will be more. They will continue until Wei Ye dies. Du Yuan is not afraid to die. He will be satisfied only when he has finished off Ye."

A shiver went down Samejima's spine.

18

The elegantly appointed condominium in Sangubashi was a league apart from Nami's small studio in Okubo. There was a glass door set in the brick-red outer wall outfitted with an automatic lock. The entrance to the building had a special key, and visitors could only enter the elevator hall after being buzzed in by residents.

At nine p.m., Nami and Yang stood in front of the entrance. Nami wore a dress, and Yang was in his suit. They had stayed in a business hotel in Shiba after they left Shinjuku Gyoen Park the morning before. This time, Nami knew what was going to happen.

Yang had been telling the truth when he told her in her apartment, *You'll see something you've never seen before, and it's going to make you sick.*

Nami had thrown up several times the day before. She would never be able to forget what she'd seen at the park. After Yang had left her in the shadow of the pump house, she had heard voices of people approaching. Then, a few minutes later she heard a scream the likes of which she had never heard before. There was only one, but it had been long and drawn out. After it was over, everything was deadly quiet.

Nami waited for half an hour, until she couldn't stand it any longer. She was sure Yang had been murdered. Just as she had begun to climb the stairs next to the pump house back to ground level, Yang returned.

On his back was a man. His nose had been broken and his face was almost unrecognizable. It took her a few moments until she realized it was Yasui. The elbows of both of his arms were bent at unnatural angles, and there was a rock in his mouth that was slightly smaller than a fist. His front teeth were gone, broken to accommodate the rock. Blood and saliva dripped from his chin.

Yang flung him on the ground in front of Nami like a sack of potatoes. Yasui cried out in pain. His eyes were wet with tears and filled with terror and supplication.

Nami stood rooted to the spot. Yasui's body twisted when it hit the ground, but his arms were useless. He looked like an insect with its wings ripped off. Yang was completely expressionless as he spoke to Nami in Chinese.

"Ask this man questions for me. I'll help him if he answers. Tell him I'll kill him if he lies or refuses to answer. I won't kill him quickly. It will be very painful."

Nami nodded as she covered her mouth. Yasui looked up at her. His eyes were pleading for his life. Nami held back the urge to vomit, and spoke.

"If you answer his questions, you'll live. Otherwise you'll die."

Yasui did his best to move his head. Yang grabbed his shoulder and roughly dragged him up to a sitting position. Yasui screamed again from the movement.

"I'm going to take the rock out of your mouth. If you scream, I'll kill you on the spot." Yang spoke and Nami interpreted it into Japanese, her voice quavering. Yasui nodded in agreement. Yang put his finger in Yasui's mouth and pulled out the rock. It hit his broken teeth, and Yasui squeezed his eyes shut to keep himself from screaming.

"...d-don't kill me! Tell him... p-p-please don't kill me..." Yasui's voice was thick with mucus. Yang put his palm over his mouth, and Yasui went silent again. Yang removed his palm.

"Ask him if he knows a Chinese man named Wei Ye. He's from

Taiwan, about sixty-five years old. He's a friend of the Ishiwa boss."

Nami nodded. Yasui's eyes went back and forth between the two of them. His face was mottled with sweat, blood, and saliva.

"Do you know a Taiwanese man named Wei Ye? He's a friend of the head of the Ishiwa gang, an older man."

"No, no, I don't! I'm telling the truth. We're connected to Ishiwa, but I don't know any man from Taiwan. I'm not lying! This guy just killed three of my men. It was so fast. Please, please tell him not to kill me. I'm telling the truth, I'll tell him anything—"

Nami told Yang what Yasui had said. A momentary look of despair ran across Yang's face.

"Ask him where the Ishiwa boss lives."

"In Yotsuya, or someplace like that. In a condo, I think. I don't really know."

"Where is the Ishiwa office?"

"In Shinjuku. There are two. The headquarters and the dorm. The address is in here." Yasui tried to indicate his breast pocket with his ruined right arm. Nami explained what he said, and Yang took out his address book.

"Do you know where any of his head men live?"

"I do, I do. Takakawa, Ishiwa's number three. Left his wife and lives with his girlfriend in Sangubashi."

"Tell me exactly where it is."

Yasui explained. He had taken the woman home for Takakawa a number of times. She used to be a hostess in a Shinjuku club, but she wasn't currently working.

"Does Takakawa go home to this woman every night?"

"Usually, I don't know, probably. One of his young henchmen is probably going there to pick him up today."

Yang looked hard at Yasui and then glanced over at Nami. "Do you think he's telling the truth?"

Nami nodded. "I do. He's scared for his life."

Yang nodded, and then picked up the stone he'd taken out of Yasui's mouth. Yasui's eyes went round with fear. He opened up his mouth to scream again, but Yang shoved the rock down his throat before he had a chance. What came out was no more than a pitiful squeaking groan. Yang picked him up again as if he weighed nothing, and flung him over his shoulder. Yasui's legs batted back and forth, like a child throwing a tantrum.

"Wait a while longer," Yang called back to Nami, as he walked down the path back into the thicket. Yasui continued his attempts to scream, but nothing more than high-pitched wheezes squeezed out from between his throat and the rock.

Nami crouched down in the weeds and threw up. She decided not to think about what was about to happen to Yasui. She felt as though she'd had a terrible nightmare. The dark green of the quiet, peaceful park was so incongruous with what had just happened. It was if it was a movie playing on a screen in her head.

Yang was back a few minutes later. He took off his black sweat suit, and was back down to his underwear again. Nami saw that he was soaking wet.

"I'm finished," he said.

Nami looked up at him. Yang was looking at the sky. The Shinjuku skyscrapers were glowing in the morning sun.

"I think it will rain later today, so the level of the pond will stay high. They're sunk down far, so it will be a while before they're found."

"Sunk?"

"Weights. I used iron gutter covers. I tied the three of them together and put the cover in their arms."

Nami was about to vomit again.

"Let's say good-bye here," he suggested as he began putting on the suit Nami had folded for him. "Just please don't go to the police."

Nami looked down and shook her head. "I'm staying with you."

185

"Aren't you scared?"

"Yes, but being alone would be even worse."

"He's dead. There is no longer anyone who can connect the two of us."

Nami refused to budge. She shook her head. "I'm not leaving."

Yang was silent as he tied his necktie. He looked like a businessman on his way to work. He was completely composed.

"Will you take me with you?" she asked.

Yang finished tying the knot and looked down at her. He seemed puzzled by her persistence, but said nothing. Picking up his sweat suit, he walked back to the tree stump, moved it, pulled the duffel bag out of the hole and shoved the clothes in. He removed the knife he had strapped to his leg and put it on top of his attaché case. Then he tied up the bag, and put it back in the black trash bag and dropped it in the hole under the stump. He filled the hole with dirt and slid the tree trunk back over it.

Finally, he put the knife into the attaché case and looked at Nami.

"Let's go."

Nami reached out to push the bell for apartment 802. There was a buzzing sound and a voice came out of the perforated stainless steel plate of the intercom.

"Yes?" It was a woman's voice.

"I'm from Club Adeli. Mr. Takakawa asked me to bring something to you." Nami said quickly.

"Okay," the woman said coldly. There was a metallic clicking sound, and the automatic door to the elevator hall opened. Yang pulled a handkerchief out of his suit and quickly wiped off the button for 802, and then gently pushed Nami through the door. A few moments later, it automatically slid shut.

Yang pressed the elevator button using a handkerchief-wrapped finger, and they walked inside when it arrived. When they got to the eighth floor, Nami got out first. Yang handed her his attaché case. She took it and walked down the hall. Yang pulled rubber gloves out of his pocket and put them on. When they arrived at apartment 802, Nami positioned herself in front of the door and Yang stood flat against the wall on the opposite side of the doorknob in the blind spot of the peephole.

Nami pressed the doorbell.

"Coming!" They heard someone come up to the door and look through the peephole. The lock was opened with a click, and the door opened outward.

In the next instant, Yang grabbed the doorknob with his left hand and yanked it open. The woman came flying out, still holding onto the knob. She had long hair and wore a sheer black dress. Yang's right hand zipped forward and grabbed the woman's cheeks, hard. His fingers squeezed her face so tightly that the insides of her cheeks almost touched. Her eyes were wide with fear.

Yang kept his right arm thrust straight out and pushed her back into the apartment. She walked backwards, helpless. He stepped up inside without removing his shoes, and Nami followed behind. Her fingers shook as she closed the door and turned the lock.

Yang continued pushing the woman, her face still in his grasp, into the living room. He looked like a magician who had just pulled a rabbit out of his top hat. He looked quickly around. From the large windows, you could see out over the Shuto Expressway. The room had a wood floor and a black leather sofa with matching chairs. A small beer bottle and a glass were set on a table with a marble top, and a subtitled foreign film was playing on the wide-screen TV.

Next to the beer was an ashtray filled with Salem Light butts with lipstick on them. The woman was here alone.

Yang pulled the woman's jaw up with his right hand, exposing her pale throat. He pulled back his left hand. His palm was flat and his fingers were bent at the second joint.

"Stop!" Nami cried. "Don't kill her."

Yang turned to look at Nami, but his expression did not change. He lowered his palm, and punched the woman in the pit of her stomach instead. She howled like a wounded animal and dropped to her knees. Yang laid her out on the floor. She was still conscious, but she was in too much pain to speak or even open her eyes.

Yang looked around and motioned to Nami to bring the attaché case. He got out a length of rope and a roll of masking tape. He tied up the woman's arms and legs, and put tape over her eyes and mouth.

There were two rooms beyond the living room. One contained a king-size bed, and the other a kitchen table. Yang lifted the woman and put her on the bed, covering her with a blanket. Nami quietly sat down on the sofa. She could hear a conversation in English from the movie playing on TV, and she noticed an empty videotape case on top. She clasped both hands together tightly on top of her knees.

Yang came back into the living room and looked around again, then walked over to a sideboard next to the wall. There was a cordless phone with an answering machine, which he switched on. They heard the recording of the woman's voice and then a beep at the end. Yang got to work inspecting the contents of the sideboard.

Nami saw Yang take his medicine once. He kept the pills in the attaché case. The dose was larger than the one he had taken before, and she was now able to tell from the way the color drained from his face when he was beginning to feel pain. He had had an attack at noon the day before, too, but he had just used ice to numb the pain. He didn't take the painkillers.

The medication was beginning to run out. He told Nami that, when he was in a safe place, he tried to handle the pain without taking any medication. The effectiveness wore off as time went on,

188

and he had ended up needing more than he had planned and was running low. He was taking antibiotics along with the painkillers to avoid getting peritonitis, but he only had a few antibiotics left.

The phone rang a couple of times, but the caller hung up without leaving a message. Yang asked Nami to read a few of the documents he found in the sideboard. She didn't understand some of the more complicated certificate-like papers, but he didn't seem particularly interested in those anyway.

About midnight, Nami began to doze on the sofa. She had hardly slept the night before. Yang had reached for her when they were back in bed after the incident in the park, but she didn't feel well enough to reciprocate, so he silently gave up. Then, near dawn, she turned to him, even though she hadn't slept at all. Yang responded and they made love. When they were through, he rolled over and went back to sleep, but Nami still had a hard time sleeping.

She watched him when he woke up. He didn't speak, but he stared at the ceiling and walls with his eyes wide open. She couldn't bring herself to ask what he was thinking. She was too afraid.

As they had been preparing to leave for the Sangubashi condo, Yang had been clear with her.

"This is the last job you and I are doing together. Once Takakawa tells me where I can find Wei Ye, I'll do the rest on my own."

Nami asked Yang about Ye for the first time. "What did he do?"

"He betrayed me," he answered simply, his face expressionless.

"Will this all end when you kill him?"

Yang got a faraway look in his eyes as he nodded gently. "I'll go home to Taiwan, if I can get back the same way I came."

"What do you mean?"

"I can't begin to explain. I came by ship on a roundabout route. I got seasick. I'd rather walk over hot coals than do that again."

"So you didn't come by plane?"

Yang smiled vaguely, and said no more.

Sometime after three a.m. the phone rang a third time, waking Nami up. As before, the caller left no message after the answering machine picked up. Twenty minutes later someone buzzed the condo from the entrance.

Yang silently pushed the button to open the automatic door. There was no further sound from the speaker. A long, narrow hallway led from the apartment door to the living room. The bath and restroom were in between. Nami stood up and headed towards the hallway. Yang stood flat against the hallway wall by the living room. He had tied an apron he found in the kitchen around his neck and held his knife in his right hand.

Nami stood on the concrete floor by the door and pressed close to the peephole. She could hear the elevator come up and stop at the eighth floor. Then she heard footsteps. From the peephole she saw a man in a green double-breasted suit. He had loosened his tie and his hands were in his pockets. His hair was slicked back and his eyes were sharp.

He took one hand out of his pocket to push the doorbell. Nami took two deep breaths and undid the lock. As she opened it, the man looked at her in surprise.

"Who are you?" He stank of liquor, and his cheeks were red.

"I'm a friend of Yukari's. She wasn't feeling well, so she asked me to come."

"What?" The man clicked his tongue and stepped inside. He roughly removed his shoes. "That idiot, no wonder she didn't answer the phone." He shoved his feet into the slippers Nami put out for him and stomped noisily down the hall. Nami watched him go, and then locked the door again.

"Yukari?" he called out as he turned towards the living room. Just as he was about to enter, Yang whipped out the knife and thrust it in the man's stomach.

190

The man's eyes bulged, and he breathed in sharply. He reached out for Yang's right arm. Yang grabbed his cheeks with his left hand.

"You scream, I slice you in half!" whispered Yang.

The man tried to move his jaw as Yang pushed him over to the sofa, the knife still in his stomach. The man fell back on the sofa. Yang sat opposite him, their knees touching. The man stared at the knife in his stomach. He blinked. He didn't seem to be in much pain even though about six inches of the knife had disappeared inside him. After he sat down, though, his breathing turned into rough gasps. Tears flowed from his eyes and snot ran from his nose. The hand he had on Yang's right arm began to shake.

Yang nodded to Nami. The man's shirt and slacks were now covered in blood. It was trickling onto the floor where it formed a pool.

"I'm going to ask you once. You could still go to a hospital and get help. If you don't answer or try to scream, he will kill you."

The man moved his jaw, which was still in Yang's grip. Yang let go, and the man began to pant like a runner at the end of a marathon. Occasionally, he let out a high-pitched whimper.

"Where is Wei Ye?" asked Nami. The man turned sharply in her direction. He began to open his mouth wide, but Yang's left hand whipped up to cover it and he pushed the knife in further with his right one. The man's cry leaked out from Yang's left hand. He moved his head up and down. Yang let go.

"H-He's in one of the boss's condos. In Wakabacho district in Yotsuya. He's got bodyguards. There are t-two apartments."

Nami quickly explained to Yang what he was saying.

"Get the name of the building and the numbers of the apartments," Yang told her, and Nami related his demand.

"Wakaba Grandheim, 1021 and 1022…"

"How many bodyguards?"

"Two of Ye's, two of ours…"

191

"Firearms?"

"Y-Yes…" The man's eyes pleaded with Nami. She felt as though she was about to faint. The back of her head went cold. Unable to stand any longer, she crouched down on the floor. The man's voice sounded far away.

"Is this him? Is he the one?" The voice was in tears. Seeing that Nami was unable to respond, he turned to Yang.

"Are…are you the Poison Ape?"

"'Poison Ape'?" Yang repeated.

"I just met a detective from Taiwan. He's looking for you. What was his name? Guo…something Guo."

"Guo?"

Nami tried to keep herself conscious as she listened to them.

"Help me, please help…" The man was in pain, and tears ran down his face every time he blinked. His ruddy complexion had gone white.

"Help me, Mr. Poison Ape…"

"Not Poison Ape. *Du Yuan!*" said Yang slowly, demonstrating the pronunciation as he pulled the knife out. The man gasped and pressed both hands against his stomach. "*Du Yuan.*"

"D-Du Yuan!" the man did his best to copy Yang, and as he did so, Yang slit his throat in a single swift move.

Nami blacked out and never saw what happened next.

19

Uniformed patrolmen from the Yoyogi Precinct stood in front of the condo. Samejima and Momoi got out of their patrol car, walked in, and went up to the eighth floor on the elevator. The entire floor was roped off as a crime scene. The two headed for the apartment where they could see camera flashes going off. Both of them took gloves out of their jacket pockets.

Inside were Hashiuchi, squad leader of Criminal Investigation Unit from HQ, and Hori, head of the Yoyogi Crime Division. They were talking to Araki in the living room.

Hori turned around and acknowledged Samejima and Momoi. "So what is Shinjuku doing here?"

Hashiuchi stopped in the middle of a conversation and gave Samejima a good, hard look.

"I asked them to come," Araki said in a subdued voice. "Our perp is probably a foreigner Shinjuku has been looking for."

"The victim's a high-ranking Ishiwa member, right?" said Momoi.

Hori, looking at Araki in surprise, nodded. "That's right. Mitsuaki Takakawa, thirty-nine."

"Cause of death?"

"Got his throat slashed. He was stabbed in the stomach beforehand and would have died eventually from blood loss from that wound alone."

"So, you're saying that he was stabbed in the stomach, and after a while, his throat was cut," Momoi said.

"It looks more like a grudge killing than the start of a gang war. Apparently the crime was committed by a man and a woman working together," Hori explained. Hashiuchi looked at Hori as if to shut him up.

"It's all right," said Araki. "Samejima is the one who first brought forward the information about the perpetrator." Samejima noted the looks of surprise on the other two detectives' faces.

Araki led Samejima and Momoi into a corner of the living room, out of the way of the crime scene investigators. When they were out of earshot of the others, Araki asked, "Have you heard?"

"Samejima told me about some of it in the car. We've got a hit man from Taiwan," said Momoi in a low voice, "and he's going too far."

"I didn't think you would come, sir."

"I just wanted him to get a look at this scene. I don't want my chief getting too involved with this case," Samejima said. Araki nodded, his eyes closed. Samejima could tell he was disappointed.

Araki opened his eyes, and asked, "Do you know the victim?"

"I saw him just yesterday. Guo called me out, and we saw him at a late-night restaurant in Kabukicho."

Araki was puzzled. "What?"

Samejima had told Momoi in the car what had gone on the night before. He related the details to Araki as well.

"So, he came back here afterwards and was killed."

"Were the perps here first?" Samejima asked.

"Yeah, at about nine, a girl came to the front and rang the owner of the apartment, Yukari Iijima. She said she was from the club where Ms. Iijima used to work. The girl said she had something from Takakawa. When Yukari opened the door, the man burst in, tied her up, and put her in the bed. She didn't get a good look at him. He was tall and wore a suit. She heard the woman speaking a foreign language, either Chinese or Korean, to him. She was there all night until Takakawa's thugs came to pick him up and found her. Takakawa was in the living room, just like we said, stabbed in the stomach with his throat cut. And…" Araki pointed to the table. A plastic marker with the letter "D" was on the marble-top table. "Hori, show him what was here on the table."

Hori, having given up trying to block out the outsiders, took a clear plastic bag out of the box of evidence they had collected.

"Is this what you mean?" Inside the bag was a carving of the three monkeys—see no evil, hear no evil, speak no evil.

"What do you think?" Araki asked Samejima. "The worst has happened, right?"

"Guo has got to see this right away," Samejima said, avoiding the question.

"Forget it," said Araki, shaking his head. "We'd just be putting ourselves in jeopardy. Let's just say we heard about this from a rat."

"He must have tortured Takakawa. We'll be getting a report of yet another murder before long." Samejima's tone was serious.

"I know. I've got a contact in Section Four. The Ishiwa HQ's already being watched."

"It won't be enough. They won't be hiding Wei Ye there."

"Shhh, come over here." Araki, not wanting to be overheard, moved the conversation out into the hallway. He asked an investigator if he was through looking for finger and footprints. The investigator nodded, so Araki took out a pack of Short Hopes. "Ishiwa must know that Takakawa is dead. Ye might be on his way to the airport."

"What do you plan to do?"

"Leave HQ to me. I'll talk to Section One and Section Four. I'll tell them that you've heard about the case from an informant. I'll say that Ishiwa is fighting with the Taiwanese, and a Taiwanese hit man is in the country," said Araki.

"What about the Poison Ape?"

"I'll leave him to you. For the time being, Section One will be following the line of inquiry based on the assumption it's a grudge killing, and Section Four will think it's a syndicate matter. We won't have a prayer if Wei Ye is killed. The perp has a woman with him, and she is serving as an interpreter as well as his accomplice. I want you to find her."

"What if Ishiwa talks?"

"That would be the best we could hope for. They'd have to hand Ye over to the International Investigation Unit, and they'd get him to confess to all of his dealings with them. Do you think Ishiwa is going to do that for us?"

"I guess not," said Samejima.

Momoi coughed. Araki looked over at him, and Momoi spoke. "I agree with you, Araki. Ishiwa will pretend not to know anything about the murders, but they aren't going to let the killer get off free."

Araki looked distressed. Momoi continued. "The Ishiwa gang is known for their combat skills. They're not going to shrug off the fact that one of their top men was murdered."

"You think Ishiwa will try to hunt him down?" asked Araki.

"Ishiwa knows who the killer is. Ye knows Du Yuan's characteristics and habits. They'll comb every corner of town while the police are out on a wild goose chase."

"But Du Yuan is a highly skilled pro. He won't be that easy for Ishiwa to find."

"That's the problem. The younger yakuza hotheads will be looking for Taiwanese blood. And how many Taiwanese do you think there are in Shinjuku? Those thugs can't even tell them apart from the mainland Chinese."

Araki blanched as Momoi continued. "Personally, I don't care how many Ishiwa members or Taiwanese bosses are killed. My concern is for the innocent Chinese and Taiwanese whose only crime is speaking their native tongue. I don't want the Ishiwa thugs threatening or hurting them. I certainly don't want them killed."

"…You're right. We'll get Ishiwa leaders to act responsibly and keep a lid on this. We'll put pressure on them."

"You're going to do that?" Momoi pressed Araki.

Araki swallowed hard and nodded. "I'll go myself," he said.

"Then I'll leave Ishiwa to you," Samejima said. "I'll go looking for the perp with Guo's help. Ishiwa has a right-hand man named Hata. He has a bad temper. Please don't let your guard down around him."

"Hata. Got it." Araki took a deep breath and nodded.

Samejima turned his attention to Momoi. "We'll be on our way. Superintendent, there's one more thing you should be careful about."

"What's that?"

"Even if Section One decides to go with the grudge killing theory, make sure you and your men are prepared for the worst. Wear your bullet-proof vests and make sure you're carrying your own weapons when you watch the Ishiwa headquarters."

"Do you think Du Yuan will go after the Ishiwa boss?"

"Not if Takakawa told him where Wei Ye is. If that's the case then he has probably already gone after his target. But if something goes awry, there's no telling what will happen."

Araki paled.

"If you find yourself in a tight spot, don't hesitate to call in a SWAT team," stressed Momoi.

"Your lives are more important than any information on Ye," added Samejima. He left with Momoi.

Samejima and Momoi got into a patrol car and asked the officer at the wheel to take them to the Sanko Hotel.

"Do you think Du Yuan knows where Ye is?" asked Momoi as he

gazed listlessly out the window.

"Probably."

"So if he kills Ye, that should be the end of it, right?"

"As long as Ishiwa doesn't go looking for revenge."

"What about Guo?"

"If Ye dies, he'll figure he deserved it. Guo is only concerned about Du Yuan. That's the feeling I get."

"That could be a problem, too."

Momoi hadn't scolded Samejima for being late with his report on Guo and Du Yuan, nor had he objected to how freely he offered information to Araki. Samejima knew he was out of line, and he had planned to apologize for it on their way to the crime scene. But Momoi had spoken first.

"I think you're more interested in helping out your new friend Guo than you are with cooperating with Araki."

Momoi was right. He was acting as Araki's gopher because of his sympathy for Guo, but he hadn't expected Momoi to figure that out.

The two were silent until the patrol car was close to the Sanko Hotel. Samejima spoke when it came into view.

"I'm sorry. I know I've been nothing but trouble to you."

Momoi spoke as the car came to a stop. "Do what you like. You'll get away with it as long as you're my subordinate." The car door opened.

"Thank you very much," Samejima replied.

"Stop by the precinct when you're done here," said Momoi. "Takakawa's dead, and Yasui, who was like a brother to him, is missing. I'm beginning to think this is all connected to the murder of the nightclub manager. I'll see what data I can find. And you follow the same advice you gave Araki—make sure you're armed."

Samejima gave his boss a quick bow of appreciation as the patrol car sped off.

198

Guo was waiting for him in the lobby of the hotel. He sat on a sofa with English and Japanese newspapers spread out. One look at Samejima's face told him something had happened.

"What is it?" he asked.

"One of the Ishiwa leaders we saw last night has been murdered. Someone was laying in wait at his home. A figurine of the three monkeys was found at the scene."

Guo blinked. "Du Yuan," he said softly, his expression unchanged. "The hunt has begun."

"It might have started a while ago. Would you mind coming with me? Bring along that picture you showed me of Zhensheng Liu."

Guo nodded and stood up. "Wait right here," he said, and got into the elevator. He went upstairs to his room and came back down to the lobby with his jacket on.

"I have the photograph," he said.

The first place they went was the office of Yasui Enterprises. Samejima had Guo wait at the entrance. He found two young gang members manning the telephone, but no one else. There was still no word of Yasui's whereabouts.

"Do either of you know what Yang looks like, the employee Yasui was looking for?"

Both of them shook their heads.

"Can you give me the list of addresses of the hostesses who worked at Fountain of Roses?"

"The boss has it." The young men certainly looked like yakuza. They couldn't have been more than twenty.

"He took it with him before he disappeared?" asked Samejima.

"Yeah."

"Had Yasui gone to talk to the hostesses to find out if they knew were Yang was?"

"Don't know," said one, curtly.

"Agi was an addict. He must have been getting it from Yasui," said Samejima. Looks of agitation crossed their faces, but they didn't seem to have any other information about where Yasui was.

Samejima tried a different tact. "What kind of car does Yasui have?"

"A Mercedes Benz."

"Color and license plate?"

"It's white, but I don't know the plate number."

"You punks drive him around. You know the license plate number."

"Nerima 33, NE65…" the young man finally closed his eyes and recited.

Samejima wrote it down. "If you hear from him, call me."

The two nodded. From the looks of them, they still didn't know that Takakawa was dead. Samejima went out, apologized for making Guo wait, and headed back to the precinct on foot. Guo smiled as they walked through the entrance. He must have felt at home in a police station, even if it was one in a foreign country.

"I have to go get some documents. Wait here for me." Samejima got Guo settled on a sofa in the lobby and turned in the direction of the Crime Prevention Unit.

Guo sat down and happily took in the surroundings. "Take your time. I'll be here."

Momoi had everything ready for Samejima, including the addresses of the hostesses. It was on file from the interrogation. Samejima thanked Momoi, who, as always, was seated at his desk, quiet as a cadaver. He was reading the newspaper. Momoi silently nodded, never turning his attention from the paper.

Samejima took the papers and went to the weapons locker. He strapped a holster to his hip, and fitted it with a .38 New Nambu. He went back to his office to give Momoi Yasui's license plate number.

"Can you look for it? It might already have been towed away."

Momoi nodded. "If it is, it'll be in the computer."

Samejima next visited a different unit to get an unmarked patrol car, and was lucky enough to find a hatchback that was available for the day. He drove the car out of the garage, and brought it around to the front to pick up Guo.

"It's so quiet. I thought the place would be full," Guo commented.

"You mean so few criminals being brought in?"

"Yes."

Samejima laughed. "If you really want to enjoy a tour of the Shinjuku Precinct, you need to be here nights on the weekends. There might not be any guides available, though."

They got in the car and Guo looked at the papers Samejima held.

"What are those?"

"Confidential papers not allowed out of the precinct."

Guo's eyebrows shot up, but he didn't say anything. Samejima looked through them until he found the list of Fountain of Roses hostesses. They lived in Okubo, Koenji, Takadanobaba, and Nakano.

Samejima turned on the ignition and headed for Okubo. As he drove he explained to Guo the case of the murder of the nightclub manager. He mentioned that the manager was a drug addict, the yakuza owner of the club had gone missing, and Takakawa, a big-brother type figure for the missing owner, had turned up dead this morning.

Guo listened in silence. Samejima continued, "This all means that there is a good chance that Yang, the missing nightclub employee and prime suspect, is Du Yuan. The only question is why he got a job like that. Why didn't he do what you did, and try to get involved in the Taiwanese community in Shinjuku and find Wei Ye?"

"Because of Ye himself," replied Guo. "Ye is no problem for me, but if the Taiwanese community learned about Du Yuan, news would get back to Ye fast, and he would flee the country. All of Du Yuan's efforts to sneak into Japan would have been for nothing."

"So you think he's here illegally?"

"Of course. If he has a passport, it is false. He knows Ye is with yakuza in Japan. You can't bring tools for fighting into the country by plane."

"Do you mean guns?"

"If it were only guns, he'd be able to get them in Japan," said Guo quietly as he looked out the windshield.

"What else is there?"

"Can't say for sure, but frogmen learn many ways to kill people and destroy cars and buildings."

Samejima shook his head. If what Guo was saying were true, Araki needed the army rather than a SWAT team.

"How do you think he got in the country?"

"Boat. One made to look like a small fishing boat. There is a route linking Taiwan, mainland China, and Japan. The boats carry drugs and guns. Japanese make money off them just like Chinese do. They take roundabout routes to avoid the Coast Guard. They sail during bad weather."

"What about money?"

"Du Yuan has money. His work earns him a great deal. He will have no trouble changing it into Japanese yen. People with money can get things done. That's true in Taiwan as well as Japan. Am I right?"

He must have come up somewhere on the Japanese coast and hired a car to take him to Tokyo, thought Samejima. "Was he in love with the girl who was killed in Taipei?"

"I don't know. If Du Yuan is Liu, he would be serious about women. He did not use women or buy their favors. Also, he hated drugs. Never used them, not heroine, not amphetamines. He would never forgive the thugs who filled his lover with drugs and then killed her."

Samejima nodded. They had reached Okubo where one of the hostesses, Kiyomi Taguchi, lived. Looking around, Samejima turned left onto a one-way street until he came to a convenience store on the right side of the road. The upper floors were studio apartments.

He stopped the car, and they got out. They walked up to the fourth floor. There was no nameplate next to the door. Samejima pushed the doorbell, but there was no answer. They waited a while and pushed it again. Still no one appeared.

Then they tried the apartments on both sides. One resident was out, but a girl, maybe seventeen, in shorts and brightly colored hair came to the door of the other. She reminded Samejima of Sho.

"The girl next door? No idea. I've never talked to her, and haven't seen her lately either."

Samejima thanked her and asked how they paid their rent. He wanted to know if each apartment had a different owner or if the entire building was operated by a real estate agency. It was the latter. She gave him the name and address of the agency.

Samejima thanked her again, and they left.

Back in the car, Guo commented on Samejima's style. "You are very gentle when questioning. Are all Japanese policemen like that?"

"Police are supposed to be kind to people who haven't done anything wrong, aren't they?"

"But that girl had dyed hair. She might use drugs. She is so young, but lives alone. You were not suspicious of her?"

Samejima smiled. He could see why Guo thought that way. He knew that the majority of Japanese detectives would feel the same way if they saw a young girl with flashy clothes and hair dyed an unnatural color. That was the way Samejima used to be, but he changed once he met Sho. She had taught him that colored hair and weird clothes didn't necessarily make one a criminal. Sho was the one who pointed out the obvious piece of logic to him. It wasn't obvious to most of the police force. Samejima wondered what Guo would think if he ever met Sho. Especially if he met her a year ago, when she had purple streaks in her hair.

Their next stop was Takadanobaba. If they had just been looking for information, they would have called ahead, but there was a possibility that one of these hostesses was working with Du Yuan, so they had opted for unannounced direct contact instead.

Masumi Kitano lived in Takadanobaba. They turned just past the Totsuka Precinct on Meiji Boulevard. Their destination was a building of studio apartments just like the last one. This one, though, was equipped with an elevator.

They rode to the sixth floor and pushed the doorbell. There was no response. Samejima shook his head, and then pushed it again.

"Yeah?" A young girl with messy hair opened the door with the chain still attached. She looked irritated. She was wearing a tank top without a bra and a pair of shorts. "Who are you?" she demanded.

"Police," Samejima flashed his badge.

"Again?" the girl groaned. "This is getting to be a pain in the ass."

"We just want to ask a few questions. It won't take more than a few minutes."

"Wait a sec." She slammed the door shut, but there was no sound of her unfastening the chain. Samejima thought about ringing the bell again, but instead pressed his ear to the door. He heard the sound of bottles clinking together; she must be straightening up. Samejima recalled the first apartment they visited. If Du Yuan were inside, the only escape would be to the balcony of the apartment next door. Just then the door opened.

"Come in," she said, still pissed off.

Samejima looked down at the entrance. A pair of men's sneakers was mixed in with the collection of pumps and sandals. The girl was

204

chewing gum. She put her right hand down the front of her tank top and scratched.

"Do you have a guest?" Samejima asked, indicating the sneakers.

"Just a friend. None of your business."

"I see," said Samejima. He looked at her teeth. There were telltale signs of paint thinner abuse.

"Your name is Masumi Kitano?"

"Yeah."

"I'm sure you've been asked this before, but we need to check again. Have you seen Yang since he disappeared?"

"Nope. Never even talked to him."

"Do you remember what he looked like?"

"Kinda."

"Would you take a look at this photo?"

Guo took the picture out of his jacket and handed it to Samejima, who displayed it for the girl.

"This man in the left-hand corner."

"Can't tell." She chewed her gum loudly and rolled her eyes in annoyance.

"Take a good look."

"I told you, I don't know. Are we done?" She had one hand on the doorknob and appeared about ready to shut it in their faces.

"Too much thinner is bad for your vision," said Samejima quietly. The girl's eyes opened wide.

"Whaddya mean?"

"I can smell it on your breath. You were just using it."

The girl tried to close the door, but Samejima blocked her movement with his left hand. "Doing thinner this early in the day, huh? What are you going to do when thinner won't do it for you anymore? Speed? Eh?"

There was a clatter of feet inside the apartment, and the sound of the back window opening. Samejima burst past the girl and into the apartment.

"What the hell!" the girl screamed out.

There was a bed in the center of the cluttered room, and a young man wearing only a pair of jeans was standing outside on the balcony. His hair was dyed bright red, and he had a gold chain around his neck. Samejima leaped out to grab him while the girl continued to scream. Just as the boy put one foot on the railing, he looked up to see Samejima, and the color drained out of his face.

"You'll fall to your death," Samejima warned him.

The boy looked down at the street below once more, and then back at Samejima. He had a deep tan. He might have been trying to pass himself off as a surfer, but it looked unnatural. He must have spent more time in a tanning salon than on the beach. He probably bleached his hair before dying it.

He pulled his foot off the railing and sulked. He shouted in a high-pitched voice, "What business you got being here?"

Samejima looked around the room. It had been cleared of the small bottles and cans that were usually used for thinner.

"Let me go, you fuckin' son of a bitch!" the girl cried, drawing Samejima's attention. Guo had walked into the room, grabbed the girl's arm with his good hand, and shoved her on the bed. He then went into the kitchen and picked up a black trash bag. He undid the opening of the bag with one hand and kicked it over with his foot. Several small bottles rolled out, and the bit of liquid left inside emitted a volatile odor.

The girl glared at Guo, "I'll have your balls for an illegal search!"

"Better not act like you know what's going on," Samejima warned her. "You can moan and groan to whoever you like, but if the Shinjuku police come in here to investigate, I wonder what else they might find?"

Samejima spotted a device for rolling cigarettes on the dresser.

"What could this be?" Samejima asked, glaring at the boy. In a tight situation, males were always the first to give in. The boy looked at his feet.

"Thinner and pot. What else? Speed? Probably got some benzies, too."

"I dunno! I don't live here." He pouted like a child, and the girl glared at him.

"Then why did you try to escape?"

The boy was silent and swallowed hard.

Samejima went back to the girl. She was quiet now, too, and stood there chewing on a thumbnail.

"Where do you work?"

"Not your business." She looked up at Samejima.

"Yes, it is."

"Charm. In Shinjuku."

"Where?"

"Charm. Kabukicho 2nd Street."

"What is it?"

"A club."

"You're moving up in the world. Did someone get you that job?"

The girl looked away.

"Well?"

"Mr. Yasui."

"I see, and just when did you last see Mr. Yasui?"

"The day after we lost our jobs, and the day after that."

"What time of day was your last meeting?"

"About four in the afternoon."

That was about twelve hours before Yasui went missing.

"Why was Yasui being so nice to you?"

The girl was silent.

"Did you tell him something about Yang?"

She took a deep breath, and looked up at Samejima as she chewed on her nails.

"Are you arrestin' me?" she asked.

"Depends what you tell us."

"Will you let me go this time?"

"What did you tell Yasui about Yang?"

"Yang took the manager's bag. Agi had something important in it that the boss lent him. So…"

"So?"

"Promise you'll let me go."

"We'll leave quietly this time. But I'll be back, and if you still have any drugs around, next time I'll search every square inch of this place."

The girl nodded. "I told him about Nami."

"Nami?"

"One of the girls from the club. Real name's Kiyomi Taguchi. She can speak Chinese. She was from one of those Japanese families left in China during the war. I told Yasui she was probably involved with Yang."

"Look at the photo again." Samejima showed her the picture once more. "Is this him?"

The girl was quiet. After a few moments she finally spit out, "Yeah, that's him."

20

Here he was, aged sixty-five, and feeling regret for the very first time. Wei Ye had never even known what the word meant until now. He realized also that one regret always led to another.

The first thing he regretted, of course, was giving Du Yuan's address to Wen Baiyin, the half-crazed young drug addict. But he knew that if he hadn't handed it over, he would have been dead already. If Wen Baiyin had murdered Du Yuan as he was supposed to, none of this would be happening.

His second regret was hiring Du Yuan to take out the Baiyin gang. He should have paid the ransom and forgotten Baiyin and the whole kidnapping business. Eventually the police would have caught up with the Baiyin gang and hunted them down like dogs anyway.

Ye's concern had been that if a Baiyin member lived and ended up in prison, he would talk. Then the world would know that Ye had not only been kidnapped, but his family had paid the ransom after he, a respected underground boss, had begged and pleaded for his life.

He had been a high-ranking officer in Sihai, a gang with origins in the fabled Tiandehui, and served as an advisor for a number of top-class companies. How could he admit that he had been blindfolded and had to beg for his life from a man whose face he never even saw?

What he regretted most of all was visiting the Taipei apartment of his lover, Lihua, with fewer bodyguards than usual. How could he have even imagined that the reckless and foolish Baiyin gang, the members of which he had never even met before, would try to kidnap him? Baiyin killed his sweet little Lihua as well as Hou, his chauffeur of fifteen years. How could he have forgiven any of them? However, it had come to this. He had been forced to flee to Japan with no more than two of his bodyguards.

This whole mess had to be cleared up as quickly as possible.

Du Yuan was an intelligent man, but the murder of his lover had driven him into a state of distraction. Otherwise, he would never raise a hand against Ye.

Ye first suspected many years ago that Du Yuan had a death wish. Not that he thought he would ever kill himself, but he didn't seem particularly interested in trying to live as long as possible. Maybe he had killed so many people that his feelings about his own life had gone numb.

Du Yuan had been ill when Ye asked him to take out the Baiyin gang. Appendicitis was usually not a major problem, but left untreated it was lethal. Du Yuan had kept at his work, not even taking the time to have a simple operation. The disease had to have progressed considerably by now. He knew that Du Yuan wouldn't take a break to have the operation until he hunted him down and killed him.

Ye knew that once Du Yuan had started an assignment, there wasn't anyone or anything that could stop him from completing it. For him, it was kill or be killed. Du Yuan was like an incurable disease. All you had to do was whisper the name of a target in his ear, and Du Yuan would latch onto him until the end. He was infamous for his diligence and incredible patience. It took more time with some, but he killed them all eventually.

Now Ye had been afflicted with this fatal illness, and he was terrified. He had never experienced regret before, but fear was something he was acquainted with. When he had been confronted with fear, he had always managed to find a way to survive.

That's why he felt certain that he would survive this time as well. He would survive, and return to his seat of power in Taiwan. He had fled to America and then to Japan all in an attempt to survive.

Ye had ordered his subordinates in Taiwan to catch and kill Du Yuan and he had put a high price on his head to speed them along. However, that didn't give him peace of mind.

There was Guo, who he'd met yesterday night. Guo was a detective from Taiwan who was on Du Yuan's trail. He was also a fool who would never take a bribe. Ye was not concerned with how rudely Guo had spoken to him. He could go back to Taiwan and have him taken care of in a matter of days. He'd make sure Guo knew that he could never get away with laying a finger on him.

The problem was that Guo believed Du Yuan was in Japan. When he had fled to Japan, he knew that Du Yuan might follow him here. That was why he had asked Ishiwa to look out for any Taiwanese they weren't sure about. Ishiwa had given him his word—if anyone heard anybody mention Ye's name, he'd have his young thugs on it immediately.

Until yesterday, there had been no one who had spoken his name. Guo's appearance was bad news for Ye. It meant there was a strong possibility that Du Yuan was in Japan. It also meant that Ishiwa had taken the issue too lightly. He had to assume that if Guo knew about his Ishiwa connection, so did Du Yuan. Du Yuan would kill every member of the Ishiwa gang one by one until he found him.

Japanese yakuza were smart and they had well-oiled organizations, but they were never fully prepared for a fight. They were certain that if their organization was tight, they had little to fear. They certainly never thought that an individual might be able to take down an entire syndicate. None of the Japanese yakuza knew how powerful and dangerous Du Yuan was. They wouldn't even be able to imagine it. They had no idea how mercilessly efficient he was at zeroing in on his target. They also didn't know how long he could lie in wait.

211

Ye planned to stay away from Taiwan until he knew that Du Yuan was dead. He was prepared to wait for years. The mess he was in would only be resolved when either Du Yuan or he died.

Ye had hoped to receive good news from Taiwan because he knew that his Japanese yakuza friends were incapable of taking on Du Yuan. Hata, Ishiwa's right-hand man, thought of Du Yuan as little more than an upstart thug. He knew that Hata laughed at Ye behind his back, calling him a coward.

He could see it in Hata's face. *If there's only one of him, what's to be afraid of?* Hata would have his answer if he ever came across Du Yuan's handiwork. As a matter of fact, it might be just as well if he did.

If something happened, and some of the Ishiwa gangsters were murdered, the gang was sure to get serious about getting rid of Du Yuan. Supposing he was actually in Japan.

Ye hoped he'd kill someone soon. Anyone but himself.

The evening before, Ye had gone out. He'd been having a good time until Guo showed up and ruined it. A Japanese detective had been with him, though he had looked awfully young for the job.

Today, Ye wasn't feeling well, so he had decided to spend the day in bed. The girl he had brought back with him wasn't too bad looking, but the events of the evening had left him so rattled that he hadn't been able to function, so he finally sent her home at dawn. She was a nineteen-year-old Japanese girl he'd met at the second club they visited. He couldn't bring Taiwanese girls home with him because they might blab and word would get out—possibly to Du Yuan— about where he was hiding out.

Ye was staying in an apartment that Ishiwa had purchased for his mistress. It was within walking distance of Ishiwa's own home, but Ishiwa had stayed all of last night. From outside, there appeared to be two separate apartments, with two entrances and separate verandas. However, when Ishiwa had bought the apartments, he ordered renovations made to connect the two. What looked like a closet in each was really a doorway to the other. Ishiwa had explained that it was a precaution in case they were attacked by a rival gang or raided by the police. The three-room apartment Ye was staying in was usually vacant.

The windows were covered with a film that made it impossible to see inside. Ye slept in the room in the back. His Taiwanese bodyguards, Huang and Ji, slept in the front two rooms. Huang was a master in Fujian White Crane, a traditional martial art. Ji was a sharpshooter. Both of them were willing to die for Ye.

Ishiwa and his mistress were supposed to be in the room next door. He only had two bodyguards when he stayed there. The bodyguards slept in the room closest to the entrance, with a room between themselves and Ishiwa. Ye imagined that he didn't want his subordinates to hear the sounds of his lovemaking.

At eleven-thirty that morning, Ji had knocked on Ye's bedroom door and looked in.

"Ishiwa called. He says he has to discuss something with you," he said. "He wants you to open the connecting door on our side."

Ye sat up. "Go ahead and open it, and then I'll have some tea."

"Yes, sir."

The hidden door was in the closet in Ji's room. Ye got up and put on his bathrobe over his pajamas. There was a chill in the air. He didn't have much of an appetite, but he wanted something hot to drink.

He went into the bathroom, washed his face and went back into the living room to find Ishiwa sitting on the sofa. He was wearing a cotton kimono that showed a glimpse of some of his tattoos. Behind him stood a bodyguard wearing a suit and holding a cell phone. Ishiwa looked terribly irritated.

"Good morning," said Ye and took a seat in a chair opposite of

Ishiwa. Ye was born before World War II, which meant he could read, write and speak Japanese.

Ji brought a hot pot of tea from the kitchen. He was wearing a sleeveless undershirt and slacks into which he had thrust a gun. It was a .45 Colt that Ishiwa had provided.

"Have some tea," Ye tried to smile as he took a cup for himself.

Ishiwa shook his head. "Mr. Ye, I have some extremely bad news," he began. "Takakawa, one of the men we were with last night, has been murdered."

Ye was speechless as Ishiwa went on. "He was killed by a man and a woman. They both spoke Chinese. They slit his throat."

Ye put down his teacup. Somehow the liquid had suddenly lost its heat.

"Before he was killed, he was apparently tortured. He might have told the killer about this place. The police are probably going to come snoop around here, too. I'm sorry, but you should probably leave."

"Where should I go?"

Ishiwa put a cigarette in his mouth. His bodyguard lit it for him. "I don't know. The airport, or somewhere out west. Hata is on his way here with some of our young men. They'll accompany you to either an airport or a train station."

Ye interpreted for Ji and Huang, telling them what Ishiwa was saying.

"Is this bastard saying he's throwing you out, Boss?" asked Ji in Chinese.

"Might be. He's afraid of the police getting involved," answered Ye.

"Was there a monkey next to the body?" Huang asked. "Takakawa could have been killed by someone with no connection to you."

"Was there a figurine of three monkeys near Takakawa's body?" asked Ye in Japanese.

"Yes, there was. One of our men discovered it near the corpse."

Ye gave this information to his bodyguards, who both nodded wordlessly.

"Mr. Ishiwa, where do you think I should go? Osaka? Kyoto? Or back to Taiwan?"

"Taiwan might be best. I've told my men to be careful, but the police are going to cause trouble. That Shinjuku detective knew about Du Yuan."

Ye nodded, thought a moment, and then asked another question. "Who might the woman with him be?"

"She's probably the lover of that son-of-a-bitch Du Yuan. Who else? She's probably Taiwanese."

Ye shook his head. "His lover is dead."

"Then I don't know." Ishiwa leaned back on the sofa and blew smoke up towards the ceiling.

"He's a rude fucker. Let's kill him later," mumbled Ji in Chinese.

"Wait," Ye told him, and turned back to Ishiwa. "Mr. Ishiwa, what do you plan to do about that woman and Du Yuan?"

"Hata is itching to move, but I told him to wait. If we panic now, we'll play into the hands of the cops. But we won't stay still forever."

"Then look for the woman. She must be interpreting for him since Du Yuan can't speak Japanese. He must have found Takakawa with her help."

"You're probably right. He died in the apartment of his new mistress. It's only been a month since he left his wife." Ishiwa looked pensive.

"I'll try to think of something, too," Ye said. The he turned to Huang and Ji. "Get ready to leave." The two bowed and got down to work. Ye went into his room to change. When he was finished, he went back to the living room.

"Hata just arrived," said Ishiwa. "He and the others are investigating the area downstairs. The police haven't shown up yet.

Leave as soon as my men say it's safe. I'll say good-bye here. As far as anyone else is concerned, we never had this conversation."

Ye nodded, keeping his real feelings from showing. He smiled. "Mr. Ishiwa, thank you for all you've done for me. I'll never forget it. I hope that when all this is over, you'll make another visit to Taiwan. I'll prepare a wonderful gift for you."

Ishiwa stood up. "I'm sorry I couldn't do more. I've instructed Hata to stay glued to you until you're safely on a plane or a train." Ye and Ishiwa shook hands, and he noticed that Ishiwa was missing the tip of his right little finger. It was the same with his left little finger.

"See him downstairs," Ishiwa ordered his bodyguard, and the man hurried for the door. Huang, Ji, and Ye followed. Ishiwa walked behind Ye with his other bodyguard. Ishiwa's man looked out the peephole and opened the door. Ye looked nervously out towards the hallway. The door was blocked by something, and the man looked down. A small cardboard box had been left next to the door. It was covered in wrapping paper. He reached down to pick it up.

It exploded.

Yellow fire flashed out, and the bodyguard's hands and face were blown away. Without even having the chance to utter a word, he fell backwards to the floor.

"We're being attacked!" It was Ji, who was walking slightly ahead of Ye. Ye turned right around to go back the way he came, running into Ishiwa who stood there gaping at the corpse of his bodyguard.

"Get away! Ishiwa, go!" shouted Ye as he pushed aside Ishiwa's other bodyguard who stood there dumbly, and ran back into the apartment. He turned back. Ishiwa was still standing there.

"Ishiwa, it's the Ape! He's here!"

Huang grabbed the knob of the blood-drenched door and tried to slam it shut, but the legs of the dead man were in the way. Just as Ji pulled out his gun to cover Huang, something came flying through the narrow gap in the door.

Ye grabbed Ishiwa's shoulder just as the room was filled with blinding light and a deafening boom. The sight of Huang covering his ears with both hands and squeezing his eyes shut was burned into Ye's brain. He stopped thinking and pulled Ishiwa away.

The door burst open, and the dark figure of a man leapt in. Ye pulled Ishiwa as far as the door to the living room. He was still seeing red, blue and purple spots.

Ji's gun went off with an insignificant blast, the result of a dying spasm.

The Ape wore a black sweat suit with the hood pulled tightly over his head. He walked calmly into the room and continued the massacre.

Ye could tell that Du Yuan had his favorite weapon with him, an Uzi submachine gun. Mechanical blasts drilled holes through Huang, Ji, and Ishiwa's remaining bodyguard. Blood spattered into a red mist in the narrow foyer.

Ye let go of Ishiwa and closed the door of the living room. He couldn't hear anything. Ishiwa's face was white as a sheet and he wore an expression of blind terror.

Machine gun fire came drilling through the living room door. Ishiwa screamed as Ye's hearing returned to him. Bullets had ripped through Ishiwa's left shoulder. He and Ye raced silently across the living room. They both knew to head for the secret door in the closet. They managed to get into Ji's room and pulled the door shut. Gunfire ripped through the door. The two men fell to the floor.

"Wh-What's happening?" Ishiwa reached out to lock the door. Ye had already reached the closet. He opened the door and motioned to Ishiwa to hurry. Ishiwa crawled in on his hands and knees. He looked like a hunted bear.

They closed the door to the closet and opened the secret door inside. Holding onto each other for dear life, they pulled themselves through to the room occupied by Ishiwa's mistress.

"Close it, close it, close it, close it!" Ishiwa repeated like a maniac. They shut the hidden door together. It was a sturdy double door made of steel that had been made to fit perfectly flat into the wall.

There in the room was Ishiwa's mistress, her eyes wide with fear.

"What's happening? A fight?" she asked.

Ishiwa, breathing hard, grabbed the phone. He dialed a long telephone number and screamed at the person who answered.

"You motherfucker! Where are you? We're up here! Upstairs! Hurry! He's going to kill us!" He threw down the receiver, and went pale as he looked at the steel door. He suddenly turned to his mistress. "Is the front door locked?"

"Yes. Are you going to call the police?"

"Wait, wait." Ishiwa began to calm down. He nervously chewed on his lip. "Over there, over there. Let's go."

They moved into the living room. On the way, they heard the sound of many feet pounding the hallway of the apartment building.

"That's Hata. He's finally here," Ishiwa mumbled and sat down on the sofa.

Then there was a loud banging noise from the closet with the hidden door. Ye froze. The Ape had found it.

"Let's get out of here," he said to Ishiwa, pointing to the front door. Ishiwa was white. His kimono was soaked in blood from the wound to his shoulder. He nodded and stood up, and the three of them headed for the door.

The entire building shook from the impact of another explosion. The steel door blew open and white smoke billowed through it. Out sprang the black-clad figure. Ye saw clearly this time that it was Du Yuan. He had a bag slung over his shoulder across his chest. In his hand was the Uzi he had used to slay their bodyguards.

Just at the moment Ye was sure they were finished, there was a shout, as Hata and more than ten of Ishiwa's men came streaming

218

through the front door into the living room. All of them had guns in their hands. They were the Black Stars Ye had supplied to Ishiwa.

There was a barrage of fire. Du Yuan met Ye's eyes for a second before he crashed through the glass in the window and leaped out onto the balcony. He jumped lightly up onto the railing and then sprang quickly, just like a monkey, over to the next-door neighbor's balcony.

"Get him!" Ishiwa screeched. "Kill him!"

Hata and the others rushed out to the balcony, but Du Yuan was nowhere to be seen.

21

Samejima, upon receiving instructions from Momoi over the radio, went with Guo to Ishiwa's condo in Shinjuku. Detectives from the Yotsuya Precinct, Section Four and Section One were conducting a joint investigation. Araki was there in the lobby. It had only been a few hours since they had last met.

When Araki caught sight of Guo, he prevented him from going into the rooms now being investigated. He led them down to the parking garage instead.

"Don't get the wrong idea," said Araki, "but if you get involved, it will confuse the other investigators." Guo showed no reaction. "We appreciate the information you've given us, but to be perfectly honest we never thought this hit man would go so far."

"We can talk about that later," interrupted Samejima. "Who was hurt? Was Ye killed?"

"No, there's four dead and one seriously injured, but Ye wasn't among them. Two of the dead seem to be Ye's Taiwanese bodyguards.

"So where is he?" asked Samejima. Araki shook his head.

"He's missing. It appears that he and Hata, one of Ishiwa's top men, lived. Ishiwa was shot in the shoulder and is in the hospital."

"Tell me about the attack," asked Guo.

Araki hesitated for a second, but with a sharp look from Samejima, he began. "Ishiwa was the only one here alive when we arrived. We're not sure about all the details, but Ishiwa and Wei Ye were in an apartment on the tenth floor, 1022. When they opened the door to leave, there was a small package in the hallway. Ishiwa's bodyguard picked it up and it exploded, killing him instantly. Next, say the crime scene investigators, a bomb called a flash-bang grenade was tossed inside. It makes a powerfully loud sound and gives off an extremely bright light so that it renders anyone in the vicinity temporarily blind and deaf.

"The killer used those moments to come into the room with a submachine gun that he sprayed the room with. That took care of Ye's two bodyguards and Ishiwa's remaining man. Apartment 1022 is connected to 1021 by a secret door, and Ye and Ishiwa escaped through there. That saved them from getting killed. When he found that door, the attacker used a different kind of bomb, probably one made with plastic, to blow it open. In the meantime, Ishiwa managed to contact Hata, who was downstairs. When he and his men got into apartment 1021, the attacker escaped out the balcony. Can you believe it? He used his own body to break through the window, ran across the railing on the balcony, and slid down the drain spout to the ground. Just like a ninja."

"What type of machine gun did he use?" asked Guo.

"Hard to say. The shells we found the most of, though, came from a 9 millimeter gun."

Guo turned to speak to Samejima. "It's an Uzi. It's what Du Yuan used to take out the Baiyin gang. An Uzi uses 9 millimeter pistol rounds."

Araki exhaled deeply and took out a cigarette. He was wearing a bulletproof vest over his white polo shirt and had a gun strapped into a holster.

"How badly injured was Ishiwa?"

"He'll live. He let Ye and Hata escape before the police got here. He didn't want us to get Ye. Hata is definitely with him."

"Was the attacker injured?"

"There was blood on the drain spout. We can't tell if he was shot by Ishiwa's men or cut on the glass."

"Were any of Ishiwa's men arrested?"

"A few were brought in for carrying arms. Ishiwa whined and begged for a uniformed policeman to be stationed outside his hospital door."

Hata was somewhere out there, and he was sure to be in a frenzied state. His comrades had been murdered and his boss was injured. The Ishiwa gang was sure to be busy hunting down Du Yuan.

"Do you have a warrant out for Hata?" asked Samejima.

Araki blew out a puff of smoke and shook his head. "He's not a suspect in this case. I'll do what I can to convince the others that they need to find him, but Section Four is in upheaval. No one had any information that something like this was about to go down."

Samejima looked at Guo. "What do you think Du Yuan will do next?"

Guo thought hard. "There are two things. First he'll go underground and wait until his wounds heal. Then he'll continue killing off the Ishiwa gang until they give up Ye."

"You think he'll keep this up?" Araki looked upset. Guo looked up at him.

"Du Yuan has never given up a target. He will not let Ye get away. He will kill him," he said.

Araki cursed under his breath.

"We know who Du Yuan is with. A woman named Kiyomi Taguchi. She was a hostess at Fountain of Roses," said Samejima.

"What?" Araki was stunned. "Why would a girl like that—"

"Du Yuan worked there for two weeks using the name Yang. His first murder in Japan was Agi, the manager." Samejima went on to explain the Fountain of Roses incident. He told Araki about Yasui, who Takakawa had looked after like a brother, and how he was missing. "I believe Du Yuan started with Agi, then got Yasui, then

222

Takakawa before he arrived here at this condo. We might as well assume that Yasui is dead, too. You need to get a search warrant for Kiyomi Taguchi's apartment. Du Yuan can't speak Japanese, so she's been helping him."

"Why does she speak Chinese?"

"Apparently her mother was left in China after the war. She was born and raised there."

Araki bit his lip. "Of all the…"

"What we don't know is whether she is with Du Yuan of her own volition, or whether she's being coerced. If he made the attack today alone, then Kiyomi would have been left on her own. If we can find her, we might be able to put a stop to Du Yuan's movements. And…" Samejima looked at Guo, who wordlessly held out the photo. "We know who he is. The man in this photo is Du Yuan."

Araki's attitude changed when he saw the photo. "Do you mind if I borrow this?"

"Yes, but I have one request," said Guo.

"What's that?"

"If you find Du Yuan—his real name is Zhensheng Liu—if you get him in a corner, you'll need someone who can speak Chinese. Let me be the one to speak to him. I know Liu. Better than anyone else in this country." Guo was dead serious. Araki looked at the picture again.

"I'll do what I can," he said.

22

"You got it, you numbskulls? No matter what the detectives say, do not leave the boss's side," ordered Hata, then he hung up his cell phone and handed it to his bodyguard. Wei Ye sat next to a window of a suite in a hotel next to Haneda Airport, watching the planes take off.

Hata came over and sat across from him. They had three bodyguards, one in their room and two others sitting in the next room. All of them were Hata's. Both of Ye's bodyguards were dead. Ye absently picked up and sipped a cup of the Chinese tea room service had delivered.

Hata was mad as hell. His partner, Takakawa, had been murdered and Ishiwa had been badly injured. Ye could understand Hata's angst, but it made him uneasy. If Hata blamed this all on him, he would probably kill him. The only thing in his favor was that Ishiwa had survived the attack, and it was because Ye himself had dragged him back to the living room. He had done it almost instinctively.

"There was a message from the boss. He wants to thank you for saving his life." Hata spoke in a vexed tone, his teeth clenched.

"It was nothing, I just did it without thinking," said Ye, "and I'm sorry he lost his bodyguards, the young men."

"Don't forget Takakawa." Hata's face was red. "Takakawa and I were different, but he was a good guy. We trained together. That's why..."

"I'm sure you are angry. So am I," said Ye.

224

"The boss ordered me to send you to Taiwan. We can't let anything happen to you here." Hata had both of his hands rolled into fists and placed on his knees. Ye noticed with discomfort that they were both shaking. Ye had done his best to sound sympathetic, but he didn't regret the loss of any of the men, including his own. They were disposable and could be easily replaced.

"What about the police?"

"They're not a big problem right now. We're the victims this time."

Ye leaned forward to grab Hata's hand.

"Mr. Hata, I was going to leave tomorrow, but I've decided not to. Don't you want revenge for Takakawa and your young men?"

A look of surprise crossed Hata's face. "Of course I do, but the police are in the way…"

"Is everyone searching Shinjuku?"

"The Ishiwa gang is out there looking for Du Yuan. We'll kill him if we find him before the police do."

"Are there many police on guard?"

Hata bit his lip. "There's a SWAT team at our headquarters. The detectives are looking for the two of us. There's still room to move at the dorm."

"The dorm?"

"We have a place for the young guys to stay if they need to. It's a pile of bedding, that's all. They've only got three or four plainclothes cops watching it. But they're checking out anyone who comes near headquarters. They're even searching food delivery boys."

"Then we can use the men at the dorm. I have a way to catch Du Yuan, and the police will never know."

Hata furrowed his eyebrows. "Are you sure?"

"I've been thinking about this the whole time I've been in Japan, but I didn't know whether Du Yuan was here, so I didn't tell Mr. Ishiwa about it. I didn't want to risk the lives of the young men."

"What do we do?" Hata's voice was intimidating.

"I'll tell you, but first we have to find someone."

"Who?"

"Du Yuan is not alone. He can't speak Japanese. Mr. Ishiwa said Takakawa was killed by a man and a woman. The woman probably speaks both Chinese and Japanese. She's his guide."

"Guide?"

"How did Du Yuan find Takakawa's place? Either the woman knew, or she knew someone who did."

Hata thought hard. "That's right. The woman told Yukari she worked at Adeli. Yukari was Takakawa's woman. Adeli is where she used to work."

"Where did they get that information?"

"The woman worked at Adeli?"

"Maybe. Or before they tortured Takakawa, they might have tortured someone else who knew about Adeli."

"It wouldn't be one of us. Nobody else from Ishiwa was killed."

"Du Yuan knows about Shinjuku. He knows the Ishiwa gang is from Shinjuku. Is there anyone else, another yakuza, who knew about Takakawa's apartment?"

Hata reached for his cell phone. "I'll ask Takakawa's driver."

Ye put out his hand to stop him. "There's one more thing. Pharmacies. We need to put a lookout on pharmacies."

"Why?"

"Du Yuan is sick. He's got a bad case of appendicitis. The woman he is with might go looking for medicine."

"But there are hundreds of pharmacies."

"Du Yuan can't go to a doctor. What would you do if you needed a strong medicine, but you couldn't get a doctor's piece of paper for it?"

"You mean a pharmacy that will give out medicine without a doctor's prescription?"

"Yes. Are there a lot of those?"

"No, only a few in Shinjuku."

"Those are the places you need to watch. The woman, Du Yuan's guide, will go looking for medicine for him. Catch her. She knows where he is."

"The woman, that's it, the woman." Hata said in a low voice.

23

Nami picked up the cigarette pack and opened it, but it was empty. Behind the heavy door, she could vaguely hear the sound of gunshots and a woman screaming.

She was in a small movie theatre near the Koma Hall. The theater showed double features of B-grade movies. There were less than twenty customers in all. More than half of them were asleep or making out.

There was no one else on the sofa in the hallway. She stood up and walked towards the concession stand to the left of the entrance where she had purchased a cup of coffee earlier. She wanted to buy a pack of cigarettes, but the stand was closed. She looked at her watch. It was seven-forty.

The final film of the evening had begun twenty minutes before. All of a sudden she was filled with dread, wondering if she was in the wrong theater. No, this was the place. Yang had given her the name of this theater. He said it wouldn't be crowded. There were quite a few theaters in the area, but not many of them were showing a double feature of B-grade action movies.

It will all be over today, Yang had said. *Forget you ever met me. If you want to go to the police, do it tomorrow. Meet the Taiwanese detective Takakawa mentioned. Guo. Tell him about me. But be sure to tell him that I forced you to do it all. Don't forget that. And don't go back to your apartment until after you've been to the police.*

No! I'll wait for you. When you're finished, come back for me, Nami had insisted, and Yang had looked at her in disbelief. Even Nami was unable to understand what she was doing. Why was she trying so desperately to stay connected to Yang? She only knew that Yang was different. He was in a separate class from the other men she had liked. She was terrified by the idea of being apart from him.

She wondered if the police were already on his trail. If the police were looking for him, they must be looking for her, too. What would they do? She had helped Yang kill twice. If Yang were executed, would she be, too?

He had given her two different places to meet up with him. If he didn't make it to the movie theater, she was to go to Shinjuku Gyoen Park. He had wanted the park to be their first option.

No, she had said. *I can't go back there again. There are dead bodies in that pond. Choose somewhere else.*

That was when he had given her the name of this theater. *Sit in the end seat of the front row, the one closest to the exit. If I don't show up there by tonight, go to the park, to the Taiwan Pavilion.*

When?

Tomorrow morning between nine and ten. If I'm not there, go back the next morning at the same time.

Nami decided not to consider the possibility that Yang might be killed. When she saw that the theater was showing action movies, she closed her eyes and tried to go to sleep. She didn't want to watch scenes of people being shot and stabbed. It would just terrify her and make her nauseous again.

She dozed off twice only to wake to some lecher touching her knees and breasts. She had hit him in the face and hands with her bag. She was afraid and wanted to move, but she couldn't risk missing Yang. Tears ran down her face when she struck the man. He had scuttled away like a cockroach.

Where was he? Was he shot or had he been stabbed? Was he lying in the dark somewhere, unable to move? He couldn't speak

229

much Japanese, but he should be able to at least hail a taxi and get to Kabukicho. As long as he could still walk and talk. But he might be injured so badly he couldn't do either. Maybe he was in a hospital. She had no way of knowing, since she had been in the movie theater all day. She tried to tell herself not to think about it.

Yang had given her three hundred thousand yen before they parted.

Use this to stay at a hotel until you can get back to your place.

But I've got money. And I can always borrow if I run out.

Don't contact anyone. Don't even call your family until I tell you it's okay. His expression had been stern then, but only then. *It's for your own good. Takakawa's associates are looking for me, and they might be looking for you, too.*

Just before dawn, they had left the Sangubashi condo and walked to a family restaurant that was open all night. That was where they had parted. More than twelve hours had passed since.

Nami hadn't thought of what she would do if he came back unharmed. So many things had happened. There was nothing she could do except follow his instructions. She couldn't think of anything else to do.

She had to wait for the last movie to end. If he didn't come, she'd go out and buy a newspaper. If there were no mention of an incident, she'd check into a hotel and turn on the news. She might learn something about Yang.

Nami left the theater just before ten. It had been light when she went in, but now Shinjuku was covered in the dark of night. As usual, the streets were full of people. Nami walked with her shoulders hunched over, and bought a newspaper at an all-night newsstand near the Koma Hall.

She shoved it into the shopping bag she carried with her and began to walk quickly. She opened the door of the first coffee shop she came to, sat in one of the booths in the back and spread out the evening paper.

"Terrifying afternoon shoot-out in residential area."

The headline on the second page leaped out at her.

"Man attacks mob boss at lover's home with bombs and submachine gun," read the by-line. Nami gasped as she read on. She didn't even notice the waitress coming to take her order. She read the article over and over until she was finally able to concentrate on the last part where it said that the attacker had fled.

Yang was alive. They hadn't killed him. Nami breathed a sigh of relief. She noticed the irritated waitress, and ordered a cup of coffee. She looked for the name "Wei Ye" in the list of those killed. It wasn't there.

There were two Chinese names, Huang and Ji, and the article said they had Taiwanese passports. The newspaper said they had been visiting the Ishiwa gang boss and got caught in the crossfire. Nami thought maybe one of the names had been an alias for Ye, but then she saw that the dead men were both in their thirties. Ye was much older.

It wasn't over yet. That's why Yang hadn't shown up at the theater.

Nami reached for the cup of coffee the waitress brought her, and her fingers trembled. At least she knew Yang was alive. He hadn't shown up at the theater because he was still after Ye. Then she remembered that there was still a possibility that he had been unable to come back for her. She told herself not to think about it, but she couldn't help remembering how he had sat on her bed, his hand gripping his stomach.

He said he had appendicitis. Left untreated, it could turn into peritonitis and kill him. She remembered when she was in junior high that a girl had fainted in the restroom at school. She had thought that pain from appendicitis was just menstrual cramps, and it had gone septic. They said she'd have died if she'd waited another few hours to get treatment.

Yang was running out of medicine.

He had antibiotics and painkillers, both of which he had brought with him from Taiwan. Even if he were uninjured, he would be immobilized from the pain of the appendicitis. She knew he had two doses left which he had to take at least once a day. Yang had said the pain was becoming more frequent, but he had been trying to make the medication last. If the pain began while he was under attack, he would be unable to defend himself.

Nami had seen him take the medicine at the family restaurant the morning before, as they were about to part.

Does it hurt? she had asked.

No, I'm all right now.

As far as she could tell he didn't appear to be in pain. He must have taken the pills to make sure he was in top condition to track down his target. Which meant he only had one dose left. He would have to take the last one today.

He's out of medicine. He's out of medicine.

Nami knew it was strong stuff. The painkiller was more than the aspirin she took for headaches or cramps. It wouldn't be available at just any pharmacy. She had to get a new supply of medicine to him. Otherwise he'd never finish the job. But how could she do it?

No pharmacy would sell anything that strong without a doctor's prescription. That would be true whether she or Yang himself tried to buy it. She had to somehow get the meds so she could take them with her when she met him at Shinjuku Gyoen Park the next morning.

Nami looked at her watch. It was almost eleven. Pharmacies tended to stay open late, but she was at a loss for how to get around the prescription problem.

What should I do? What?

Then she remembered Kazuki, one of the other hostesses at the club. Her oldest child had asthma. The asthma medication was powerful, and if she ran out she had to get the prescription refilled at the hospital. But she didn't always have the time to visit the doctor, and sometimes she'd buy it directly from a certain pharmacy.

You're supposed to have a prescription, but there's this one place that will sell it to you without one.

Nami looked around the coffee shop. There was a pay phone next to the door. Nami stood up.

"Welcome!" called out a waitress as two boys suddenly walked in. They must have been about fifteen or sixteen.

"I'm gonna make a call. Order ice cream for me, will you?" One of them said. He walked right in front of Nami and picked up the receiver. He put some coins in the phone and leaned on the counter as he dialed.

"Hey, it's me. What? So you found it, that's great! You don't want to get mixed up with someone like that. What?"

Nami stood there biting on her lip. The boy noticed her standing there, but ignored her, turning away to chat. "Hm? I don't care, anything'll do. Look, I told you—you might as well just steal one." Nami took a deep breath and went back to her seat. She sat there staring at the boy. He stuck out his rear end and leaned on his forearms, compulsively bouncing one leg up and down. He eventually pulled out a cigarette and blithely asked the waitress to bring him an ashtray.

Nami gave up. She'd have to find a public phone outside. She picked up her check and went to the register to pay.

It would mean breaking her promise with Yang about not contacting anyone, she thought as she walked towards the station. She'd do it just once, to find out the name of the pharmacy. She wouldn't tell Kazuki what she needed it for.

She found another pay phone, but someone was on it. The third one was broken. She finally found a phone booth near the station. She saw a man with his suit jacket tossed over one shoulder and his tie loosened heading for the same phone. Nami picked up her pace and got there first, closing the door behind her. The man clucked his tongue in annoyance.

She opened up her purse to look for her address book. She knew Kazuki wouldn't be home at this hour if she'd already started a job somewhere else. She put a telephone card into the slot and dialed Kazuki's apartment.

Please be there. Please, Kazuki-san.

The phone picked up on the fourth ring.

"Hello." It was the voice of someone who obviously didn't want to be bothered.

"Hello, Kazuki? This is Nami." There was a pause. "Hello?"

"Nami! Where are you calling from?"

"I'm out."

"Look, um, yeah, Nami…"

Nami realized from the tense sound of her voice that the police had been looking for her.

"Kazuki, please, give me the name of that pharmacy!"

"Pharmacy?" Kazuki's voice went up an octave. "Are you hurt?"

"No, but my friend's sick. I'm looking for a pharmacy that'll give me medicine without a prescription."

"Hey, are you sure… are you okay with that?"

"What?"

"You know…" Kazuki hesitated.

Just then somebody began kicking the door of Nami's phone booth.

"Hurry up!" There was a man waiting outside making a fuss. He had a mean look in his eyes and he yelled at her again. People walking by noticed the commotion.

"Come on, Kazuki. I'm in a hurry! Tell me about that pharmacy you went to when you had to get medicine for your kid."

"Fine, I'll tell you, but you know, you ought to at least go see the police. You're going to be in trouble too if you don't. You don't want them on your bad side."

"Yeah, I'll go, I swear." The man outside began to beat his fist against the phone booth.

"That pharmacy is right there, by the club. You know, Fountain of Roses. You go straight and then turn left when the road ends. There are two guys there. A bald one and a young one. The bald one will give you what you want."

"Thank you."

"Nami, do you want me to go pick you up? I'll go with you to the police if you're afraid to go all by yourself."

Nami's eyes brimmed with tears at her friend's kindness. "Don't worry. I'll be fine. I'll call you later."

"Nami—"

Nami put down the receiver. She turned around to see the man standing there waiting, his hands in his pockets and his feet spread wide apart.

"How the hell long you plan to talk? It's not your personal phone, you stupid bitch!"

Nami had had enough. She walked up to him and yelled in his face.

"Shut up, you drunken piece of shit!"

The man's eyes opened wide, and some people waiting for a traffic light snickered. Nami walked off without looking back.

24

Wei Ye returned to Shinjuku, sitting in the back seat of a Mercedes with two layers of blackout film on the windows. The car didn't stop. The driver just kept circling the Kabukicho area.

Next to Ye was Hata, who was busily making calls on his cell phone. The car was equipped with a phone, but no one was allowed to touch it—it was left open to receive incoming calls.

The mobility of the Japanese yakuza was surprising, thought Ye. The horizontal relationships, especially, were adroitly used to gather information. He thought their organizational skills were probably superior to both the police and the military.

All afternoon, a flood of information had been coming through on Hata's phone. The most important had concerned the condition of his boss, Ishiwa, and the movements of the police. Hata knew exactly how the Ishiwa gang was being observed. Ye also learned that he and Hata were the focus of a police search. Their driver had been instructed not to go near either the Ishiwa headquarters or the dorm.

The second-most important information had to do with the woman Ye suspected was working with Du Yuan. Takakawa's driver was serving as one of Ishiwa's bodyguards at the hospital. Hata had drilled him about the names of Takakawa's friends, whom he then ordered the young thugs at the dorm to contact one by one. This was how they had learned of Yasui, who had been like a brother to Takakawa, and that he had been missing for several days.

Hata immediately began calling the men who were in positions directly above and below Yasui. He found out from them that Yasui's gang was involved in drugs, and that Takakawa had been responsible for the route they controlled. Hata followed the trail of Yasui's drugs and discovered that Ye's syndicate had exported them.

Hata had learned from someone at Yasui Enterprises about the murder at Fountain of Roses. Agi, the manager, had gone to Yasui to beg for some speed the day he died, and he should have had several fixes worth of it still on him. When the body was found, though, Agi's bag containing his drugs and hypodermic needle was gone. Yasui had panicked because his fingerprints were on the bags of speed. Yasui thought that Agi's murderer was a Chinese man they had hired just two weeks prior. Yasui had gone to try and get the bag back before the police found it, but now he was missing.

What the police didn't know was that Yasui had received a call from a Fountain of Roses hostess who was close to Yang, the Chinese employee, and she had asked him to meet her somewhere. Yasui Enterprises had been trying to find the hostess since then, but were having no luck.

As soon as he learned which one—Nami—Hata had one of his men find her address. That night, he sent two of the Ishiwa gang members to her apartment in Okubo. They arrived just as the police were in the middle of searching it.

Ye seemed satisfied to hear this when Hata told him of developments. The facts were beginning to fall into place.

"Excellent. The Ishiwa gang has discovered the woman helping Du Yuan get around."

Hata, on the other hand, wore an expression of hopelessness. He realized that he never would have gotten this far without Ye's instructions.

Ye derided Hata in his mind. *It's all so obvious, you idiot. The only thing you can think of is getting revenge for your boss and your comrades.*

Your pride is all you have. You've got no brain, just a mindless thirst for blood.

However, he simply said, "We've caught up with the police investigation. Now it's time to get ahead of them."

"How?"

"First of all we need to find someone who can identify this Nami. Takakawa's mistress saw her, but the police have her in custody in case they need her to identify Du Yuan."

"Wait a moment." Hata made a few more calls. It wasn't long before he found someone that could help. "There's a club called Charm in Kabukicho." He told the driver the location. "One of Yasui's girls is there."

25

When Nami found the pharmacy, the shutter was halfway closed. The man pulling it down with a long pole was the one Kazuki had told her about, a bald man in a white lab coat.

"Excuse me!" She ran under the shutters and into the shop.

The shopkeeper was obviously surprised at this late-night visitor. He wore glasses and Nami could see that his lab coat was stained in places. "Uh, welcome," he said.

"Um…" Nami began as she looked around the shop. The shopkeeper had brought in the tissue and toilet paper, which he usually kept stacked outside, so the shop was cramped. It smelled of paper products, medicine and detergent. The man turned sideways to wade through the piles of things and headed back into the pharmacy.

"Can I help you with something?" He spoke with a bit of a lisp and his glasses made his eyes look enormous.

"I have a friend who's planning to leave on a trip tomorrow, and it looks like he suddenly got appendicitis…" Nami told him the lie she had thought up.

"Has he been to a doctor?"

"Once, a while ago. He got medicine…"

"Has it spread?"

Nami didn't know what he meant, but nodded anyway.

"He can't leave it like that, he'll have to have surgery."

"He'll do that as soon as he gets back. But he really wants to take this trip."

"A doctor would tell him to have his appendix out."

"Please."

The man exhaled loudly through his nose.

"Is your friend in a lot of pain? It's not you, is it?" he said looking Nami up and down.

"No, it's not me."

"He'll need a painkiller and antibiotics…"

"Please!"

"Hang on a sec. I'm really not supposed to give anything so strong to you without a prescription," he continued as he went into the back behind a wall with a large glass window.

Nami was relieved. She'd be able to get the medicine to Yang. He'd be so pleased with her when they met at Shinjuku Gyoen Park the next day. She was certain he'd be there.

She looked around the shop as she waited. They were having a special on condoms. Flyers for energy drinks hung from the ceiling like fly paper. Then she peered through the glass window where prescriptions were filled. The pharmacist was on the phone. He kept glancing at a memo or something that was posted on the wall.

He finished his call. Then he started opening and closing drawers looking for the medicines.

Nami was suddenly worried. She hoped he hadn't run out of the ones Yang needed. No, it couldn't be. Still, it was taking him an awfully long time back there. She could hear the rattle of the drawers. Finally, he seemed to find what he was looking for. He glanced over at her, his hands still moving out of sight.

He leaned out past the window into the shop, a white paper envelope in his hands. "This is enough for three days," he said.

"Can't I have a bit more?"

"Five days?"

Nami nodded, and the man went back behind the glass. Nami took a few deep breaths—it was taking a long time, but she would get what she needed.

The man returned to her, opened the paper envelope and began explaining the medications. Her friend needed to take two of the red pills and one of the white capsules per dose. He could take two white ones if he was in a lot of pain. However, if it hurt that much he really needed to see a doctor, because that was a sign of a dangerous condition.

Nami nodded and took out her wallet. The man gave her a high price, but Nami paid it without a word of protest. She didn't know if he had seen through her lie, or if the medications were really that expensive.

"Here you are. Thank you." The man handed her the change from the cash register and gave her a hard look. Nami stuffed the paper envelope into the bottom of her bag so she wouldn't lose it.

She walked out of the pharmacy. She looked to the right and left, trying to decide which direction to go. She had to find a hotel to stay in. On either side of the road, there were men who looked like yakuza, but she didn't give them a second thought. Yakuza were always all over this area.

Wishing to avoid walking past Fountain of Roses, Nami headed in the opposite direction. She knew the shutters were down on the club and a sign was posted saying it was closed for the time being.

Then she remembered a section of Kabukicho that ran from 2nd Street to Shokuan Boulevard, the heart of Koreatown. There were a number of hotels in that area. Most of them were "love hotels" that were rented by the hour, but she supposed they would put a single woman up for the night. She wanted to get away from Shinjuku, but at this hour it would be difficult to flag down a taxi, and she didn't want to go to a station where there would be even more people, maybe even police looking for her.

She kept her eyes down and walked as quickly as she could. It seemed as though she were being followed, but she was too frightened to turn around and look. She just wanted to check into a hotel, lock the door of the room, and watch the news on TV.

She turned into an alley next to a restaurant that was famous for letting customers choose their fish, still alive and swimming in a tank. The cook would then prepare the fish to order. The glass-walled building looked more like a disco than a high-priced restaurant. It was closed for the day and there was no one around.

"Excuse me…"

Nami was certain it was some guy trying to pick her up, so she didn't stop.

"Keiko, is that you?"

Nami turned around. It was a man she didn't recognize in a dark blue suit. His black shoes were beautifully polished. She recognized him as one of the yakuza she had seen in front of the pharmacy. She was petrified.

Opposite the man was a white Mercedes, parked with its side facing them. Nami glanced over just as the back window was closing. Behind it was a woman with a pale complexion, but Nami didn't get a good look at her.

"Sorry, I thought you were someone else," said the man.

For an instant, as Nami looked at the car, her heart froze in fear. She was so relieved when the man said he had mistaken her for someone else that her knees almost buckled. She began walking again. She was finally in the hotel area, but she couldn't figure out where to stay and it was very dark.

Suddenly she was jumped from behind. A few people surrounded her. Her arms were grabbed, her mouth covered, and someone pulled her hair.

"I'll kill you if you try to scream," someone whispered next to her ear. Then she was dragged backwards and shoved into the car that had followed her. Her bag was wrenched away and her shoes removed. In the process, her head banged against the car door, and she could feel herself blacking out.

"Okay, drive," said a voice. She was in the back seat with her face pressed down and her arms pinned behind her. Before she knew what was happening, she heard a ripping noise and her mouth and eyes were covered with masking tape. Her hands were tied behind her with something that felt like wire.

"Good!" a man's voice said. "Get her down."

She was pushed from the car seat onto the floor. She felt the breath being knocked out of her as she landed on her chest. That and the pain in her head brought tears to her eyes.

"Give me the phone!"

"Hurry up and hand it over!"

"You know the number?"

"It's the dark blue Mercedes, isn't it?"

"Yes."

"I know it, asshole. Shut your face."

Nami heard buttons being pushed and, after a few moments, the first man spoke again.

"We've got her. Yes. We're fine. How are things over there?"

There was a pause.

"Yes. What about the director? Okay."

She heard the sound of the phone being hung up.

"Hey, drive slower. You know what you're supposed to do."

"Yes."

"Are we going to the director?"

"Yeah, they want her there."

Someone laughed.

"Stop laughing, you fuckin' moron!" a voice rang out.

The inside of the car went silent.

26

When the car phone rang, the Mercedes carrying Wei Ye was on a narrow street driving along what looked like a large open sewer. They were still close to Shinjuku.

Hata answered, asked about the police presence, and said, "Take her to the freight building," and hung up. Then he looked over at Ye. "We've got her."

"There is no mistake?"

"A girl from her old club identified her from the car. It's her."

Ye nodded. "How did you get her?"

"The one who made the ID? We got her at the club where she works now. We had to pay her—she had the balls to ask us for five hundred thousand yen," Hata clucked. "The club stays open until two, so they took her back and two of our men are keeping an eye on her until closing time."

"Where are we going now?" asked Ye.

"We're almost there. This area is North Shinjuku. It's part of our territory. There's a freight company that went under a while back, and we got the building as part of the settlement. It's built on this river, and there's a room that's partly underground. It's a great place for convincing people to talk, and when we need to get rid of the corpses, we just back a truck in for the pick-up."

"Is this a river?" Ye had thought it was a sewer.

"Yes, the Kandagawa River. This is what it looks like. In the summer it can flood its banks."

A river, thought Ye. When he was young, he used a warehouse on a canal as a hideout. There had only been one window, and part of the embankment had been lower than the road. That had been before he had joined the Sihai gang.

Ye and some of his friends had rented the place, and they worked for the Kuomintang (Nationalist Party) army, which had recently escaped from the mainland with their leader, Chiang Kai-shek. It was about five years after the end of the war.

The Kuomintang had been anxious to create a base that would keep them securely in power, and they had systematically killed off the intelligentsia—professors and thinkers, communists and liberals. Ye's job had been to go after the names on the list he got from the secret police, threaten them with guns and then torture them.

The targets had all been born and raised in Taiwan before the war. They were the ones who rebelled against the Japanese colonists and headed the movement for an independent Taiwan. They were doctors, politicians, and students.

When Chiang Kai-shek and his army retreated to Taiwan, these intellectuals, wary of another occupation, stood up as the ideological leaders of the native population.

Torture often went on for two solid days. Ye and his cohorts would force the rebels to give up the names of their fellow conspirators. Some gave up names and others did not. In either case, at the end of the session, Ye would put a gun to their heads, pull the trigger, load the bodies into cotton bags, and toss them out the window into the canal. The water carried the bodies far away to the Danshuihe River.

The Kuomintang was made up of the youngest sons of mainland Chinese farmers scrambling to make a living. Most were illiterate. Some had never even heard of electricity or running water until they came to Taiwan. When they first arrived, the country must have seemed much more wealthy than the one they grew up in.

Wei Ye was a native of Taiwan, but he had managed to live through the post-war confusion by occasionally posing as a mainland Chinese. The Japanese, Ye realized, weren't very aware of what had happened during those years in Taiwan.

The Mercedes pulled up to a lot surrounded by a chain link fence with its entrance chained shut. On the other side of the chain was a concrete parking lot with a three-story building in one corner. There were no lights on, but the headlights of the car revealed a concrete slope at the farthest side of the parking lot that led into the basement of the building.

The man sitting in the front passenger seat got out, unlocked the padlock keeping the chain in place, and let the Mercedes in. The concrete was dotted with weeds that grew from cracks here and there. The man who left the car hurried over to the building, ran down the concrete slope, and pushed up a shutter. The Mercedes slid underneath.

Inside there had been no effort made to panel the concrete walls. To one side was a pile of old desks, chairs and telephones. Next to them was a sofa with its stuffing poking out of the upholstery next to a glass table that was partly shattered.

While the car headlights were still on, the man found a breaker that turned on three lights that hung suspended from the ceiling. There were black oil stains here and there on the concrete floor. The man opened the back door of the car to let Ye out, followed by Hata with his cell phone in hand.

"Close the shutter when Tani's car gets here. Does the phone work in here?" He shook it in the other man's face.

"It'll work," said the man.

"Good. Hold onto it, then. And get some chairs here. We're going to have her sitting."

"Right away." He and the driver began rushing around to set

246

things up. Ye took out a cigarette. Hata lit it for him.

"Let her live until Du Yuan is dead. We might need her later if things don't go as planned," Ye said. He felt strangely excited as the old memories began to come back to him. He had often used oil burners for torture. Another method had been cutting off the toes of the prisoner one by one with a knife.

"I understand."

"No one can hear us, right? Even if she screams?"

"Not when the shutter is down. The river is behind us. It's an isolated place."

Another set of headlights flooded the space as a white Mercedes descended the slope.

"As soon as you get the woman out," ordered Hata, "Tani's driver should back it up to the lot and keep a lookout."

"Right."

The car rolled down the ramp with four men inside. As soon as it came to a stop, they dragged out the woman. Most of her face was covered in masking tape, so it was hard to see what she looked like.

"Put her on that chair," said Ye.

They put her on a metal folding chair and the men surrounded her. The driver got back in the white car and backed it up the slope. As soon as it was gone, they closed the shutter.

Ye looked at the men left inside. There were Hata, the two men who had been in his car, Tani, who had kidnapped the woman, and two of Tani's thugs. That made six, not including himself.

Hata looked over at Ye, who nodded.

"Take that tape off," Hata ordered. The men removed the tape from the woman's eyes and mouth. Even after it had been ripped off, she did not try to open her eyes.

She had a long face and white skin. There was nothing defining about her features. She had a bruise on her forehead, and she wept quietly, her eyes still closed.

One of the men opened his mouth and walked towards her. He pulled back his right hand and made as if to hit her face. Ye put out an arm to stop him. No one said a word. The only sound in the underground room was the echo of the woman's sobs.

Ye looked at her as he took a drag on his cigarette. Eventually she slowly opened her eyes. Ye was surprised to see how wide and beautiful they were. She looked around at all of them, her body shaking. She stopped when she saw Ye.

"Are you afraid?" he asked her in Chinese.

She didn't respond. She just kept trembling from head to foot.

"We want to help you. A man you know is a murderer," he continued. "Do you know where he is?"

She shook her head. This was proof to him that she understood Mandarin. "So, you're Chinese?"

"Ja-Japanese..." Her voice shook. She was terrified, naturally. "Let me go."

"Of course we will. Now let's start speaking in Japanese," Ye said, switching languages in mid-sentence. "Why can you speak Chinese?"

"I-I-I was raised in China."

"How old were you when you left?"

"Thirteen."

"Are your parents Chinese?"

"M-My father. My mother was raised in China. She's Japanese."

"I see." Now Ye understood. He had heard about people like this. When Japan lost World War II, there were still many Japanese living in mainland China. They thought they owned it. The army of Mao Zedong drove them out. As the desperate Japanese tried to escape, they left behind their babies. This woman's mother was probably one of those babies.

"So you and Du Yuan both speak Mandarin."

"Du Yuan?"

"Yes, as in Poison Ape. He is a very bad murderer. He has killed dozens of people."

The woman was silent.

"And you saw him do it. You were there when he killed Takakawa."

She looked down, staring at the stained floor. Ye realized that this might take longer than he thought. This sort of woman could be difficult.

"I'm not angry at you though," he said, taking a new tact. "That man, he's the bad one. Tell me. Where is he?"

"I don't know." She spoke listlessly, still looking down.

"It's not nice to lie. You bought medicine. That was medicine for the Poison Ape."

She bit her lip. Her face turned white.

"I don't like violence," said Ye. "If you just tell us where he is, we won't hurt you."

She was silent.

Ye exhaled loudly. "What is your real name?"

"Qing Na."

"Qing Na? Even though you are Japanese?"

She nodded. There was a glint in her eyes.

Ye was dumbfounded. He recognized that look. She was in love with Du Yuan. Those were the eyes of a woman protecting a man she loved.

Ye clenched his teeth. "If you won't talk, I will have to leave you to these men. It will be painful for you. Very painful."

Her expression was unchanged.

"This is the last time I will ask you. If you help a killer, you will be hurt. That would be a very foolish choice. Now, tell me. Where is he?"

She wasn't listening to him anymore. She was as expressionless as a doll. Now Ye was angry. He nodded to Hata. Hata nodded back, walked up to the woman and punched her several times in a row in the face. Blood flew out of her nose and her split lips. She moaned, but still would not say a word.

Hata stared into her face and growled in a low voice. "You bitch, you're gonna wish you were dead!"

The woman began to shake again and she squeezed her eyes shut. Hata kicked her chair. She gave a small scream as it tipped over and her face hit the floor.

"Strip her!" Hata ordered his thugs.

27

Samejima and Guo were in the car in the parking lot of the emergency hospital on Shinjuku 5th Street. It was just about midnight. The wind was blowing hard, occasionally rocking the car. They were looking up at the ward of private rooms on the third floor where Takezo Ishiwa was recovering.

Takezo refused all visitors. Detectives from Section One were allowed in for a few moments soon after he was admitted, but that was all. A few uniformed cops were posted in front of his room and around the hospital, but they were far outnumbered by the members of the Ishiwa gang. Some of them were ignoring the doctor's orders and going in and out of Ishiwa's room.

Predictably, there had been a number of skirmishes already between the gangsters and the cops and hospital staff. Hata had not put in an appearance. Samejima took this to mean he was on the move with Ye.

Samejima and Guo were riding in an unmarked patrol car rented out from the Shinjuku Precinct. It was equipped with a two-way radio, and all evening they had been listening to reports of fights and other incidents that had been called in.

The first one was at about five p.m. A Chinese transfer student had called from a public payphone in a park on Shinjuku 7th Street. He had been surrounded by what appeared to be yakuza who then harassed him and eventually beat him up. He had sustained serious head injuries.

A while later, a Chinese cook who worked in an upscale hotel restaurant had gone out with his girlfriend, and he too had been punched and kicked by a group of thugs.

By nightfall, similar calls were coming in fast and thick from the Kabukicho area. Almost all of the victims had been Chinese, Koreans and other Asians who had been strolling through town, chatting in their native tongue.

Once again the radio signal was coming through.

"HQ calling all units in Shinjuku. Reporting an incident involving bodily harm. Calling all units in the vicinity of West Shinjuku, 7th Street, Daiko Park Building. Over."

"Shinjuku 7 calling from the front of the Seibu Shinjuku Station. Over."

"HQ reads you, Shinjuku 7. Are there any other units?"

"Metro Police 310, near the scene."

"HQ reads you, Metro 310. Metro 310 and Shinjuku 7, head for the scene. A man has been reported injured and bleeding in the employee parking lot behind the Daiko Park Building. One Sakurai, an employee in the building, made the report. Make an immediate investigation of the scene."

"Shinjuku 7 reads you, HQ."

"Metro 310, on our way."

"HQ, roger. A witness reported seeing several yakuza-type suspects running towards Kabukicho just after the victim was discovered. Metro 310, Shinjuku 7, please cooperate on this matter, and call in to report any suspected criminal activity to Section One. Shinjuku?"

"This is Shinjuku. Over."

"The number for this call is 1286. The order came down at 23:53. Kikuchi in charge. Please send officers and stand-by patrol cars."

"Shinjuku reads you, HQ. Hamada in charge. One stand-by car and officers from Shinjuku 18 are already on their way."

"HQ, roger. We will be controlling communication about the incident until we know more about details."

Samejima stubbed out his cigarette in the ashtray and turned on the engine. "The hunt is on."

Guo was silent. They had been waiting for Hata, Ye or possibly even Du Yuan to show up at the hospital.

"Let's head back into town," Samejima said, and Guo nodded. Samejima raced towards Yasukuni Boulevard. The Ishiwa headquarters was in Shinjuku 7th Street, the neighborhood of the incident that had just been reported. He decided to go there first.

They knew they were close by when they saw the bus carrying the SWAT team. The team, outfitted in bulletproof vests, helmets and duralumin shields, guarded the office. Cars entering the area were stopped and questioned.

Samejima pulled over so they could watch what was going on. "Do you think he'll still try to attack their headquarters, even like this?" he asked. There were spotlights illuminating the building.

"If Ye is inside," Guo responded matter-of-factly.

"I'm sure he's not. Otherwise we would have seen Hata somewhere," Samejima said, and turned the car around and headed for Kabukicho. Before heading to the emergency hospital, they had gone to see the other Fountain of Roses hostesses. In the meantime, warrants had been issued for Kiyomi Taguchi and Zhensheng Liu. The police had searched Kiyomi's apartment, and they finally had a picture of her.

All of the hostesses they interviewed had last seen Kiyomi at the Yasui Enterprises office. None had heard from her since.

"Why don't we walk?" suggested Samejima, and parked the car near the Seibu Shinjuku Station. He didn't think they'd be so lucky as to run into Du Yuan on a cloudy night while walking around, but there didn't seem to be any point in continuing to drive on the congested roads of Kabukicho.

Samejima had a feeling something was going to happen that night. Du Yuan was wounded, but as Guo had said, he would make an attack on Ye and the Ishiwa gang as soon as possible. Unless he had been forced to go underground.

They got out of the car and walked into the Kabukicho district. Samejima could feel the tension crackling through the air. There were several nights a year like this in Shinjuku. One didn't have to be a yakuza or a cop to sense the difference. It was a different "smell," something anyone who had been to Shinjuku a few times would notice.

On the surface everything would look normal. But there was something dangerous lurking underneath, and it would manifest in the air and in the pulse of the town.

There were fewer pimps on the street. Yakuza were walking more quickly than usual. Porn shops that were usually open most of the night were closed early. No one could ignore the menacing atmosphere. With such a degree of tension, all it took was a single spark to set it all ablaze.

Samejima didn't think this sort of thing happened in other parts of the city. Whatever happened below the surface in other parts of Tokyo rarely affected an entire area. It was something peculiar to Shinjuku itself.

The yakuza they came across were quick to move away when they saw police coming. Gangsters who would usually greet them with "Good evening" were careful not to lift their eyes or even pass by on the same side of the street.

On the other hand, they weren't trying to hide. They were out and ready, but for what, it was not clear. All of the gangs who claimed territory in Shinjuku had their antennae out.

Guo deftly pulled out a cigarette and lit it, all with his good hand. "Lots of yakuza tonight. There are always many, but there are more tonight."

They ran into two in front of the Furin Hall, and Samejima nodded in agreement. Yakuza usually traveled in packs of four or five, but tonight they were moving in smaller units. They all had their cell phones in their hands.

"The hunting dogs are out," Samejima answered. "They're looking for the same man we are."

"They could never catch him. He would kill them first," commented Guo in a low voice. A group of seven or eight came out of a nearby coffee house. They divided up into three groups and went in different directions.

"Very strange," said Samejima. He clapped his hand on the shoulder of one of two men that passed by. "Yo."

The man glared suspiciously at Samejima, and then his expression turned quickly to one of surprise. He had a cell phone in his hand, too. It was one of the men from Yasui Enterprises.

"You all are working unusually hard this evening," said Samejima, indicating the phone. "Have you heard anything from Yasui?"

The man shook his head. "Nothing. What can I do for you?"

"Drop your 'what can I do for you' crap. Why are you still on duty tonight?"

"I'm not...not on duty."

Samejima gripped the man's shoulder. "Did Ishiwa call for reinforcements?"

"None of your business."

"Then why is everyone so spread out? Looking for someone?"

The other man spoke up. "Sir, give us a break, please."

"Shut up!" said Samejima with a glare, and the man quickly closed his mouth.

"Talk to me. Who is giving you orders?"

"We don't know."

"From above? Your gang and Ishiwa are in the same syndicate."

The man lowered his eyes. He realized he was in dangerous

255

territory now. "Arrest me if you want to talk to me. But I haven't done anything to deserve it!"

Samejima gritted his teeth and let go of the man. He was obviously under a tight gag order.

"Finished?" the man asked. Samejima nodded. The man clicked his tongue and he and his partner walked on.

Guo watched Samejima see the two off, and asked, "Is there something strange about them?"

"Those two are not Ishiwa members. They're with Yasui."

Yasui and Ishiwa were under the same syndicate umbrella. But it was odd that Ishiwa would be borrowing Yasui members to look for the man who attacked Takakawa and the Ishiwa boss.

"They know Yasui is dead," said Samejima. "They're somehow getting information from Ishiwa."

"Ishiwa?" Guo asked.

Samejima looked at his watch. "The mass media has not yet reported a connection between the murder of the club manager, Takakawa's murder, and the attack at Ishiwa's mistress's home. Only a few cops know about Yasui. If they aren't getting information from the police, we have to assume it's coming from Ishiwa."

"Why?"

"They've got someone who figured out the connection between Takakawa and Yasui. Someone knows both of them were killed by Du Yuan."

"You think it's Ye?" Guo asked in a low voice.

"I do. Hata and Ye are underground, but they are still in contact with the others. Ye is trying to use Ishiwa to get his revenge on Du Yuan."

"It is possible."

"Which means…" suddenly Samejima looked up at a signboard posted on a nearby building.

"What is it?" asked Guo.

"Ishiwa knows about Kiyomi Taguchi. When Ishiwa told the Yasui gang about what had happened, they also learned about the woman who Yasui had suspected of being involved with Yang. Yang is Du Yuan."

Yukari, Takakawa's mistress, confirmed that the woman in the photo the police confiscated from Kiyomi's apartment was in fact the woman with Du Yuan. Kiyomi used the name of Yukari's old club to get into the condo. The police did not give Yukari the woman's name or the connection she had with the suspect. They knew she would give the information to Ishiwa if they told her.

"The Ishiwa gang is looking for Kiyomi Taguchi. That means that sometime during the day, Ishiwa learned about her from their contacts with Yasui."

"That woman…"

"The one using thinner. Masumi Kitano."

"They would need her to find Kiyomi," agreed Guo.

"We'd better get in touch with her again and ask if she's had any contact with Ishiwa."

He recalled that Masumi mentioned that Yasui had found another job for her at a club called Charm in Kabukicho 2nd Street. It was late, but it might still be open. They walked around a little longer until they found Charm listed on the signboard of a building. It was on the sixth floor.

Samejima and Guo took the elevator. It was just past one a.m. As soon as they got to the sixth floor, Samejima could tell that Charm was still open for business. He could hear a karaoke duet coming from behind the door where the club name was posted.

He opened the door.

"Welcome!" called out a man in black near the entrance. Samejima could see inside past the man's shoulder. There was a narrow walkway leading from the entrance that made a turn into an L-shape further in the back. At the corner was a stage and monitor for karaoke.

About sixty percent of the booths were filled. There were a dozen or so customers, and just about as many hostesses to accompany them.

"Excuse me," Samejima called the man back and gestured for him to come out into the hall. The man had already recognized he was a cop without seeing his badge.

"What's the problem? We've got a license…"

"I just want to know if you've got a woman named Masumi Kitano working here. Probably just started recently."

"Masumi?" The man didn't recognize the name.

"Introduction from Yasui Enterprises?"

"Ah, Yasui. Right. She goes by the name Ikuko here."

"Is she here tonight?" Samejima gestured to the door.

"Yes, she was out for a while, but she's back now," the man said before realizing he'd said too much.

"What do you mean, 'she was out'?"

"Uh, nothing. Some shopping," he said quickly.

"Tell me the truth."

"That's the truth. She was shopping."

Samejima glared at the man, who finally looked down in defeat. "A couple of customers took her out. It was something she couldn't turn down."

"What couldn't she turn down?"

"Look, don't ask me any more questions. We try to keep our customers happy…" The man was anguished.

"Are those customers still in there?"

"Uh, well…"

"Are they here?"

The man nodded wordlessly. Samejima pushed him aside and opened the door.

"Wait—"

"Don't worry. I won't make any trouble for you. Where are they sitting?"

"In the back. The second to last booth."

"Wait here." Samejima left Guo outside, went in and peeked at the customer seats from behind the wall of the walkway. Masumi Kitano, wearing a pink mini-skirt and matching jacket, was sitting in a booth with two men, one on either side of her, clapping to the music. A bottle of brandy was set on the table in front of them.

Neither of the men looked like they were enjoying themselves. They weren't even looking at the stage. Samejima recognized one as a member of the Ishiwa gang and backed away before the men could see him standing there.

He went back outside and nodded to Guo. "It's the Ishiwa gang, all right." Then he spoke to the man at the entrance. "Would you mind asking those three to come out here a minute?"

"Don't make me do that!" The man was in obvious distress.

"I'm sorry, but I can't hang around here until you close, and I'm sure you don't want me going in there and causing a ruckus."

The man was at a loss.

"Please," said Samejima. "You don't have to tell them I'm a cop. Just say there's a customer who wants to see them."

"All right." The man, looking utterly despondent, disappeared back into the club. As the door closed, the sound of karaoke faded. Samejima looked around. There were clubs on either side of the elevator. Charm was on the left. The places in the middle and on the right were already closed.

Guo was a few steps away from Samejima, leaning against the wall.

"It might get rough," he warned Guo in a low voice. Guo nodded and almost smiled. The door opened and the music got louder again.

The two yakuza came out. Samejima was unfamiliar with the first one. Both appeared to be in their mid-thirties. One was wearing a suit and the other wore a light jacket and knit slacks. Samejima knew the latter. Masumi brought up the rear.

When the man in the knit slacks saw Samejima, his eyes opened wide.

Under her breath, Masumi muttered, "Cops!"

The man in the suit turned on his heels to go back inside, but Samejima grabbed his shoulder.

"Let go, you son of a bitch." The man pulled his arm away.

"Don't try to run," Samejima warned, pushing him in Guo's direction. He then grabbed Masumi's arm.

"What's the big idea?" she fumed. The man in the slacks didn't hesitate. He leaped towards Samejima to get his hands off of her. Samejima let her go and grabbed the man by the front of his jacket.

"What the fuck!" he growled.

Out of the corner of his eye, Samejima saw the man in the suit reach out for him. Guo moved in. He grabbed the man's cheeks with his right hand and banged his head against the wall. The man howled in pain. Samejima backed the other man up against the wall.

"Asshole!" The man tried to grab Samejima with his right arm, but Samejima caught it with his left, and kneed him in the groin. He cried out.

Samejima looked over at Guo, who was making mincemeat of the man in the suit with his one good arm. He had shoved his face against the wall and pinned his right arm behind his back. The sheath of a dagger was visible under the man's coat. With a flash of his leg, Guo had the man on the floor. The dagger came loose and flew out.

Guo had his right foot on the man's throat. The man choked once and then lay still. Samejima turned back to his man and pulled back his right wrist. He could see the black butt of a gun. He quickly grabbed it and pressed it against the man's face.

"What do we have here?"

Guo looked over at Samejima. "It's a Black Star."

"What's a low-life like you doing with something so nice?"

"How should I know? Just take me away!"

"Don't fuck with me!" Samejima kicked him in the groin again. The man doubled over. Samejima grabbed his hair and banged his head against the wall. The man closed his eyes and opened his mouth, gasping for air.

"If you won't talk, I'll ask that nice man in the suit over there."

Guo was lifting the other man up by his necktie. The instant the man tried to beat him away, Guo knocked him in the chin with his right elbow. The man fell to his knees. His lip split open and blood began to flow.

Samejima looked over at Masumi who just stood there.

"What did they make you do?" he demanded.

Her eyes opened wide and she shook her head violently. "Nothing. They didn't make me do anything!"

"Stop fucking around!" Samejima yelled, and Masumi went white. "Their boss was attacked. They've got to be mad as hell. What are they doing just sitting around drinking? Eh?" Samejima shook the head of the man under his grip.

The man's eyes opened, and he looked to the side at Masumi.

"I-I don't know anything. You talk, you die, bitch!"

She shrank back.

"You're full of it, aren't you?" said Samejima as he kicked the man's legs out from under him so he fell on his knees.

There was a howl of pain. It was the man in the suit. Guo was standing on the back of his right ankle, about at his Achilles tendon. At the same time he pulled him up by his lapels.

"What are you doing?" Masumi asked, covering her mouth in horror.

"Ow, fuck, that hurts! Ow, ow, ow…" The man in the suit was in so much pain he lost his ability to speak. He screamed instead.

"Stop! Stop right now!" Masumi yelled at Guo.

Guo didn't budge, nor did his expression change. The eyes of the man under him were opened as wide as they could go, and sweat stood out on his forehead. Guo released the man's lapel and his foot from his ankle. The man rolled around on the ground cradling his foot.

The other man went chalky white. His lips shook as he tried to speak. "Why are you doing this?"

Guo walked over to the man in the slacks as Samejima handed him over. Guo pulled him to his feet and stared into his eyes. "Got anything to say?"

Samejima walked over to put handcuffs on the man in the suit. The man in the slacks did his best to avert his eyes from Guo's icy gaze. "Just arrest me," he pleaded.

Guo pulled his head back and bashed his forehead into the man's nose. The man screamed as blood spurted from both nostrils.

"Got anything to say?" Guo repeated.

"Who is this guy?" cried the man in the slacks, tears running down his face. Guo took hold of the man's right wrist with his right hand, and pulled it up. The man moaned in pain. Guo's fingers dug into his wrist like a vise.

Samejima walked over to Masumi. She stared at Guo as if in a trance. "What did they make you do?" Samejima demanded of her again.

She shook her head. "I can't say anything."

"Tell me!"

"They'll kill me if I tell you."

Samejima indicated Guo, who was stringing up the man in the slacks. "It's your turn next."

"No, you can't. Please."

"Then talk! They can't kill you. Tell us what you did. Look at them. You know they're not a threat now."

Tears spilled out of Masumi's eyes. "I'm sorry... don't make me..."

262

"Don't expect any sympathy from us. Talk!"

"I told them it was her. I told them it was Nami. That's all!" She cried out and sank to her knees. She covered her face with her hands. "Why is this happening to me?"

"Where did it happen?"

"In that area where all those hotels are. I looked at her from the car. I just told them who she was."

"Then what happened?"

"I don't know! It's the truth!" She twisted her body to hide her face.

"Was she alone? Was Nami alone?"

Masumi didn't reply.

"Was she alone?" Samejima shouted.

"Yes!"

Samejima looked back at the man in the slacks as he groaned in agony.

"Did you take her away?"

Guo tightened his grip.

"Yes!" the man screamed in pain.

The waiter from the club came out of the door with a ringing cell phone in his hands. He stopped, speechless at the scene before him.

"Sorry to, uhm…"

"Is that their phone?" Samejima asked.

"Uh, yeah."

Samejima took the phone and put it up to the man's face.

"Speak."

The man turned his face away. Guo squeezed harder.

Samejima put the phone up to the man's left ear, and pressed the button to receive the call.

"…yes… no… in Okubo…" the man spoke listlessly. "What? Wh-When? I see. All right, I see…" He looked up at Samejima, who took the phone away. He could hear the dial tone. The caller had hung up.

"What was that about?"

The man in the slacks spoke in a defeated tone. "Our dorm was attacked. Three men were killed. Right there, with the police guard…" Then he turned and glared at Samejima. "What are you fuckers doing? Why can't you catch him?"

Samejima looked over at Guo, who scowled.

"Where did you take the woman?" asked Samejima.

28

Nami could hear the sound of the men talking as if from far away. Her tears had stopped and the pain had subsided. It went on like some sort of demented ceremony. Once one man finished raping her, he punched and kicked her for good measure. Then the next one climbed on top of her to do the same thing. One after the other, they were all the same. It didn't matter whether it was one or a hundred of them. It just kept going on and on.

The only one who did not participate was the old Taiwanese man. He sat in a chair and watched as each of the men toyed with her, defiled her and beat her.

As each new one huffed and puffed and writhed, Nami, detached from the reality of what was happening to her, let her eyes wander around the basement. She looked into the old man's eyes several times. But she couldn't keep her eyes on him because the men twisted her around, her head flopping back and forth.

The interminable ritual finally came to an end. They had all—all except that old man—had their turn. When the last man got off of her, the old man stood up from his chair. She looked into his eyes again, and she realized that he had been waiting.

Nami lay on the sofa like a broken doll. She knew there was blood on her face and blood seeping from the lower part of her body. That was all it was to her. What did it matter? The thread connecting her body to her mind had snapped.

"All right then," said the old man. Nami saw a young man hand him a dagger. The old man pulled it out of its sheath and he knelt down at her side.

"You don't have to talk until you want to," he said in Chinese. He gently picked up the calf of her left leg. "I'm going to cut off your toes, one by one." The bottom of her left foot touched the cold concrete as he set her leg down. In the next instant, a hot current surged through her little toe.

Nami screamed. The pain that had finally grown duller was back with a vengeance. At the same time, her mind, having left her for some far-off place, leaped back into her body.

Nami began to sob. Her throat ached and she couldn't scream anymore. The men held down her limbs so she couldn't flail about. One of them even held her eyelids open so she was forced to watch. The old man held up Nami's toe to show her. Then he rested it lightly between her breasts. He peered into her face with a look of concern.

She heard a phone ring from far away. The sound seemed completely out of place. One of the yakuza answered the phone, but the old man kept his eyes on Nami.

"…Mr. Ye!" The man with the phone was standing behind the old man. He turned around with a start.

"What is it?"

Sobbing, Nami watched him. The man with the phone was the one who had punched her at the beginning. He had been the first to rape her.

The old man stood up, still holding the bloodstained dagger in his right hand. "Who is it?"

"It's him," the man said in a low voice.

"Who?" Ye asked again in irritation.

The yakuza's voice was puzzlingly low, and it seemed mixed with fear. "He said he was the Poison Ape. How did he get this number?"

Nami's eyes grew wide.

29

Ye felt as if a knife had been thrust into his back. Why? Why was Du Yuan calling here? He looked down at the woman. She was bloody and filthy. He couldn't believe she wasn't pleading for her life. He switched the dagger to his left hand and put the phone to his ear.

"This is Ye," he said in Chinese.

"I kill traitors," the voice said. Ye's back broke out in a sweat. It was unmistakably the voice of Du Yuan. He had talked to him on the phone many times—every time he ordered him to kill someone.

Even though it was a cell phone, Ye felt a pang of terror at the thought that Du Yuan might know where he was.

"You're making a mistake," he said slowly.

"It's no mistake," the man on the other end said. "Wen Baiyin pleaded for his life. He had to die, of course, but I won't even give you the chance to beg."

Ye suddenly realized that his voice had the slightly high-pitched tone of a man in pain. "Let's meet," Ye suggested. "We'll straighten all this out."

Du Yuan laughed. "That will be fine. Tonight, when you wake up, I'll be standing there next to your pillow."

"I don't think so. I've got a friend of yours here. Someone who would like to see you."

"A friend?"

"A woman named Qing Na."

267

Ye enjoyed the silence that followed. He'd let Du Yuan know who had the upper hand.

"I…don't know who you're talking about. "

"Is that so?" Ye put the phone up to the woman's mouth. "Say hello." The woman's lips shook. She looked at the phone and then at Ye. Tears began to pour from her eyes. Ye put the dagger up to her cheek and pressed it ever so slightly. There was a spurt of blood.

"Yang…?" she said tearfully.

Ye was satisfied. He took the phone back. "So?"

"I don't know her." Du Yuan spoke as if he were trying to control himself.

"Well, then there's no problem. By the way, how did you get this number?" Ye changed the subject.

"I killed a few more of Ishiwa's men. I cut them open, one by one. They screamed out all kinds of things, but I couldn't understand much of what they said. One wrote a number on a piece of paper. We won't have time to chat when I see you, so I'm giving you that information now."

"Then you won't have time to talk to this woman either. I really wanted a chance to straighten things out between us." After he spoke, Ye put the dagger in the woman's mouth. "Du Yuan is not interested in seeing you, Qing Na. He says he doesn't know you." He spoke loud enough for both of them to hear.

The other end of the line was silent. When Ye pulled the blade out of her mouth, he made a deeper cut in her already-injured lip. The woman sobbed.

"Don't you want to see him, Qing Na? No? You'd be better off forgetting an unfaithful man like that," Ye said gently.

Du Yuan's silence was dark. Ye could sense him torturing himself in that silence. "I guess we'll give you an injection, Qing Na," he said.

The silence broke and there was a voice like a sigh on the other end of the line.

"Come to the Taiwan Pavilion in Shinjuku Gyoen Park. Bring the woman with you."

The line went dead.

30

The Ishiwa dorm was in West Shinjuku 4th Street, a distance from the gang's headquarters. The area near the Shinjuku Central Park was residential, and as Samejima and Guo got closer to the dorm, they passed a block of small apartment buildings and condos. A large crowd of onlookers had assembled. The crowd and a fire truck blocked the road. There must have been a fire caused by another bomb.

Samejima and Guo got out of their car at the edge of the crowd, waded through it, and passed the policemen trying to direct traffic. Samejima explained Guo's presence to a cop who tried to block him from entering, and the two reached the crime scene.

Araki was talking to a fire fighter at the entrance to the condo that housed the dorm. Araki's hair was a mess and there was a bruise on his cheek. He'd obviously seen a medic as his right sleeve was torn and a bandage had been wrapped around his arm up to his elbow.

Guo and Samejima stepped over a fire hose, and Araki turned back to look at them. The look in his eyes told Samejima what he had just been through.

About a year ago, Samejima had been following a gunsmith all by himself. The gunsmith had captured and confined him, bringing his experience with fear to an entirely new level. Looking in a mirror after his release, Samejima had seen the vacant glint in his own eyes that he now saw in Araki's. Sho was all that had kept Samejima from going over the edge and becoming a raving lunatic after the incident.

The anger Sho had for his captor had eased his pain, even though he knew he would never be able to forget what had happened.

As he walked over to Araki, Samejima wondered if there would be anyone to help him out with his trauma. A moment passed as the men quietly looked at one another.

"He was here," Araki said shortly. "I underestimated him. I talked it over with Section Four, and we decided to only post a few men here. We wanted to give him the impression that it would be vulnerable. We had a SWAT team at the gang headquarters, but only plainclothes detectives here."

Araki didn't wait for them to ask questions, the words just spilled from his mouth. "I don't know when or how he got into the building. This is just a regular condo. There's only one entrance. It's right next to another condo rented out to corporations. There's not even a foot between the buildings. The Ishiwa dorm is a three-room apartment at one end of the fourth floor. When he attacked, there were two guys there to answer the phone and one who was asleep.

"When we got there, they were all dead—sliced through the stomach. We were just in time to hear the last one screaming in pain, I think he made him scream for our benefit. I was downstairs in a car with two others from Section Four. We heard the scream and ran upstairs. When we tried to open the door, it exploded from inside. An officer from Section Four died. Another is in critical condition. The door was unlocked. The bomb was set to go off when the door was opened."

"What about the Poison Ape?"

"He left. Walked right over us as we lay on the floor. I had a gun, but I couldn't move my arm. Can you believe it? He was dressed all in black with a hood over his head. He just stood there looking down at us. I think he was trying to decide if he should let me go with just a minor wound. He would have killed me if he thought I was Ishiwa's man. I couldn't move a finger. It was like I was possessed. I closed my eyes when he bent over me. What do you think he did then?" Araki's pale lips were trembling. "He put a monkey figurine in my hand and squeezed it shut. Then he left. I-I've never seen a criminal like him before."

Guo spoke in a subdued tone. "A policeman died." He looked as though he had suddenly aged several years. He shook his head, gritted his teeth and whispered, "Du Yuan!"

Araki tried to move his right hand, grimaced, and then used his left hand as best he could to pull something out of his breast pocket. "Here's the photo you lent me." It was the picture of the Taiwanese frogmen. "I was going to give it back as soon as I had it duplicated." Guo accepted it with a nod.

Araki's breath was ragged. "He's still out there. He'll continue to kill until he gets Ye. He'll kill, and kill, and keep on killing. I don't know how many more men we'll lose trying to stop him."

"Don't worry," Guo said, and Araki looked up at him.

"What? How can you say that?" he asked.

"Du Yuan and Ye are getting closer to one another. Very soon, they will meet." Guo turned to Samejima. "We're running out of time. That other man told us they have the woman. We have to find where they took Kiyomi Taguchi."

Samejima turned to Araki. "Can you call for back up? Ishiwa's men have kidnapped Kiyomi Taguchi. We know that for a fact."

Araki swallowed hard. "I'll call, but it'll take time. Both HQ and Shinjuku have their hands full. And there are other crimes as well. There won't be anyone available until tomorrow."

Samejima nodded. He understood the situation. He had contacted the Kabukicho police box for someone to arrest the two Ishiwa thugs at Charm for possession of firearms, and they were told it would be at least thirty minutes before anyone could show up.

The precinct chain of command had not had enough time to order all men to duty as they spent the day responding to one incident after another. It would take another day to catch up. In the end Samejima and Guo had taken the two yakuza to the nearest police station themselves.

"I understand," Samejima said to Araki. "Take care of yourself."

"Wait a minute," Araki said, startled, "you're not planning to go now, are you? Wait just a little longer. Don't go in yet!"

"We don't have time. Kiyomi Taguchi's life is in danger."

"But, alone..."

"He's not alone," Guo spoke up.

Araki was dumbfounded. "No! If anything happens, you'll be charged with abuse of authority."

"We'll see you later." The two left Araki standing there and walked off.

When they got to the car, Guo asked, "You're taking me with you, right?"

Samejima nodded. "You're the one who provided the information. My report will specify that I wouldn't have found the crime scene without your instructions."

Guo smiled. "I've got your back!"

They got into the car.

31

The long three-story building stood on the edge of the Kandagawa River. There were no lights on, but driving by, Samejima saw a white car parked in the concrete lot in front.

The sign in front said "Owuchi Transport." It was just as the yakuza they caught at Charm had said. Samejima continued on past the building and then stopped the unmarked car. He and Guo got out as quietly as they could. The air was dank. Samejima felt tension creep up as he breathed in the smell of the river.

If they were holding Kiyomi Taguchi here, both Ye and Hata were bound to be here, too. It wouldn't be like the time they had spoken with them at the late-night restaurant. This time there was a crime in progress. There was also a strong possibility that Ye, Hata, and the other Ishiwa men were armed and waiting for Du Yuan's attack.

"Wait here," Samejima instructed Guo, "I'll check to see what's going on."

He started walking back towards the deserted building. It was a residential area, and the narrow streets wound in all directions. He finally got near the fence surrounding the lot. The white car was a Mercedes Benz, and it was parked alongside the building. There was a chain across the entrance of the fence. He couldn't tell if anyone was in the car. If a lookout was in there, he'd be sure to see him climbing over the chain.

Samejima stood for a few minutes by the fence of the house

next to the building, watching the Mercedes. Most of the lights in the surrounding houses were out. Of course they were dark. It was almost three a.m.

Samejima took a deep breath. If he were seen, the lookout would have time to warn Hata so he could make his getaway. Samejima put his hand to his holster and felt for the handle of his New Nambu pistol. His palm was sweaty.

Then a light glowed in the Mercedes. There was one man inside. He was sitting in the driver's seat and seemed to be lighting a cigarette. Samejima looked back to where he had left Guo, but he wasn't there anymore. Surprised, he looked back towards the Mercedes. Sure enough, there was Guo, crouched behind the car like a shadow.

Samejima stood watching in amazement. How did he get back there? He must have run along the bank of the river. He couldn't comprehend how he could have done that with only one good arm for balance.

Guo had seen that Samejima knew he was there, and he made a move. He wanted to get the driver's attention. Samejima waved, and moved out from the shadow of the fence. The glowing red tip of the cigarette in the car moved. Samejima feigned ignorance and stepped over the chain and into the parking lot. The door of the car opened and the man inside put one foot out.

"Uh—" he said, but it was too late. Guo already had him on the ground. By the time Samejima reached him, the man was out cold on the concrete. He handcuffed him and used his necktie as a gag.

Samejima whispered, "How did you get here?" Then he saw that the legs of Guo's slacks were sopping wet. He also had a pungent odor about him.

"I was a frogman," he replied simply.

They searched the lookout. He had a Black Star stuck inside his belt. Guo pulled it out.

"I'll return this later," he said. Samejima thought for a few seconds and then nodded his assent. Guo pulled back the breechblock and set the first round in the chamber. They rolled the man over on his stomach and stepped around to the other side of the car.

It was then that they noticed that the car had been parked sideways to hide a concrete ramp leading to the basement level. The entrance was closed with a shutter. Samejima took off his shoes. He walked softly down the slope. He could hear people speaking inside, and a tiny streak of light leaked out from underneath the shutter.

Samejima walked back up to the top of the ramp. The shutter appeared to be the only entrance into the room. "They're in there," he said. "We've got to find another way in."

Guo nodded and went over to the first floor of the building. Half of the wall was shutters, the other half were frosted windows. The windows were set in a regular frame.

Samejima took off his jacket, put it up against the lower part of a window near the lock, and hit it with his pistol. The broken glass clattered onto the floor inside, but it was not as loud as he feared it might be. The gangsters would never have taken a hostage into a place where they could be easily heard from outside, which meant they probably couldn't hear what was happening outside either.

Samejima put his gun back in his holster, reached inside the broken window and opened the lock. He opened the window and stole inside. It was empty. There was just a bare concrete floor and a strong stench of mildew. Flicking on his lighter, he saw a pile of old wooden palettes.

Guo climbed in after Samejima. They quickly investigated the area. The length of the building was divided by three walls and connected by a single hallway. There was a stairway leading to the basement at the end of the hall.

They could see a landing at the end of the flight of stairs that must have connected to another flight leading further down, but it was partially blocked with a bunch of old steel lockers. Samejima leaned over the banister to get a look. At the bottom of the next flight was a steel door with a small window in it. He could see light coming from the other side. There was a tab on the doorknob.

The two men looked at each other, and Guo whispered, "I'll go around to the front. I'll bang on the shutter to get their attention, and you enter from here."

"That would be too dangerous for you. I'm the policeman in this country, so I'll do that part."

Guo smiled, but shook his head. "That's true, but I can't use my left hand. I can't get back behind those lockers."

Samejima looked at Guo. "All right then…"

"You go down to the door," Guo instructed him. "Count slowly to a hundred, and then go!"

Samejima nodded, and pulled back from the banister. It was slippery with dust, and had blackened his sweaty palms. He would make a lot of noise climbing over the lockers, so he decided to cross over the banister and jump directly onto the landing below.

He pulled himself up. The banister was made of concrete and was angled and didn't give him good purchase. He turned towards it, put one hand on either side and swung his left foot over. He was still a distance from the floor. He felt pain shoot through his toes as he swung his right leg over and jumped down to the hard floor below.

Samejima stood next to the door to the underground room. He looked up and nodded at Guo. Guo pointed to his watch and then to his mouth, indicating to Samejima that he should begin counting. Samejima moved his lips silently as he began. *One… two… three…* Guo turned around and headed up the stairs.

Samejima crouched on the bottom step and pulled out his gun. His entire body was cold and sticky from sweat and dust.

The tab on the doorknob was horizontal. Samejima assumed it was the "lock" position. Given the circumstances, that was the natural assumption. His count reached fifty. The glass had wire embedded in it, and he couldn't see anything on the other side of the door. Based on the light coming through, though, he felt it was safe to assume there was nothing large blocking the way.

Eighty. Samejima leaned over and put his ear up against the door.

"How long will it take?"

It was a man's voice.

"Probably ten minutes," was the response.

"What's this for?"

"When he's dead, we'll bury him."

The conversation stopped.

"What was that?"

"Probably just Takao."

"He's tired of being lookout and wants his turn, eh? Who is it?"

Samejima could hear the faint sound of the shutter being shaken.

"That wouldn't be *him*, would it?"

"Don't be stupid, he said he was at the park. Lift it up a little."

Samejima wiped his left hand on his pants and reached for the knob. He could hear the shutter going up. He turned the lock, and pulled on the door. It made a sound, but didn't open.

He heard the sound of gunfire from inside. Samejima ground his teeth. The door hadn't been locked. He turned the lock back to horizontal and opened it. That was when he heard the second shot followed by a scream.

Samejima aimed his gun over his head, crouched low and flew inside. The room had a bare concrete floor. To the right was the shutter. It had been lifted about two feet. Next to it was a man rolling on the ground in agony, his arms around his knee. At the furthest corner of the room, there was a pile of furniture. One man stood between the furniture and the wall. He was trying to behind the furniture. In front of the pile was a sofa on which he saw a pale naked

278

body.

"Police! Freeze!" Samejima aimed his gun at the man hiding behind the furniture. The man fired his gun.

Samejima dropped to the floor and took a shot at the ceiling. He couldn't see Guo anywhere. The man with the gun was white with panic. His first shot had been aimed at the shutter, but now he was aiming for Samejima.

"Police! Damn it!" Samejima hollered out, but the man was not listening. Samejima hesitated to make a second shot. Between himself and the man was a woman, her body bloody, lying on the sofa. From his low angle, he was in danger of hitting her.

The man began to fire wildly. Samejima prepared to die as he heard the bullets ricocheting off the wall and the floor and the ceiling. The sound was deafening.

All of a sudden, Guo appeared from under the shutter. He ran between Samejima and the man, dropped to his knees, and fired two shots. The man turned away and fell over onto the pile of desks then slid onto the floor. Samejima stayed still for a few seconds. It wasn't the first time he'd ever been shot at, but no one had ever fired at him with so many bullets. The man must have taken four or five shots before he fell, but none of the bullets had hit Samejima.

Swallowing hard several times, Samejima got up. Guo, still on his knees, looked over at him.

"Thanks," Samejima said. Guo just nodded. Then his right knee gave out from under him, and he fell forward. He was trying to support himself with his right hand, which still held the gun.

"Guo!" Samejima yelled. Guo's shirt was covered in blood from his chest to his stomach. "I'll call an ambulance!" Guo's hand let go of the gun, and reached out. Samejima grabbed it. He was trying to move his lips, and his voice was barely above a whisper.

"Du... du... yu..."

"Guo, stay with me!"

Guo licked his lips.

"Catch… him…" He let go of Samejima's hand and reached into his coat pocket. Samejima supported his shoulders so he wouldn't fall. Then he heard the sound of moaning. It was the yakuza that Guo had shot in the knee. Guo managed to pull out the photo. His face was quickly losing color as he pressed the picture into Samejima's hand and then pressed it to his chest.

"Hang in there, Guo."

Then he reached up his right hand to Samejima's neck and pulled it towards him with strength unthinkable in a gravely wounded man.

"Catch… Du… Yuan. You… catch… him. You…"

Samejima breathed in deeply.

"You…" Guo seemed to want him to promise.

"I will. Don't worry."

Guo arched back his neck. He opened his mouth and let out a roar. It sounded sorrowful. After that he was quiet.

"Guo?" Samejima could still hear the moaning behind him, but the detective was motionless.

Samejima used the car phone in the white Mercedes to call the police and an ambulance. Going back into the basement, Samejima saw Guo slumped against the wall, his head drooping down. Samejima felt the inside of his nose burn.

He looked down and walked towards the woman on the sofa. She was naked, and had terrible injuries to her face and left leg. He could see that she had been the victim of intense and extended violence. She was breathing, but her eyes were not focused, and her face was blank.

Samejima gently helped her sit up, and he took off his jacket to cover her. "I'm from the Shinjuku Precinct. You are Kiyomi Taguchi, if I'm not mistaken."

The woman just stared in Guo's direction.

"Miss Taguchi?" He didn't expect a response. She was obviously in shock. It was difficult for him to speak as well.

Her lips moved. "I am Qing Na Dai."

Samejima watched her, but her focus did not change.

"Qing Na. Dai," she repeated.

Samejima took out the photo Guo had given him, and showed it to her by putting it directly in front of her face. Her eyes finally moved, and when they found Zhensheng Liu, they froze. She stared at the photo.

"Where is he?" Samejima asked.

"The Taiwan Pavilion," she replied.

"Taiwan Pavilion?"

She nodded almost imperceptibly.

"Where is it?"

She had no response.

It was not long before they heard the sound of the ambulance and patrol cars. Samejima tried to ask the woman a few more questions, but she had nothing more to say.

The emergency vehicles poured into the parking lot of the deserted building. Medics carrying a stretcher and two uniformed officers peeked under the shutter.

"Oh my god," said one. Samejima turned around and identified himself. The officers stood up straighter.

"What happened here?" one asked.

"We came on the scene to find this woman kidnapped and confined against her will."

The medics approached Guo and the yakuza he shot.

"Two are dead. This woman was the victim. The corpse over there and the one shot in the leg were perpetrators. There is one more perp handcuffed behind the car outside."

"And this one?" The policeman indicated Guo.

Samejima closed his eyes to keep the tears from running down his face. "He was an informant. He was killed while assisting in the arrest."

Kiyomi Taguchi was the first to be carried out on a stretcher. When they came back for the wounded man, Samejima stopped them from putting him on the stretcher.

"Where are Hata and Ye?" he asked him. The man didn't speak but continued to scream in pain.

"Where are they?" Samejima grabbed the man's shoulder.

"Hold on, there," said the medic, pulling back Samejima's hand. Samejima glared at the medic, who quickly let go.

"I won't be long," Samejima explained. "I promise." Turning back to the injured man, he demanded again, "Where?"

"I don't know. Get me to a hospital. I'm gonna die!"

Samejima pulled out his gun. The yakuza went pale. "Whoa!"

Samejima cocked the gun and pointed it at the knee of his good leg.

"What the fuck are you doing? Stop!" the yakuza yelled.

"Inspector!" said a medic. The cops were all frozen in place.

"Where is he?"

"Back off, man, gimme a fuckin' break!" The yakuza's eyes were wide in fright as they went from Samejima's face to his gun and back again. "All right, all right!" he finally caved, his voice tearful. "The woman said it. It's in Shinjuku Gyoen Park. The Taiwan Pavilion. Mr. Hata went there to take care of that son of a bitch. They're gonna tear him to shreds."

"When did they leave?"

"About forty minutes ago. That fucker called here."

Samejima looked over at the policeman whose face was frozen in fear.

"You heard what he said. Contact the unit investigating the attack on the Ishiwa gang office."

"Yes, sir!"

Samejima put his gun back in its holster and walked outside.

"Uh, Inspector?" one of the officers called out. "What about this... this crime scene?"

"Later," Samejima said and ran off.

32

It wasn't supposed to happen like this. It wasn't supposed to, thought Ye as he sat in the back seat of the Mercedes parked in front of City Hall, sandwiched between two of Hata's bodyguards. One was named Tani, who was in the white Mercedes that brought the girl to the transport building.

After they had spoken to Du Yuan on the phone, Ye was sure that Hata and his men would take the woman with them and go to Shinjuku Gyoen Park. He had planned to wait in the underground room until he got word that they had taken care of Du Yuan.

But right after the Ape's call, the phone had rung again. It was the Ishiwa gang headquarters saying that Du Yuan had attacked their dorm, backing up the claims Du Yuan himself had made.

As soon as Hata heard this, he was livid. He ordered every available Ishiwa gangster to mobilize.

"The police are guarding headquarters? Then get everyone out of there! Listen carefully. If everyone leaves at once, the police will be suspicious. Have the men go a few at a time. Make sure someone stays to answer the phone. Bring all the flashlights and guns you've got! Contact everyone at their homes! Ring the pagers of all the rest out on patrol! This is war!" Hata hung up and turned to Ye. "Mr. Ye, please come with us."

As he had feared, all Hata could think of was getting revenge on Du Yuan. Now that he had his chance to do so, he didn't care who or what had to be sacrificed. He wanted to slay the Poison Ape.

284

Ye tried to hide his discomfort and asked, "What about the woman?"

"There'll be plenty of time to deal with her later. She'll only get in the way if we take her with us. We'll decide what to do with her after that bastard is dead."

"How many men have been contacted?"

"There'll be about twenty. All armed."

Twenty? That's all? thought Ye. However, Du Yuan was sick and they had captured his woman. If they let this opportunity go by, they might never get another one. Ye would have to go back to Taiwan and continue to live in fear.

Hata waited for him to make up his mind. He could barely keep his rage from boiling over. "You're coming, right?"

Ye knew that if he refused, Hata might kill him on the spot. It was clear that Hata had come to the realization that all of their current problems began with Ye.

He tried to sound cheery. "Of course, I will. This old man might come in handy yet."

If only Ishiwa were there. He never would have allowed this to happen. Ye was a key person. If he were arrested or harmed in any way, it would devastate the Ishiwa gang's drugs and gun route from Taiwan. Not only would they lose their own supply, they would no longer be able to spread the goods to other gangs in their syndicate, and their position would be badly compromised.

However, Ishiwa was in the hospital and Takakawa was dead. Hata was calling the shots in the Ishiwa gang.

Ye looked behind him. Hata had ordered his troops to assemble in front of the Tokyo City Hall in West Shinjuku. He ordered them to avoid drawing suspicion by riding no more than four to a car. There were about seven cars in all.

The dark, futuristic façade of City Hall was covered in blinking red lights, adding to Ye's bleak feeling of foreboding. There was a line of cars brimming with gangsters. All of them were silent and looked grim, but their eyes glowed with the prospect of drawing blood. No one was in the mood for small talk.

Hata checked the cars one by one to make sure everyone was armed. He advised them on how to take on Du Yuan. Ye was slightly comforted that, despite Hata's state of anxious distraction, he was not foolish enough to go into battle without giving detailed instructions.

The spot they had picked was one where taxi drivers usually stopped to take a nap, but the thugs had little trouble getting them to move elsewhere. Hata finally returned to the white Mercedes and got into the front passenger seat.

"Drive," he said.

As the lead car left, the rest of the Ishiwa gang pulled out like a formation of fighter jets.

"I asked someone who knows the park. The Taiwan Pavilion is in the center near a pond. It's a large area. I've organized the men into four groups of five so they won't shoot each other by mistake. That bastard will be alone, right?" Hata looked back at Ye.

"Yes," Ye confirmed, "he always works alone." As he spoke, he tried to keep his voice from betraying his fear.

Hata nodded. "The men in the cars behind us will go in first. The park is closed, so we'll have to climb the walls. The first to go in will set up ladders. The fact that it's closed is in our favor—the place is huge."

"What about…us?" Ye asked tentatively.

"After the first group goes in, we'll climb over the wall and head for the Taiwan Pavilion. He told us to bring the woman, but he'll be dead before he figures out she's not with us. He used the submachine gun again to attack the dorm. There's some who think he must be out of ammo by now."

286

"That's hard to say." Ye shook his head. Hata nodded and turned his eyes forward.

The car phone rang.

After he had answered and hung up, Hata ordered the driver, "Go around to the Sendagaya side. It's easier to get in that way."

Ye took out a cigarette. Even after he had it in his mouth, neither of the bodyguards on either side of him offered a light. The goodwill of the Ishiwa gang for him had obviously been put on hold. After this was all over, he'd have to say something about this to the boss. Gently, of course. He'd just mention that Hata's influence on his subordinates might have an adverse effect on Ishiwa's friendly ties to Taiwan.

It took no more than ten minutes to arrive at their destination. They saw a car with its hazard lights blinking, stopped near an iron fence about six feet high.

"Let's get started," muttered Hata as he got out of the car. He went over to talk to the occupants of the first car.

On one side of the narrow road ran the spike-tipped black fence. On the other side of the road were small buildings and houses.

Two more Mercedes passed Ye's car and lined up along the road near the first one. Hata put his hand on the roof of the first car and watched the others pull in. There was a thick, dark forest on the other side of the fence as far as they could see. Leaves and small branches poked out from the fence, and some of the trees were easily more than twenty-five feet tall.

It's so dark in there. Ye's mouth went dry with fear.

Two men got out of the first car. One had a fold-up ladder on his shoulder. The other held a cell phone. The two walked softly towards the fence. Hata watched them go, and then came back to the car. He sat down in the passenger seat leaving the door open, and put his hand on the receiver of the car phone.

The phone rang, and he quickly picked it up.

"Speak!" he demanded and listened as the man on the other end spoke. "Got it," he replied, and hung up.

He got out and signaled the men in the waiting cars. They got out all at once. Some were in battle gear. None of them said a word. Following Hata's gestures, they walked in the direction of the first two that were already climbing over the fence.

Hata got back in the car. "Drive," he ordered. "Go that way and drive around for about ten minutes."

The driver pulled out slowly, passing the group on foot. They had found a place where they could climb over the fence without being seen from the road. From there they could enter the expansive park.

Ye had only been here once before. It was when he had come to Tokyo for sightseeing about four years ago. There was a Taiwanese guide who had taken him to the Taiwan Pavilion. It had been a present from Taiwan to the Showa Emperor on the occasion of his marriage in 1927, just about the time Ye was born. It was built of Taiwanese cedar, and Taiwanese workers had come to Japan to construct it. When he had first seen it he had wondered what such an old Taiwanese-style building was doing in Tokyo.

The guide said that the enormous park was a waste as it had so few visitors, especially on weekdays.

This is one of the most valuable pieces of real estate in the city, his guide had told him. *The Japanese are strange. They should tear this down and use the property for something more relevant. You can see that almost no one comes. The only time it gets any use is during the flower-viewing season.*

She was right. There were a number of ponds, an English garden and a formal Japanese garden. It was covered with a rich, thick lawn and surrounded by dense woods. Over a hundred acres of land, and no more visitors in it than you could count on both hands.

And they close it at night, so it's not even a place for young lovers to meet. Even in New York where they have so many crimes, Central Park stays open at night. The guide had shaken her head. She lived in Japan, but she didn't seem to like it much. She, of course, had no idea that Ye was a prominent gangster, and she freely shared with him her plans to move to the United States.

The car phone rang, and Hata picked up. "It's me. Okay. I'm on my way. Is the ladder in place? …All right, wait for me there."

Hata ordered the driver back to the original location. "Stop when you get to the place where they went in." It was a block of houses that had all been abandoned.

As they got out, Hata gave instructions to the driver. "Keep moving, but stay in the area, and keep an eye out for the cops. Come as soon as I call." Then he turned back to the three men in the back seat. "Let's go."

Ye got out, the bodyguards still on either side of him. They walked single file to where the fence warped behind the houses. At the back, Ye saw that the iron fence changed to a concrete wall. The ladder was set up, and several men with flashlights were waiting for them on the other side. One climbed up the ladder and jumped down to the other side, followed by Tani.

"Mr. Ye, you're next," said Hata when the two of them were the only ones still outside the wall. Ye wanted to spin around and run off.

"I'm so old," Ye said. "Mr. Hata, please go ahead of me."

Hata shook his head slowly. "Quickly, please!"

Ye stared at him. Hata's right hand was drifting towards his hip. Ye nodded, and put his foot on the first step.

"Guys, help him down!" Hata called out to his men. The concrete wall was as high as the iron fence. Ye climbed up. He could see that there was a flat surface on top, less than a foot wide. Ye used both of his hands to pull himself onto it. The gangsters below reached out and helped him down.

There was a narrow dirt path covered in fallen leaves along the inside of the wall. Branches reached out through the fence, but the trunks themselves were set three to four yards back. Weeds covered the base of the trunks. The path was plain dirt, and fallen leaves covered it.

Hata climbed up the ladder and onto the wall. He pulled up the ladder and set it down on the other side, then climbed down into the park.

"Where are the others?" he asked.

"We spread out, just like you told us. The rest are on the main path, a little farther up."

"What does it look like up ahead?"

"This path follows the fence and then turns toward the center of the park. As soon as we get through these trees, there's a wider path," explained one of the men.

Ye tried to look through the trees. He could just barely see flashlights flickering among the dark trunks. There was some wind, and he could hear it rustling the leaves overhead. Compared to the outside, this park was a world of darkness.

"Turn on your flashlights and let's move out. Make sure the first man and the last have their guns out. Just don't trip and blow us all away, though."

Ye walked on, four men in front of him and four behind. As expected, they came to a spot along the fence where a dirt path about six feet wide turned off to the left. Not long after that, they reached a large park road made of gravel. This road was wider than the other, and it ran in both directions, winding its way through the park. The rest of the men were waiting there for them.

"Is everyone here?" asked Hata.

Each of the men announced themselves. Hata had all but one turn off their flashlights.

"Good. Now, which way to the Taiwan Pavilion?" asked Hata.

One of the younger men came forward and explained the way.

Outfitted in combat gear and boots, he appeared to be the one who knew the park best. "First we follow this road to the right until it forks. Take the left-hand road, and after a short walk, the pavilion will be on the left."

"Can't we get there if we go to the left here?"

"Yes, but it will be the long way around. We can go around the chrysanthemum nursery, and then back through…"

"What about the right-hand road at the fork?"

"It leads to the Sendagaya Gate. It gets wider, so you'll know it's near an entrance."

"Can you come back to the Taiwan Pavilion from there?"

"If you go straight into the park from the Sendagaya Gate, you'll come to a pond. Head back in this direction on the path along the pond, and you'll end up in front of it."

"Why do you know so much about this place," Hata asked with a hint of admiration in his voice.

"He grew up near here," spoke up Tani. "He spent most of his childhood playing in the park."

"Yeah? I thought maybe this was where you fucked your broads," Hata said. A few of the men snickered, and the tension eased somewhat.

"All right. We'll go to the right from here, and you and Kubo's group take the road to the left. That way sounds more confusing." The guide in battle gear nodded. "The other two groups go back to the Sendagaya Gate and take the path along the pond. Got it now? The four of us will go down the center, and you two squads of ten take the right and left. We'll get there first, so we'll leave after you do. The bastard's alone, but he's smart, so be careful. Take out anyone you see that's not one of us. If you end up killing a bum, that's his problem."

"What about cops?"

"Don't worry about them. Even if they arrest us, they'll never figure out which one of us shot a cop. Divide a twenty-five-year sentence among all of us and it'll be just one year for each. What would happen if we backed off because of cops? The infamous violent Ishiwa gang will be the laughingstock of the whole country. Got it?"

"Yes, sir!" the men shouted out in military-style unison.

"Take out your guns, and get the hell out of here!"

33

Samejima knew exactly what he was getting himself into. Not only was Du Yuan in Shinjuku Gyoen Park, but also a platoon of armed Ishiwa yakuza. It was reckless, but he had to go. Guo had saved his life. If Guo hadn't taken the bullet, he would have been the one lying in a pool of blood in that underground room.

Guo begged him to capture Du Yuan right before he died. Samejima knew why he had asked him and no other to do it. He couldn't forget what Guo had told him in that tiny business hotel room.

Liu was my best friend in the army. I want to be the one to catch him. If a SWAT team ever surrounds him, they will shoot him. I don't want that.

Guo had wanted to go one-on-one with Du Yuan. Whether that meant killing or arresting him, he wanted to be the one to take him on. That's why he had taken time off from work to come here, to Shinjuku. He knew he could easily be arrested for exceeding his authority.

He had failed in his goal because he had died to save the life of a Japanese cop. He entrusted that cop with his last request, asking him to carry on his mission since that cop was able to carry on with his life. Samejima had to fulfill Guo's request or he'd never be able to hold his head high as a cop ever again. He'd spend the rest of his life regretting his failure to keep his word.

He didn't want that to happen.

Samejima had joined the police force for his own sake, not for his country. He had explained this to Guo, a fellow cop, and the Taiwanese had understood despite the differences in their cultures. That was why he had revealed to Samejima what he was trying to accomplish in Japan.

Guo wasn't there working to protect his country or uphold the law. He was there on a personal mission. He was trying to become the type of cop he idealized.

Samejima didn't know everything there was to know about Guo or his methods. He would never know if he was the sort of detective he would have been comfortable working with. But he and Guo had very similar reasons for staying in the profession.

He had liked the man and supported his fight. He was sure Guo had felt the same way about him. Samejima had seen Guo's expression of shock and dismay when he had learned that Du Yuan had been responsible for the death of a Japanese policeman.

Samejima had to go. Someone had to carry on Guo's mission. His mission had to be completed by a cop who worked for no higher purpose than to be true to himself.

Samejima sped along Koshu Road and over the Shinjuku overpass. He turned off the siren of the unmarked patrol car, but continued flashing the red lights. If he had called for reinforcements from the crime scene in the abandoned building in North Shinjuku, it would have taken more than thirty minutes to assemble a unit, get them suited up and armed, and appoint someone as commander before heading to the Shinjuku Gyoen Park.

Samejima fully expected armed conflict, so asking for a back-up patrol car would not be sufficient. If he had decided to wait any longer, it would all be over by the time police arrived on the scene. He slowed down as he neared Shinjuku High School, and then approached the park.

He drove along the fence surrounding the park. There were four entrances: Main, Okido, Shinjuku, and Sendagaya. The Main Gate was typically closed except for formal events during the cherry blossom season.

At this time of night, all of the gates would be closed and locked. The one nearest at hand was the Shinjuku entrance. Shinjuku Gyoen was the only park in Tokyo run by the national government. In the old days, there had been sixty employees with someone on duty every night. Budget cuts had halved the grounds crew, which left it unmanned at night. It was open from nine in the morning until four-thirty in the afternoon. Yotsuya Precinct patrol cars made night rounds during the cherry blossom season only.

When the Shinjuku Gate came into view, Samejima made a sharp turn and stopped the car in the small space in front of the gate. He didn't know where he'd find the Taiwan Pavilion, so he took a flashlight from the glove compartment, left the red light on the car flashing, and got out.

He checked his watch. It was four-twenty. The sun would begin to rise in about an hour. He hopped on top of the hood of the car and jumped onto the gate. The gate, made of iron and stone pillars, was about six feet high. He pulled himself to the top and swung a leg over. The black park sprawled out before him. He stopped to listen, but heard nothing. He didn't know whether or not Du Yuan and the Ishiwa gang had begun to fight.

If it had already begun, the silence he heard meant one of the parties had been unmistakably victorious. Samejima pulled his other leg over the gate and jumped down. Inside, to the right of the entrance, was a solid stone booth for ticket sales. It was small but well kempt.

Samejima looked around and found a map of the park. He went over to it, and shone his flashlight on it. From where he stood, the park spread out in a long, oblong shape in front of him. To his right was the Japanese Garden, and to his left was the English Garden. The park was over half a mile long from east to west. The breadth was about seven hundred yards. If one were to walk around the edge, it would be almost two miles.

The Taiwan Pavilion was right about the center of the park, on one of the long, oblong ponds that ran through the park from east to west. Looking at the map, it was about five hundred yards away, past a garden and a stretch of woods. Samejima committed the map to memory and turned off his flashlight.

He took his gun out of its holster, and checked his remaining bullets. He had used one in the underground room, and he had four left. He hadn't brought a supply of spares with him.

Samejima took a deep breath. He had to find Du Yuan.

It was then that he heard the sound of gunfire coming through the woods.

34

Planning to circle through the chrysanthemum nursery, the young guide in combat gear lead his squad of ten along the left-hand side of the park road. Next, Hata sent the other group of ten men back towards the Sendagaya Gate. They would wind back along the pond. He watched as the second group turned right at the fork. Hata waited until he couldn't see them anymore, and then signaled his party to move.

"Let's go," he said.

Tani and another yakuza got out their guns. They had two weapons each and gave one to Hata and another to Ye. Ye cocked the gun; it had been a while since he had actually held one in his hand. Ji, his bodyguard, had always been armed, so he hadn't needed to carry one himself.

The gun felt heavy. In his youth, he had excellent aim, but it had been so long now that he wasn't sure if he could hit anything. He hoped to avoid having to use it at all. He never wanted to see Du Yuan again until he was presented with his corpse. Mortally wounded would be satisfactory, too.

The four men walked to the right along the gravel road, their shoes making a crunching sound at every step. Ye was drenched in sweat. His palms were almost dripping. Since they had turned off their flashlights, they had only the light of the night sky to guide them along.

A strong wind occasionally came up, and it made a ferocious

sound as it whipped the trees back and forth. Nobody said a word. Ye kept a grip on his gun as his eyes moved constantly around him, to the front, to the right and left.

Tani was in the lead, followed by Hata, then Ye, with the last man bringing up the rear. Ye felt goose bumps on his skin, and turned to look behind him. The man behind him also appeared terrified, constantly turning around to check his own back.

"That bastard's really just sitting there waiting in the pavilion?" Tani asked in a low voice.

"Probably," Hata answered, and Ye noticed that his voice was wrought with tension. Ye felt, however, that no matter how scared the rest of them were, he was more afraid than all of them combined—he was the only one who knew what Du Yuan was truly capable of.

When they got to the fork in the road, they took the left-hand path. The Taiwan Pavilion was just over a hundred yards away. Just then, he heard the staccato rat-a-tat-tat of a fully automatic weapon from somewhere on the right. It wasn't that loud, and sounded far away, like firecrackers going off.

"It's Okishi and his group." Tani turned around to Hata.

"Don't panic—" Hata started to say before he was interrupted by a blood-chilling scream. It didn't come from a single man. There were many screams from men under attack. When the continuous automatic weapon fire stopped, it was followed by two single shots, and then there was silence.

"Hey!" yelled Hata.

On the road in front of him he saw a black shadow flit from the right to the left. There were dense stands of trees on both sides, and the gunfire had come from the right, from the direction of the pond. Someone had crossed the road about a hundred yards in front of them, and was now in the trees to the left.

Ye quickly aimed and fired three shots in that direction. Tani and the man bringing up the rear followed suit. They fired seven or eight bullets into the trees in the direction of the Taiwan Pavilion.

"Was that him?" asked Hata.

Ye was about to reply when another shadowy figure appeared to their right. He held his stomach with both hands and walked unsteadily as if he might keel over at any moment. When the figure caught sight of the four of them, he tried to call out, but gave up, moaned, and fell to his knees.

"It's Kokubo," said Tani. They ran towards him. Kokubu's face and torso were covered in blood. His breath came in shallow bursts. Hata ran up to him and cradled his head in his arms, looking like a father cradling a wounded child.

"What happened?"

"Shit…shit…" Kokubo sputtered. "Sneaky goddamn bastard… hid in the pond…" Kokubo coughed and then vomited a huge amount of blood. Hata moved to avoid it.

"Hey, hey!" Tani grabbed for the wounded man, but it was too late. He fell forward on his face into the gravel. His eyes were wide open, but he no longer moved.

Hata stood up suddenly and howled. Then there was the sound of an explosion that resonated in their guts as the entire area lit up for a long moment. Ye looked up to see a flash of yellow fire race across the canopy of the trees.

"What the hell?" said Tani. The explosion came from the direction of the Taiwan Pavilion.

"Holy shit!" muttered Hata, gritting his teeth. "Let's go!" Hata took off at a run. The other two men followed close behind. Ye, consumed with fear, could do no more than stumble behind them.

They came to the path along the pond, and there, on the side of the path, lay the Ishiwa men. It was as if some giant had come along and tossed them about like so many dolls. Ye stopped in his tracks. It was the men who had come from the Sendagaya Gate. As they had walked along the path to the pond, Du Yuan had stood up in the water where he had been hiding, and sprayed them with bullets from his Uzi. It must have been like shooting ducks in a row.

Ye wrenched his eyes away from the pile of corpses and looked to the left. Through the narrow openings between the tree branches, he got a glimpse of the white walls of the Taiwan Pavilion. There were round windows next to each of the glass doors. Hata and the other two men stood frozen to the ground where the road divided. They had a flashlight trained at their feet.

"Hata!" yelled Ye, intending to notify Hata of the corpses, but none of the three moved. Ye walked over to them. At the end of the path was the Taiwan Pavilion, surrounded by trees. To the left was a narrow path that went around behind it. From the back, it looked as though the pavilion jutted out over the pond. Small fires burned along the narrow path. There was a smell of a detonated bomb and the air was filled with a haze of smoke.

Then he heard moaning, and saw shapes of men here and there. These men had not been merely tossed about by a giant, but torn apart by one. There was blood everywhere, and body parts—hands, feet, and bits of torsos.

Tani vomited. Ye closed his eyes.

Du Yuan had set bombs along the path to the Taiwan Pavilion. Upon examination, the human remains as well as the ground were covered in something metallic that reflected light. They were nails— hundreds and thousands of them.

Du Yuan had packed the bomb with nails and then booby-trapped the path with a wire to trip the fuse. It must have been set for a delayed reaction that set off the bomb several seconds after the lead man stepped on the wire. The nails had exploded over all of the men along the path. The moans they heard now were from the few who barely survived.

Hata looked at Ye. The eyes of the Japanese had lost all trace of sanity. He opened his mouth and tried to speak, but instead of words, a horrible sound came out of his throat followed by the watery contents of his stomach.

Twenty men had been murdered in no more than a few minutes. Ye felt his body begin to quiver. "Ha-Hata… Let's run!"

Hata's eyes, wet with tears from vomiting, were suddenly filled with anger. "No! We've got to hunt him down!" He mustered his strength and yelled, "Where are you, Poison Ape? Come out where I can see you! Don't make us kill your bitch!"

They waited. The moaning voice they heard was replaced by a low groan. A few of the men were still alive, but none were able to stand and fight with them.

"Du Yuan!" Ye called out in Chinese. "We've got Qing Na. Come out!" The four men stood back to back, one of them facing in each direction. The only response they got was from the wind in the trees.

The groan turned into sobs. It was the only sound they could hear.

"He's here!" Hata's third man, standing between Ye and Tani and facing the Taiwan Pavilion, shot his gun into the trees.

"Shit! Motherfucker! Sneaky son of a bitch!" Hata's man grasped his gun with both hands and ran into the trees. They continued to hear him cursing incomprehensibly and shooting his gun, but the sounds suddenly stopped.

Then a second later, a scream: "You bastard!"

Hata and Tani looked at each other, and leapt into the darkness after him. Ye watched them go, and as soon as they disappeared, he heard howls that came from the very depths of their beings.

Ye gripped his gun with both hands. He heard a rustle from among the trees and shot twice. He felt the kick of the gun and saw the burst of the bullet. He heard one bullet hit a branch, followed by the thud of someone falling over. He kept the gun in front of him and moved towards the dense foliage. Poking out from behind a bush was a pair of black shoes. One leg pointed straight up and the other was twisted to the side.

He used the gun to push the branches aside, and moved forward. Hata had both hands pressing on a hole in his throat that spurted blood, and his entire body shook. He looked as if he were strangling himself. His eyes were wide open and blinking rapidly.

Ye looked straight ahead. There was a small clearing deeper in the grove, and Tani and the other man lay in a pile. Both of their stomachs had been slit open. They were still alive, but their bodies were convulsing in the throes of death.

Ye whipped around.

35

The sound of gunfire continued for a while after the bomb, and then everything went deadly quiet. Samejima, gun in hand, was just about through the Japanese Garden with its teahouse. The gravel road wound its way through the neatly trimmed lawn and the bushes cut into oval shapes. When he had found his way out of the woods and into the garden, he had seen beyond it a pointed roof on the edge of a black pond. It looked mysterious set against the dark trees.

The outer columns, supporting a platform with railings along the edge, looked like a Noh theater. On the platform were more columns that supported the roof, which curved up into points that stretched towards the sky. The shape and the fact that it was built on the edge of the water reminded Samejima of the Golden Pavilion temple in Kyoto.

Samejima walked over the grass and towards the building. He knew immediately that it must be the Taiwan Pavilion. It could be reached from the left or the right. The road to the right was a short-cut that crossed over a narrow spot in the pond, while the one to the left wandered across a stretch of land between two ponds and around to the front of the pavilion. Samejima took the left, the longer of the two. The path to the right would take him through a stand of trees where someone might be hiding.

The area around the Taiwan Pavilion was particularly thick with greenery. Trees over thirty feet tall loomed as one overwhelming darkness over the edifice.

Samejima walked along the path that twisted its way through the bushes. He saw a long, narrow pond to his left. It was a large one, more than fifty yards across at some points.

When Samejima got close to it, he could see human forms lying on the opposite bank. He counted seven or eight that were visible between the bushes. He stood for a few moments holding his breath. He couldn't hear anything except the wind rustling the leaves and rippling the surface of the pond.

He figured that the entrance to the Taiwan Pavilion was a little further down the path, to the right. When he came to a fork in the road, he saw ahead of him the shape of someone rolled up into a ball. The dark figure looked almost like a person at prayer, his forehead scraping the ground.

Samejima cocked his pistol and lifted it as he drew nearer to the figure. A few footsteps before he reached it, he called out softly, "Hey!"

The figure, his back rounded, didn't even flinch. Samejima walked slowly around. One side of his face was pressed against the ground, and his body was folded in two. The face was covered in blood, and his eyes were wide open. Both hands were pressed to his stomach.

There was no doubt the man was dead. Samejima took a deep breath and lowered his gun. He went back the way he had come until he arrived again to the fork. On the other side of the trees was the white wall of the pavilion. It was fit with a horizontal row of round windows.

Samejima stopped again. The smell of blood there was strong enough to make him want to vomit. He looked towards where the white wall ended. Anyone coming from the other route across the pond would proceed along the tree-lined path beyond.

He saw a group of corpses, all covered in something that sparkled. There were body parts here and there, too. Arms and legs with bits of clothing still attached hung from the trees and the fence around the building.

Samejima did his best to overcome a wave of nausea. This was a massacre the likes of which he had never seen before. He must have seen at least twenty bodies. He looked over to the right. A gate made of straw and bamboo had toppled over towards the inside of the building. Beyond stood a double door with glass panes. One door was flung inward, with the glass shattered.

Built on the edge of the pond, the Taiwan Pavilion appeared from this angle to be a single-story structure. From the other side of the pond, one could see two floors built onto the foundation.

Samejima walked closer to the mangled gate. It was no more than a couple of feet high. He stepped over it, and dipped under the overhand. He could smell the scent of dry wood peculiar to old buildings. The Taiwan Pavilion was constructed with white walls and thick cedar columns.

Samejima could see nothing inside, nor was there any sound. He took a deep breath and stepped up to the entrance. A glass shard crunched under his foot.

At that instant, a flash of gunfire came from deep inside. The bullet snapped through the glass pane in the door and Samejima could feel it pass less than an inch from his skin. He instinctively pulled himself into the shadow of the wall.

A second bullet flew into the cedar doorframe, scattering a spray of wood. Samejima turned and put his back flat against the wall and crouched down. He could hear someone inside screaming in Chinese. Then came a third bullet, once again hitting the glass in the door.

Samejima slowly stood up in the shadow of the wall. He pulled out his gun and cocked it. The space around his feet lit up as he shot a round.

"Police! Freeze where you are!" Samejima yelled.

There was a moment of silence, followed by, "Police? Is it really police?" The speech was accented.

"Yes, I'm Samejima of the Shinjuku Precinct!"

There was a sudden clatter against the floor as a Black Star revolver was thrown out of the interior, still cocked and ready to fire. It scattered the broken glass as it slid across the floor and stopped at Samejima's feet.

"Don't shoot! I have nothing more!"

Samejima raised his gun, held it with both hands, and jumped out of the shadows.

Inside, he could now see a man standing with both hands raised. Samejima pulled out his flashlight and shined it into the man's face. He squinted in the light, and Samejima could see that his hair was gray. It was Wei Ye. He wore a black double-breasted suit.

"Mr. Ye, right?" said Samejima. He walked through the door and inside the pavilion.

"That's right." Ye's voice shook in terror. On his face, though, was a look of relief.

Samejima was about to ask what had happened to Hata when his flashlight passed over another figure. It appeared from behind Ye, along the handrail of the walkway extending over the pond. The figure leaped over the handrail and into the building.

Ye never even saw him as he continued to stutter in relief.

"I-I'm saved!" he barely got out. Before Samejima could warn him, a white gleam streaked sidewards behind his head.

Ye's mouth opened. It reminded Samejima of Saji, the yakuza who had been selling thinner in Shinjuku station, the instant he was stabbed. Blood sprayed in the light. Ye put his hand to the back of his neck and spun around. The face of a man in a black sweat suit, the hood pulled tightly around his head, was visible in the light. His sunken eyes were vacant. They looked like the ashes of burnt charcoal. His cheekbones jutted out of his emaciated face, and his chin was covered in stubble.

He was soaking wet and drops of water sparkled as they flew

off. There was a double-edged dagger in his right hand. Ye fell to his knees, in a pose of supplication. He gave a high-pitched scream as he looked into the eyes of his attacker.

The man let out a shout as he pulled both of his elbows to his waist. His right knee flew up, and in the next instant he kicked up his boot-covered foot as if he were aiming for his own forehead. He brought his heel down with incredible, fearsome force, crushing Ye's skull.

Samejima heard a sharp crack as Ye's head sunk into his shoulders. Ye's screams stopped, and he fell slowly backwards. His opened eyes were raised towards Samejima, but there was no longer any life in them.

Samejima shifted his gaze from Ye to the attacker. At the same instant, the man looked from Ye to Samejima.

The man had a submachine gun slung over each shoulder along with a bag made of gray fabric. Wrapped around his leg was a sheath that housed the dagger.

Samejima shined his flashlight on the man's face—it seemed devoid of any sanity. The man leaped over Ye's body, and in the blink of an eye, his left foot struck Samejima's chest with a force that sent him flying. He crashed through the door that had still been shut, breaking the glass. He tumbled backwards out of the pavilion.

Samejima's gun and flashlight were both gone. He landed on the ruined bamboo gate. He tried to stand up, but he couldn't catch his breath and sharp pains shot through his ribcage. The other man appeared, stepping on the broken door Samejima had crashed through. His ember-like eyes stared at Samejima, and Samejima was unable to move as he lay on the ground with his arms spread wide.

The man took one step closer to Samejima and then stopped. He bent his head backwards, and shook it from side to side as he looked up towards the night sky. It looked as though he was trying to hear something—and in a few seconds, Samejima heard it, too—the sound of sirens of dozens of police cars and SWAT vans. They echoed throughout the crisp, pre-dawn air, all of them heading for the park. He looked back at Samejima.

"Zhensheng Liu?" Samejima did his best to squeeze out the words.

The man's eyes stopped and grew wide.

Samejima licked his dry lips and tried to speak again.

"You're...under arrest."

The man's expression remained unchanged. Samejima did his best to slowly raise his left hand. He knew the man had his weight on his left foot in preparation for another kick.

At that instant, the man suddenly grit his teeth and bent over, his left hand pressed to his lower abdomen. Something had happened inside his body. He must have been seriously wounded. He grabbed onto a column that supported the roof, and tried to keep himself upright. His eyes opened wide as he threw away the dagger and reached for his submachine gun.

Samejima knew this was his only chance. He overcame his own pain to pull himself up and threw himself at the man headfirst. The man let go of the column and fell over backwards. His head hit the step to the entrance, but he still managed to keep Samejima at arm's length by thrusting his right elbow into his left shoulder. Samejima groaned from the pain.

Samejima hit the man's face with his right hand before the other could let his elbow fly again. The man twisted his body away before he could score another hit, but Samejima could see that he was growing sluggish. The man tried to roll over and stand up, but Samejima leaped for the submachine gun.

Since the strap was still attached to the man's shoulder, he began to fall over again. He pulled himself free of the strap, but when he did so, Samejima got possession of the gun. Yet, a second later, the man's left leg whipped around like a whirlwind, knocking Samejima's feet out from under him. Samejima fell over backwards, the submachine gun still in his hands.

The man tried desperately to stand up again. He grabbed the column and pulled his feet in. Samejima was still on his back, trying to recover from the blow. He could see the man preparing to kick the submachine gun out of his hands.

Samejima got his right hand on the trigger. He aimed for the ceiling, and let off a round of shots that went right through the roof, breaking the tiles on top of it.

"Freeze!" Still on his back, Samejima aimed the gun at the man's chest. The man froze. Samejima inched back and re-aimed. His hands shook with pain. "Do not try to resist!"

The man looked at Samejima with an almost dejected expression. His left leg collapsed and he fell to his knee. His breathing was ragged, and was occasionally interspersed with a low moan.

By this time, Samejima had finally made it to his feet. He pulled the photograph out of his back pocket and tossed it over to the man. He was rolled up in a ball, still in pain. He didn't even try to look at the picture.

Samejima looked around for the flashlight he had lost when he had been kicked out of the pavilion. By now, however, the sun was rising, and he would be able to see the picture without a flashlight.

Samejima did his best to speak in English to get the man's attention. He assumed that since he had been part of an elite army unit, he would understand English.

"Look! Look at the picture!" he yelled.

The man lifted his face and reached weakly for the photo.

"It's Guo! Your friend Rongmin Guo!" Samejima said. Just saying the name made his nose burn with the threat of tears.

The man stared at the picture and then looked back at Samejima.

"Guo…?"

"He's dead." As Samejima tearfully spoke the words, something finally flickered in the man's eyes. "But he saved Qing Na. She's alive."

The man looked up.

"Qing Na…" he said sadly.

"She's in a hospital."

The man nodded his head slightly.

"You are Du Yuan?" Samejima asked.

The man looked at Samejima, his cheeks slack for a moment before they lifted in a weak smile.

"Are you hurt or sick?" Samejima continued.

The man's pale lips moved and he spoke in a voice almost too low to hear. "Sick. Sick kill me. Nobody kill me."

After that, his neck went slack and he stopped moving.

The sirens were coming closer. The patrol cars must have driven through either the Okido or Main Gate straight to the pavilion. Samejima couldn't move. He kept the gun trained on Du Yuan until the cars crunched along the path to the front of the Taiwan Pavilion.

Du Yuan, or Zhensheng Liu, died on the way to the hospital in an ambulance. The autopsy revealed gun wounds in his right thigh and in his upper left arm. The cause of death, however, was peritonitis caused by aggravated appendicitis.

Twenty-two members of the Ishiwa gang were killed in Shinjuku Gyoen Park, including Hata, one of the top Ishiwa men. One of the survivors was blinded by the bomb. Yasui and three other members of Yasui Enterprises were found at the bottom of Nakano Pond. All of the corpses had their throats slit, were tied to iron gutter grates and lay face down in the pond.

According to a report by Section One, the victims of Du Yuan were as follows: thirty-six dead, seven wounded. Of the dead, three had Taiwanese passports. One police officer was killed and four were wounded.

Takezo Ishiwa, the head of the Ishiwa gang, promptly dissolved his organization after he was released from the hospital.

Rongmin Guo, a squad leader in the Criminal Investigation Divison of the Taipei City Police Department, was reported in a Taipei newspaper as having been killed in an accident during a vacation in Japan. Later, though, Tokyo Headquarters sent the Taiwanese police a report of the entire incident, and his status was changed to "death in the line of duty."

As is often the case in Japan as well, he was promoted two ranks posthumously.

He became Superintendent Guo.

36

Nami sat in the waiting room at the hospital. It was where she usually went when she wanted to be alone at night. Samejima, an officer from the Shinjuku Precinct, had just left. It was the second time he had come to see her. The first visit had been to question her about her role in the Du Yuan incident. The second time, he had merely come to see how she was doing.

He had wanted to tell her about Yang. He told her that Yang had been worried about her. She also gave him his real name, Zhensheng Liu. Just before Samejima left, he handed her a white envelope along with a bouquet of flowers.

You can keep it if you like, but if the memories are too painful, just throw it away, he said. He also mentioned that he had made a copy for himself. He said that he would keep it forever, that he would never forget.

Nami had opened the envelope after Samejima left. It was a picture of a row of men in wetsuits standing shoulder to shoulder in a small boat. It looked like a military ship. She found a young Yang among them.

He looked so much younger than she herself felt now, Nami thought.

She sat in the darkened waiting room under the light of the emergency exit, and looked at the picture over and over again. She tried to go back to her room, but as soon as she picked up her crutches to walk back, she found herself wanting to look at it again.

She didn't cry; she was certain she would never weep again as long as she lived. She hadn't even shed a tear when she learned Yang was dead.

Instead, she wanted to take a trip. She knew, of course, that she would go to trial and they would send her to prison. Samejima had said she wouldn't get the death penalty, which meant she might be let free some day. If that happened, she wanted to travel to Taiwan. She wanted to see the beaches where Yang had dived and caught fish.

Eventually, a nurse came looking for her and sent her back to her room. She got into bed and lay there thinking about the beaches of Taiwan, an island in the southern seas. There was a boy on the beach. He was tanned a dark brown. He dived into the marine blue sea and came up with a fish.

The child had the face of Yang, the face that had been printed on her mind. She realized that she was crying. She turned her face into her pillow and sobbed quietly. She decided that the next time she shed tears would be the day she stood looking out at the sea, from the shores of Taiwan.

About the Author

Arimasa Osawa has received the Eiji Yoshikawa New Writer Award, the Japan Mystery Writers Association Award, and the Naoki Prize for his *Shinjuku Shark* novels. Many of his other hardboiled works have also been awarded prizes and adapted to the screen.